Ro

Contents

Roman Wall

Book 12 in the Sword of Cartimandua Series
By
Griff Hosker

Roman Wall

Published by Sword Books 2014
Copyright © Griff Hosker First Edition

*A CIP catalogue record for this title is available from the British
Library.*

Dedication

This is dedicated to all those readers who have e-mailed with comments.
I read them all – the good and really good! Thank you for your interest
and your support.
Rich, Alison, Carole, Christian, David, David, Dick Jenkins, Fred, Ian,
Jim, John, Phil, Philip, Pieter, Rod, Sam, Stephen, Pr. Tom, Walt, Thomas

Prologue

Camulodunum 60 A.D.

He looked at the half-finished mural on the wall of his new home and wondered if he would ever see it finished. It seemed to take the artist forever. So far only half of his body had been completed. He winced as he touched the blue toga the artist had chosen. The dull constant pain in his stomach would not disappear despite what treatment he tried.

Prasutagus, king of the Iceni and husband to the fiery Boudicca had sent all of his servants away as he awaited his friend Sallustius Lucullus. He wanted no prying eyes and ears present. As the son of the former king Amminus and the grandson of the great Cunobelinus he was one of the few men that this beleaguered king could actually trust. King Prasutagus was surrounded by factions who either wanted him to fight Rome or curb his hotheads.

He deeply regretted the money he had accepted from Emperor Claudius. To him and the Iceni it was seen as a gift but he now discovered it was deemed a loan against his kingdom. He had wasted too much of it in generous gifts to warriors whom he now saw were self-serving. He had distanced himself from them but now he wondered if it was too late for such gestures. He could not give the money back for half of it was gone. And then there was this constant and grumbling pain deep in his body. He had taken it to be too many lampreys, but as he had forsaken them for a month it might be something else. He wondered if he had been poisoned. He had a taster but one never knew. There were many who wished his increasingly belligerent wife to rule in his stead. He knew her love for him would not allow her to be a murderer but there were others who saw the overthrow of the Romans as a way to increase their own power.

The door opened and his young friend entered. He had known Lucullus since the time before his father had fled to Rome. He was an honest young man who was now without lands and power. All that remained to him was the monies his father had been given by Rome to remain a loyal British noble. He lived well but for someone who should have ruled the Catuvellauni this was but second best. They were in the capital of what would have been his lands had things gone better. Prasutagus felt guilty that he now owned the largest house in this newly Romanized town.

Lucullus was respectful and bowed to this most senior of kings. "Your majesty."

"Rise, Lucullus. We are friends. Let there be no formality between us. You and I have known each other too long for such titles. I have watched you grow into a fine young man and you are someone whom I can trust. Sit, please. Time presses and I have much to tell you."

Lucullus was intrigued. He admired Prasutagus, who managed to balance his dignity and power with the ability to work with the new masters of the land, the Romans. It had been some months since he had seen him and he did not look well. The young man felt concern.

"I have a cousin, Ban of the Votadini. He is, like you, a young and trustworthy man. He has recently visited with me." He shrugged, "The Votadini can see that the Romans will move north eventually and he was anxious to have my opinion on how to defeat them." He gave a self-deprecating laugh. "Why my opinion should be sought is beyond me."

"You have done all that you could. My father and grandfather saw the folly of trying to defeat this mighty war machine. Queen Cartimandua of the Brigante has done the same. Look at those who oppose the Romans. They are either dead or fled beyond the reach of the Roman eagle. And even in the far reaches of this island, they will not be safe."

Prasutagus shook his head. "There will come a time when the Romans will stop. They will have to but that will be long after I am dead and gone to the Allfather. I gave Ban a chest for safekeeping. It contains the last of the money the Romans loaned me as well as my torc and royal regalia."

Lucullus was no actor and could not disguise his shock. "But why?"

"I want my girls protected after I am gone. Their mother is a woman I love dearly but she has a passion beneath her breast which will erupt one day and I need you to promise that, if things go awry, you will recover the chest and protect my children." As Lucullus nodded the King of the Iceni handed over a ring. It was made of gold and had the image of a boar upon its face. "This ring will be the surety for the chest."

6

"You can trust this Ban?"

"I can. He should be king but there are others who plot and scheme. He was sent here by his uncle who is king. Ban's cousins are ambitious and warlike." He shrugged, "I told him to leave the Romans well alone. They are like a dog which is sleeping. So long as he sleeps then do not poke him with a stick. I told Ban that the Romans will not move north for a while. Queen Cartimandua is their ally and they have no need to enlarge their Empire. They tax the Brigante and give them protection." He looked earnestly at the young noble. "What do you say?"

"I promise that I will do all in my power to protect your children."

Prasutagus stood and clasped Lucullus' forearm in the Roman style. He nodded and smiled for the first time. "My heart is easier now and I am grateful to you."

As Lucullus rode back to his estates he could not foresee the firestorm which would sweep the land of the Iceni and Londinium. He could not know that his promise would be one he could not keep as Boudicca and her daughters would perish in the slaughter of the Boudiccan revolt.

Chapter 1

Britannia 127 A.D.

This was the fourth time that Briac, chief of the Brigante, had ventured to Manavia to consult with the followers of the Mother Cult. The first time was a few years earlier when he had fled the wrath of the Romans who were seeking him after an abortive revolt. He had been both desperate and alone. He had also been fearful. The Druids who were the leaders of the cult were ruthless. Human sacrifice was still a feature of their religion. Fortunately for him, he had been accepted and welcomed. He knew that most of the Druids disapproved of him but the unofficial Queen of the island, Caronwyn, appeared to take a special interest in him. He could not see that he was being used as a tool to further her ends. She was waging war against the Roman culture. This was a religious war as far as she was concerned. The personal element was that her mother and sister had both died at the hands of a Roman and her grandmother had been crucified. She burned with hate.

She was a striking woman with flaming red hair but it was her eyes which terrified Briac. They were bright green and seemed to bore inside a man and his head so that she appeared to know his very thoughts. If she became an enemy then all hope would be gone. She was, at present, his friend. She had persuaded the council of priests that they should invest time in fermenting the struggle against Rome. As the granddaughter of Fainch, the witch who had killed Queen Cartimandua and the daughter of Morwenna who had so nearly ended Roman rule north of Eboracum, she had many who had faith in her.

Briac had been given money and contacts to take back to the land of the Brigante where he gradually formed alliances with other like-minded leaders. Through Venutius he held sway with the Carvetii. With two tribes on his side, he had visited with the Novontae and Selgovae. Unlike the Carvetii they were not committed but he had not been rejected out of hand. Caronwyn had been forceful about the need to be subtle. He had ordered his warriors to cooperate with the Roman invaders and to pretend to be defeated. The difficulties he had encountered could be measured in the men he had had to kill. As a hunted man his life had been difficult but now he spied a sort of hope.

As he stepped ashore, flanked by his oathsworn, he was greeted by Caronwyn's handmaidens. They were taken to the hall that Caronwyn had built in the shelter of the mountain. It faced the land of the Brigante for, as she told Briac, it was ever in her heart. Briac had heard how her mother had been killed by her son, a Roman and Caronwyn's half-brother. It seemed bizarre to Briac but he did not dare to question it. The Roman warrior was dead but hatred still burned in the heart of the priestess.

As they approached the hall Briac's hand went to his sword. There were Romans waiting outside. They were not soldiers, their dress was not uniform, but their hair and their weapons marked them as legionaries.

"Fear not, Chief Briac, they are friends. Sheathe your weapons."

The ex-legionaries glowered at the tribesmen. There was no love lost there. Briac was curious as well as slightly annoyed. They were trying to rid the land of Romans what was Caronwyn doing bringing them here?

He turned to his oathsworn. "Stay here and cause no trouble."

Maughan shook his head, "But they are Romans!"

Briac saw that the Romans did not react. They had not understood Maughan. "This is not our land and we are guests. Do not dishonour me." The deferential nod told Briac that his wishes would be obeyed.

The hall had no external light but terracotta bowls burned scented oils. Caronwyn regarded herself as a queen. It was a delusion inherited from her mother. As a result, she surrounded herself with regal accoutrements. She had had a small dais built within the hall and she draped herself upon a carved throne. There were just two servants within. Briac had been there enough times to know that the curtain behind the throne hid her sleeping quarters. As he abased himself and then approached the witch queen, Briac idly wondered what was to stop a Roman killer from entering her hall and ending her life. He shuddered at the thought. Not the thought itself but the fact that Caronwyn might be able to read it!

"You are welcome in my home, Chief Briac. Sit at my feet and tell me how our plans progress." Caronwyn had been taught well by her

9

mother. She knew how to control men. By placing him at her feet she was showing her superiority and her dominance over him.

He did as he was told and spoke respectfully to this woman who was a legend to the people for her passionate desire to overthrow the Romans. She and her family had fought the Romans since before the time of Cartimandua and Venutius. They were the only hope remaining to Briac and the Brigante. "We have done all that you suggested. We have smiled at the oppressors and ensured that no Roman is harmed in our lands. The Roman legion is now busy building their wall and they have only left a few auxiliaries to guard the bridges." He looked up expectantly, like a puppy which anticipates a treat. "Should we attack soon?"

She smiled but it was a cold smile which chilled Briac's blood. "No, Briac. You attacked too early the last time and it caused you to lose many warriors." Her eyes bored into him. "It is your young warriors who wish to be bloodied, is it not?"

He started. She was reading his thoughts. "It is true that they are ready for war."

"Or they think that they are ready for war. The truth is that your weapons are poor and your men have had no chance to try their skills against the Romans." Briac nodded. "I have some help for you then." She clapped her hands and two figures emerged from behind the curtain. Briac jumped to his feet for one was a Roman; at least he looked so from his severe haircut, complexion and the gladius which hung from his waist. He looked just like the ones he had seen outside the hall.

Caronwyn laughed, "Fear not, Chief Briac, this is no trap. These are two people who will help us. This is Severus Catullus, former Optio in the Ninth Hispana and this is Flavia Gemellus who is descended from Old King Cunobelinus. As you are descended from King Venutius you have much in common."

Briac was far too unsophisticated to see the machinations of the witch of Manavia. Flavia, in contrast, was not only fully aware of Caronwyn's plan, but she was also party to it. She smiled sweetly and held a perfumed hand out for Briac to kiss. Severus hid his smile as the awkward warrior rubbed his dirty hand on his tunic before putting the delicate hand proffered to his lips.

"Sit, Prince Briac." The unearned title was carefully chosen to flatter Briac whom the two women needed if their plan was to succeed.

Caronwyn waved away the last two servants who remained. "Flavia here is willing to provide weapons for your warriors and Severus will train and lead them for you."

Briac's eyes narrowed, "Why should I let a Roman deserter lead my warriors?"

Severus snorted, "Perhaps because your warriors have a habit of dying when led by your leaders."

Before Briac could react Caronwyn's voice rang out, "He is right, Briac, but Severus be careful of your tone. There are three of us in this room who are from this island. You insult one of us and you insult us all."

Severus knew he had to obey the two women. One frightened him and the other paid him. He bowed. "I apologise."

Briac nodded, honour satisfied by the apology. "How will you get the weapons to us? The Romans control the entire roads in my land."

Flavia spoke, "True but my ships come to Eboracum with many goods. They are the luxuries the Romans want. My vessels can smuggle your weapons into the heart of your lands."

"Now do you see why I want the land of the Brigante to be peaceful? The Romans need to be lulled by the docile Brigante. Fear not, Briac, this will not take long. By next spring your warriors will be well-armed and Severus will have taught you and your leaders how to defeat the Romans and then we will strike."

Briac was impressed. This was far better organised than he would have expected. "What kind of weapons can you get for us?"

Flavia smiled and, for the first time, Briac seemed to see how attractive she was. She reached out and touched his rough hand with her smooth and perfumed white one. "Whatever weapons you wish then you shall have them."

"My men do not like the gladius the Romans use. Can you acquire longer swords for us?"

Roman Wall

Flavia deferred to Severus who had adopted a more neutral face. "We can get you the spatha used by the cavalry. I personally think it is a little long to be used by men on foot."

Briac smiled. "We like a longer sword. We can manage the weapon. Axes and spears would be useful if you could get them for us."

Severus smiled, "We can get those." He hesitated, "Armour and mail shirts?" He knew that the Brigante liked to fight half-naked as a sign of their manhood. Severus could never understand it himself.

"My men do not like such weapons."

Caronwyn spoke for she had been listening carefully. "Perhaps you and your leaders could wear it. This might encourage others to adopt the style. We would not want you killed through a chance blow. I have seen too many brave warriors die to a wound which could have been prevented by mail."

Briac was convinced, "For my leaders then." The three seemed relieved at that.

Severus stood. "My lady I will go to see to my men." He looked at Briac. "I will have to travel south to secure your weapons. I will meet you in a month. Where will that be?"

Briac did not yet trust this Roman and he did not want him to come to the secret places he and his men used. "If you reach Eboracum then you can travel to the fort of Stanwyck."

"I remember it," he grinned. "I helped to destroy it."

Caronwyn flashed him an irritated look while Briac reddened at the humiliation heaped on his people by the Ninth legion. Caronwyn waved a dismissive hand. "Then go and take your tongue with you!"

He did not seem discomfited by the censure. After he had gone Caronwyn asked, "What is his story, sister?"

Flavia settled herself into the chair. "He was an optio in the Ninth. He beat a prisoner to death."

Briac looked up in surprise. "And for that, he was punished?"

Flavia smiled and shook her head, "Not really. The prisoner was about to divulge some information and so he was demoted and had to rejoin the ranks. He had been, shall we say, a little harsh with his century and he killed one of the legionaries who tried to exact revenge. He fled

12

the legion just before they sailed for Germania and I found him hiding in Londinium. I discovered he has many skills. He is useful and he is grateful to me." She turned to Caronwyn. "He bears no love for Rome. He feels he was betrayed. He will serve you well, Briac, and he might just make the difference when fighting the Romans."

Caronwyn clapped her hands three times and, almost within moments, a servant appeared with a jug of wine and three goblets. Briac was not used to such things; he would have preferred beer but he joined the two women. In truth, he was a little overawed by the two of them. In his village, the women were subservient to the men but these two seemed to be almost superior beings. Caronwyn was a witch and to be feared but this Flavia appeared to be such a controlled and powerful woman too.

He became aware that they were both studying him and he was uncomfortable with the attention. They seemed to be hunters assessing whether to make a kill to not. This was not the world of Briac but he knew he had to endure it. This might be his only chance to gain the throne of the Brigante. He knew that he had more of a claim to the throne of the Carvetii through Venutius, his grandfather, but there was little chance of power there; the Romans had the land of the Carvetii under tight control. He would have to trust his new allies and take the chances when they came.

"How many men do you have Briac?"

"I can field two thousand warriors, Lady Flavia."

"And how many of those can you depend upon?"

"All of them!" Briac bridled a little at the veiled insult.

Caronwyn laughed, "Let us have honesty. How many of those two thousand would stand against a Roman cohort?"

He did not answer for he knew that a cohort, let alone a legion, would walk through his men.

Flavia reached over and touched his hand once more. "Caronwyn does not mean to demean or belittle your men but it is a point well made. You need allies as well as weapons. We need success first to draw in other tribes like the Votadini and the Parisi. Too many of them now realise that they have made a bad bargain with the Romans but we need success."

Now that the Roman had gone Briac felt, strangely, more comfortable talking about his plans. "If the legions are not on the wall then we can attack and defeat the Tungrians and Batavians who guard the forts but their cavalry, Marcus' Horse, they are to be feared. Their leader wields the Sword of Cartimandua and that is worth a thousand men in battle."

He suddenly noticed that Flavia's eyes narrowed and anger raced across her face. "I will pay a bonus of a hundred gold pieces for the warrior who kills the leader who wields the sword."

Briac was taken aback by such passion. "It is said that he is of Brigante stock."

"I care not if he is descended from the Emperor of Rome I will pay handsomely for his head."

Caronwyn reached over to put her arm around Flavia. There are many ways to kill a man that do not involve battle. Let us use our minds sister. And, Briac, the trick with cavalry is to use the land to help you. The Mother does not like the Roman presence. The land of the Brigante has many places where you can ambush and slaughter the Romans. You do not need a pitched battle. Lure them close and use the land and your numbers to kill them. Whittle them down little by little. The sea does not destroy a cliff in one night; it takes years. Be patient."

Chapter 2

Decurion Marcus Gaius Aurelius reined in his mount. He sensed danger ahead. He looked up in the sky to see if the hawk was there. It was not. The spirit of his stepbrother sometimes hovered close by when there was danger but the air was free from birds of any type. That, in itself, was a good thing. They would not, as they had last week, come across the bodies of ambushed Roman soldiers. The land to the south of the wall was strangely peaceful but here, in the land of the Selgovae, there were still murderous attacks. The heads of the soldiers, their arms and their armour were always taken by the attackers but the bodies could always be recognised as Roman. The caligae were a clear mark. He sniffed the air. Drugi and Felix, the two scouts they used in the Dunum, were always able to smell an enemy. If the wind was right then Marcus could too. He detected nothing.

I held up his hand and waved it forward. Gnaeus, his Chosen Man, trotted forward. "Send Titus to the right with Decius and the buccina; have them come around to the north of us. I want them to meet us just beyond the trees ahead." He pointed to a stand of trees a mile or so in the distance.

"Something ahead, sir?"

"Let us say I have an itch which I can't scratch."

Gnaeus laughed, "Then there will be danger ahead." He turned and rode down the line. "Weapons at the ready lads, the decurion has an itch."

Marcus heard the sound of spatha being loosened in sheaths. He continued to stare ahead at the woods in the distance. The road they travelled would pass close by to the trees and it would be a good place for an ambush. The IX had built this road and the VIth maintained it but since the wall had been built it was patrolled less often. There had been a time when the auxiliaries would have had a daily patrol to the isolated forts which guarded it. This was the first such patrol in a week. Most of the outlying forts had been dismantled and abandoned. All the efforts of the ala were aimed at protecting those who were finishing off the wall.

Once the wall was completed then Marcus hoped they would finally subjugate this wild land.

He heard the hooves of the two troopers as they headed across the turf to the north. He kicked into Raven's ribs and the horse began to trot forward. Mindful of Gnaeus' instructions to the rest Marcus slid the Celtic sword, the Sword of Cartimandua, from its sheath. Its familiar hilt reassured him and he felt, oddly, better. He laid it across his saddle and put his left hand through the straps on his shield.

The land dipped a little which afforded him a better view and he saw that the dry valley to the west of the road fell away steeply. He frowned. Whoever had built this road had not followed the instructions of the legate. The road should have been built further east and away from such danger. Marcus felt guilty for his thoughts. The road had been first built in the time of Agricola and had been laid under fierce opposition. They were trying to get north as quickly as they could to destroy the Caledonii and Pictii. He would have to use his mind and experience to outwit the Selgovae.

It was the lack of animals and birds which confirmed his suspicions of danger. There should be a host of birds ahead. At this time of year, they were busily feeding for the shorter days ahead. There were none. Raven's ears pricked. There was danger ahead.

"Stand to!"

He reached down and lifted his shield. H moved his sword down to his side. Without looking he knew that the rest of the turma were all doing the same. With the shield protecting his left side he lifted his sword and waved the troop forward. As they trotted along the road he stared intently at the dry valley. There were bushes and scrubby windblown trees. Any and all of them could hide warriors. He sensed that the attack would come from that direction.

Perhaps one of the Selgovae was nervous or excited, or both. Whatever the reason Marcus saw the movement in the elder bush closest to the road. "Lines of eight!"

Seven troopers trotted their horses next to Raven. Without looking Marcus knew that Gnaeus would have done the same behind. There would be three lines of eight and a reserve of six.

The first javelin was hurled at Marcus. He had already lifted his shield and the sturdy, well-made shield easily deflected it away. Their cover blown, the Selgovae roared from their places of concealment and charged the troopers. It was their first mistake. There were many of them and they were spread out. The eager and fitter ones began to outstrip the others.

"Charge!"

While the rest of the first line hurled their javelins, Marcus held his sword before him. He calmly counted the half-naked, tattooed warriors. There were over fifty, probably sixty of them. They held a variety of weapons from swords and axes to spears. Only one or two had shields although Marcus noticed that one of them was a Roman cavalry shield. The seven javelins took out four warriors. One young warrior with his hair limed and spiked charged Marcus screaming his war cry. He held a long axe above his head and he began to swing it. Using his knees Marcus changed Raven's direction slightly. The axe head began to slice towards Marcus' unprotected right side. Pulling his sword across his body Marcus swept it towards the axe head. The warrior looked in amazement as the razor-sharp blade chopped the shaft in two. As Lucius' javelin was thrust into his throat he died with that same look of amazement etched forever on his tattooed face.

The horses of the turma were well-trained animals of war and they did not flinch as the warriors swung and sliced with their weapons. The troopers' javelins easily despatched the Selgovae. They were used more as spears now. The length of the javelins and the height of the horses gave every trooper a distinct advantage. Marcus felt a hand trying to wrench his reins around. He lifted the shield and chopped it down on to the skull of the warrior. The thin metal rim split the unprotected head into a bloody mess and he fell to the ground.

To his right Marcus heard the sound of the buccina. The Selgovae looked in horror. They were in danger of being outflanked. They did not know it was just two troopers. They were indecisive and that was their second mistake. The turma had now enlarged the front so that there were sixteen troopers who were racing towards the Selgovae. A chief tried to rally the demoralised barbarians. His torc marked him as a leader and he hefted the captured Roman cavalry shield and spatha. Urging Raven

towards him Marcus drew back the Sword of Cartimandua. The chief
saw him and he pulled his own shield around for protection. His problem
was that he was static whilst Marcus could go left or right. The decurion
feinted left, towards the spatha and then whipped the reins to the right.
Swinging overhand the mighty sword smashed into the shield. Roman
cavalry shields were well made but the blow was so hard that the chief's
arm was damaged by the strike. Marcus saw the pain on his face.
Savagely turning Raven to the left Marcus stabbed at the neck of the
chief. It was not a clean blow but the edge sliced across his shoulder. The
wound opened like a ripe plum. Jerking Raven to a halt Marcus lifted the
sword and swung it across the neck of the chief. His head leapt from the
body, which seemed to stand unsupported before it fell to the ground.

All resistance ended and the Selgovae fled down the dry valley.
Marcus shouted. "I want prisoners!" His men began to pursue the
Selgovae. He slung his shield on his saddle and patted Raven. "Good
boy!"

He dismounted. He noticed a warrior bleeding to death on the ground
close to the chief. The javelin was in his stomach. Marcus took the
Sword of Cartimandua and, as he ended the warrior's pain, spoke to him
in his own language. "Go to the Allfather."

Sheathing his sword, he examined the shield. As he had expected it
was marked on the back with the former owner's name and turma. It had
been a Thracian trooper's. Marcus remembered a report the previous year
about two turmae which had disappeared north of the wall. It had
probably been an ambush such as this one. Perhaps the Selgovae had
been emboldened by their success and they had tried it again. The
Thracians were new to life on the frontier. It was in the blood of every
trooper in Marcus' Horse.

He looked up as Titus and Decius rode up. "It looks like we missed
the fun, sir."

"Well done, Titus. They thought you were another turma coming to
our rescue. Check the bodies and take anything of value." He handed the
shield to Decius. "We'll take this back too."

Gnaeus led the rest of the turma up the dry valley. There were ten
Selgovae warriors tethered from the horses of ten troopers. The ten

looked defiant but there were men back at Cilurnum who were past masters at extracting information from prisoners. Marcus did not approve but it yielded results and saved Roman lives. He was half Brigante and understood the desire for freedom which was in the heart of every barbarian. He was a Roman officer first and last; he would do his duty.

"Right boys let's get back." He glanced around and saw no empty saddles. There were wounds in evidence but no dead troopers. With twenty dead Selgovae and ten prisoners, it had been a good day's work and Marcus was content.

Prefect Livius was vaguely disturbed. The tribes both north and south of the wall had been quiet of late. That was never a good sign. They did not accept the Roman imposition of order nor did they approve of the buildings the Romans erected. To them, it was an abomination. It destroyed the Mother that was their Earth. They would fight until there were no men left to fight. They were up to something. He had his turma out each day and they were given clear instructions to report back any sign that the tribes were planning something. So far they had not seen anything of merit. That did not mean that the tribes were subservient. He knew that revolt was being fermented just below the surface.

As he headed towards Coriosopitum, the largest fort north of Eboracum, and a meeting with the Legate, Julius Demetrius, he wondered if they would ever succeed in conquering the land north of the wall. He had met the Emperor and knew that the wall was just a stage in the advancement of the Empire. It allowed the clerks to collect taxes and stopped both slave and cattle raids. It had cost many lives already and it was still unfinished. When the eastern wars were over they would move north again.

"Ah, Livius, is the northern patrol back yet?"

Livius shook his head. "No sir. But it is young Marcus so I am not worried." He had sensed some anxiety in the Legate's voice. "Is anything wrong, sir?"

"No, but since we lost those Thracians last year I have been keeping a check on patrols and there seems to be a pattern to all this. They have stopped attacking anything larger than a turma or a half-century."

19

"We have been sending out single turmae and none have been attacked."

Julius smiled. "Your Ala is Marcus' Horse. They still have a reputation. The trouble is that when we send out a century or two turmae it restricts us. We have too few men to patrol a larger area. I want to know what they are up to. The land to the south of the wall has been quiet and north feels to me as though something is brewing."

The legate waved to a seat and Livius sat. "I agree. I have a nagging feeling at the back of my neck too. What about the other Prefects? Have they anything to report?"

"The trouble is that they are happy that they are not losing any men. The wall, to them, means security."

Livius snorted. "We both know, sir, it is not. Forts like this one and Vercovicium are the only defence we have. And, of course, the VIth." The VIth Legion was putting the finishing touches to the wall and its defences. They were a powerful force and more than a match for any barbarian army.

"And it seems likely that they will be pulled back to Eboracum soon or perhaps withdrawn to Germania."

"Surely not, sir. That would just leave three legions for the whole of Britannia."

"The feeling is that Britannia is now conquered and can be controlled by the auxilia. That was always the view of Agricola you know."

"I know but there are still too many armed warriors for my liking." He decided to bring up an idea which he had had in his head for some time. "Sir, I would like to arm the troopers with a long spear. The javelins are fine but once you have thrown them then the barbarians can throw them back. They have begun to lie on the ground when we charge. They know our horses won't stand on them and we have no weapons long enough to reach them when we have discharged our javelins."

"Good idea. Put in a requisition and I will get them for you. How are the new helmets working out?"

The ala had been recently sent the newer helmets with a small metal peak. It afforded more protection from blows to the head and was a better helmet in every way. Livius had been unhappy that the rest of the auxilia in Britannia had had the improved helmets for ten years while they had had to wait for them. "They are good sir. I just wish we had had them sooner."

"I know. Come on, let's go and watch for your patrol." He chuckled. "When I was Prefect I was always desperate to be either with my men or else I was waiting, anxiously, for them to return."

"And I am the same, sir."

As they approached the northern gate, they saw the Decurion Princeps, Metellus, already watching the road to the north. The Batavian sentries were giving him enough space to pace up and down. Metellus was not a man to cross.

He saluted as they approached. "Any sign of our patrol yet?"

"No sir, but Marcus was going as far north as he could." He smiled ruefully, "He is worried that we are not keeping a close enough watch on the Selgovae."

Livius rubbed his chin. "I think he is trying to be two men, himself and Macro. He works twice as hard as any other officer; me included."

"I know. I thought becoming a father would have settled him."

"No sir. Duty is more important to Marcus than anything. If you sliced into him you would see Marcus' Horse running through his veins. Besides, Drugi and Felix more than make up for him in his absence. They are like a grandfather and a big brother. Those boys could not have better protectors and teachers."

One of the sentries shouted, "Patrol approaching, sir."

The three of them all breathed a collective sigh of relief when the thirty-two troopers hove into view. The fact that there were prisoners was a bonus. "Well, let us go and greet the successful decurion."

Marcus dismounted and led his turma on foot through the gate. It was part of his regime and it helped the horses to cool down quicker. When his troop saw the three senior officers they stiffened to attention.

"Gnaeus, take the prisoners to the cells and then see to the horses."

"Sir." Gnaeus took Raven's reins.

As Decius passed Marcus took the Thracian shield and proffered it to the Prefect. "We took this from a dead Selgovae. It is from the Thracians who disappeared."

21

Julius nodded. "It seems they are bold enough to attack Marcus' Horse now. How many were there?"

"About sixty sir. It was a good ambush but we managed to avoid walking into it."

Livius shook his head, "Do not disparage yourself; it means that another turma might be headless corpses and the Selgovae might be celebrating their success."

As they strolled through the fort towards the bathhouse by the river Julius asked. "Prefect, do you wish to double the numbers of your patrols?"

"No sir. This will put my men on their mettle."

"Sir, if we had scouts like Felix with us then this sort of thing might be avoided."

"Are you sure that you wish him to rejoin us? I thought he was looking after your boys."

"Drugi can manage that."

"Then send for him." Livius looked at Metellus. "I daresay you will be sending another missive to your wife soon. It can go with that letter."

Metellus nodded. Communication with their homes was vital but sometimes messages went astray and the messengers' bodies were a savage reminder that even the land south of the wall could be dangerous. "It might be useful sir, for someone to return to the valley and find out what the Brigante are up to. They have been remarkably quiet."

"I know. Are you suggesting yourself or Marcus for that? I know that your families would appreciate it."

"No sir. Marcus and I are needed here and it needs someone who is not as well known. I was thinking of Rufius."

Rufius had been an Explorate along with Metellus. He was a superb tracker and had the ability to blend into a settlement and be unseen. "A good choice. Brief him and write your letters. Autumn will be here soon and I would like to be prepared. This will be our first winter with a finished wall. I cannot believe that the Selgovae will let us enjoy peace."

"Surely the presence of the VIth will deter them sir."

Roman Wall

"I have just heard from the legate, Metellus, that they are to be withdrawn to Eboracum for the winter. It will be just us, the Tungrians and the Batavians."

Chapter 3

Rufius' hopes of a speedy journey south were thwarted when the legate decided that Julius Longinus, the ala clerk, and Titus Posthumous, the Quartermaster should go to Eboracum and arrange for the shipment of spears and other urgently needed supplies. Metellus' Chosen Man, Gaius Paulus, led the half turma escort. Rufius knew he could be at Marcus' home within four or five hours if he travelled alone but they were forced to travel at the speed of the wagon. They would take all day to reach Morbium and the crossing of the Dunum. Rufius was anxious to reach the farm as soon as possible. He would be going into the Brigante heartland and he needed to establish himself for his journey undercover.

Julius Longinus was just unhappy about the journey itself. "At my age, I should not have to endure the privations of the roads; no matter how well built."

The Legate had been insistent and Rufius suspected that Julius would be doing some secret work for the Legate whilst in Eboracum. Julius Longinus was a very astute man who could not only read, he could read people too. Not all of the Roman officials in Eboracum had the best interests of the Province at heart.

Looking on the positive side Rufius realised that the delay would allow his beard to grow a little more. Although many Brigante now affected the clean-shaven look of the Roman army far more wore a beard. Rufius would just need a few days to acquire enough growth to pass unnoticed amongst the Brigante.

It felt strange to be back in the guise of an Explorate again. He did not wear the armour and uniform of a cavalryman; instead, he wore breeches, a tunic and a cloak. The sword at his waist was not the standard-issue; he had acquired it during his travels in Gaul. It was the attention to details such as that which sometimes made the difference between survival and discovery.

He rode next to Chosen Man Gaius. He had served with him and liked the young warrior. He had a background like Rufius. He had joined in

Britannia. He was an Atrebate but, like Rufius, he was now Roman
through and through.

"Decurion Atrebeus, I do not know why we need a sixteen-man
escort. These lands have been quiet for many years."

Although Rufius secretly agreed with Gaius he was an officer and he
put forward the argument Livius had used with him. "The tribes may not
be in revolt but there are still bandits and deserters who would seize the
opportunity to steal the horses and the wagon if we had a smaller escort."

"Perhaps but they would have to be desperate bandits to take on
Marcus' Horse."

"They attacked Decurion Aurelius the other day and he had a full
turma."

Gaius dismissed that argument. "They were Selgovae and they are all
as mad as a fish! The Brigante are a cowed people. I will bet you ten
sestertii that the only trouble we will have will be old Julius moaning."

Rufius laughed. Julius' was known as a grumpy old man; well-liked
but irascible. "You are on."

The southern road from the wall was well maintained. Just five miles
from the fort they passed a working party of Tungrians who were cutting
back the new growth of trees which had sprung up over the last year. The
reassuring wave from the optio made them all feel happier. It was a
tedious journey for the cavalrymen who normally travelled at least three
times faster than the slow wagon.

They halted for food and to rest the horses at the hill surrounded by
the Vedra Fluvius. It was still just a wooden bridge which spanned the
fast-flowing river and Rufius wondered how long it would be before it
was made a more solid and permanent structure. Julius Longinus showed
his knowledge and military acumen when he identified the features
which would make this a good site for a fort.

Gaius asked, "Why is there not one here already?"

"That was General Agricola's decision. He destroyed the tribes
around here so swiftly and was so keen to come to grips with the Picts
that he did not bother. And he built Vinovia; that eliminated the need for
a fort here. Now that we have the wall it is unnecessary. Still, it would be
an impregnable fort."

Rufius smiled at the old man's mind. Rufius had passed by this site for many years and had not even dreamed that it might be used as a fort. Now that it was explained Rufius began to question why it had not been made into one. As he mounted his horse to continue the journey he answered himself; the land of the Brigante was at peace.

The bandits under Carac hid in the woods which lined the hated Roman roads. The roads were an affront to the gods and to the Mother Earth herself. They did not call themselves bandits. They thought that they were fighting for the freedom of their land. In their minds they were heroes. They were a band of Brigante who had refused to follow the orders of Chief Briac. They would not bow to the will of a man who was not pure Brigante. His father had been half Carvetii. Carac had been disappointed when just thirty of the warriors followed him. Perhaps if he had left flagrantly and blatantly under the eyes of Briac there might have been more. That might have been seen as a challenge but Carac, and those who followed him, left in the dead of night. The ones who remained felt that there was no honour in this.

It had been some months since they had left the village and their pickings had been slim. They had waylaid a few solitary wagons and riders but the Romans who had patrolled this road had been too numerous to attack. His men, he knew were restless. This was not the glorious revolt they had anticipated. They had dreamed of fighting hand to hand with the Romans and defeating them. He worried that soon they would drift back to their villages and he would be left alone.

Now Carac spied a kind of hope. His youngest warrior had been scouting to the north and he had seen the wagon with the handful of horses guarding it. The swiftly moving scout had taken a short cut through the forest to reach their camp. Carac was animated as he spoke with his men. For the first time, they outnumbered the Romans.

"Today, my brothers, we have a chance to rid the land of some Romans. They are coming down this road and we will attack them and destroy them here."

One of the older warriors, Scanlan, was sceptical. He was already thinking of returning to their village. "These are horsemen, Carac. What if they are Marcus' Horse?"

Carac frowned in irritation. The name of the horsemen always inspired fear in the hearts of Brigante. They feared the wrath of the sword. He waved a dismissive hand. "It matters not. We outnumber them by two to one. We will have surprise on our side. Scanlan, take half of the men and go to the other side of the road. When we attack and their attention is upon us then you can fall on their unguarded backs. It will be a slaughter."

If Carac intended the task as an insult it did not work. Scanlan spat on the forest floor and picked up his shield. Unlike some of the others he knew the value of a shield and a good sword. He had fought the Romans before. He pointed to the warriors he wanted and they loped off across the road. He shook his head in disgust. None of these had shields and the weapons they held were of poor quality. He hoped the Romans who were approaching were equally poorly equipped.

Rufius was not complacent as they reached the marker which told them that it was a mere ten miles from Morbium. He had operated behind enemy lines too many times for that. He knew the potential of an inattentive warrior. They might be close to a bed for the night but that didn't mean they could relax. Gaius was a good leader but he was not the tracker that was Rufius and so when Rufius turned and said quietly, "Ambush ahead!" He was surprised.

"How do you know?"

Gesturing with his head Rufius said, "Forty paces up the undergrowth on both sides of the road has been moved and the vegetation trampled. It has not moved back yet and so it is recent. I will go to the left." He turned his horse and said to Julius and the Quartermaster, "Ambush ahead, prepare yourselves. Whatever happens, driver, you keep moving."

"Sir!"

Everyone, the Quartermaster included, respected Rufius and no-one questioned his word. Acutely aware that whoever was waiting was now but thirty paces along the road, Rufius wheeled his horse around and drew his spatha. "Troopers on the left with me. The rest on Chosen Man."

Once again the troopers obeyed instantly. They hefted their javelins and watched to the left.

Carac was neither an experienced leader nor a warrior. He did not notice that the soldiers looked prepared and were alert. He thought that they had remained hidden. When the wagon drew level, he led his warriors forward screaming their war cry which he knew would instil fear into the Romans. Of course, he did not take into account that the tree line had been cut back to thirty paces from the ditch at the edge of the road. Neither did he anticipate that the auxiliaries would be ready for him. Gaius and his troopers wheeled as one and hurled their first javelins as soon as the barbarians left the woods. Even as three men fell to the ground another eight javelins followed. Not waiting to see the effect Gaius and his men used their last javelins as lances and charged the surprised Brigante. Carac was speared by Gaius himself. The javelin struck his unprotected middle. Gaius twisted and pulled it out. Carac's dreams of glory ended, along with the lives of his fellow warriors.

Scanlan son of Osric the brave was more cautious and experienced than Carac. He saw the troopers turn to face the woods and knew that they were expected. He had chosen the three men with bows. "Aim for the horses. You men with the spears make a hedgehog." The three arrows sped towards the Romans. Two of the arrows were taken on the Roman shields but one horse was struck in the rump. It reared and screamed its pain. The trooper jerked on the reins so that it turned away from the threat and, more importantly, did not frighten the other horses.

Rufius leaned forward over his horse's neck. He charged for the archers. Even as they prepared to loose a second Rufius' horse thundered towards them. He chopped down on the closest warrior, the long spatha almost severing the man's neck. Behind him two other troopers despatched the other two. Had the spearman stood they might have had a chance but the sight of three of their comrades lying dead and the javelins of the others hurling towards them showed them that their element of surprise had evaporated like morning mist.

28

Roman Wall

When Gaius and his troopers appeared, Scanlan knew that the attack
had failed. He would return to Briac. Pausing only to throw his spear at
the trooper who charged him he turned and disappeared into the woods.
The trooper pulled up his shield to take the spear. It cracked into the
wood and he shook it free. When the young trooper looked for the
warrior he saw only trees. He wheeled instead to despatch the warrior
fleeing Rufius. It was all over within a short time. The only survivor,
Scanlan, hid in a dell and watched as the Romans eased the pain of the
dying and collected the weapons. He idly wondered why they did that.
Their weapons were patently better. He suspected it was to deny the
Brigante weapons of any type. When the wagon and its escort moved
south Scanlan stood and headed slowly west. He would face Briac and
whatever punishment was coming his way. When he passed Carac he
noticed the surprised look on the reckless warrior's face. Scanlan had
made a mistake but he was a man and would own up to it.

The prefect at the fort was not surprised by their encounter. "We
suspected there was a band operating and we sent regular patrols along
the road but they saw no signs."

"Well they are all dead now. They were Brigante."

"That surprises me, Decurion. They have been as good as gold around
here. We have a good relationship with them. Of course, we put that
down to the family of Decurion Aurelius. They live close enough for us
to benefit from their friendship."

Rufius nodded, "Well Gaius, I will leave you here and go to the farm.
I doubt that you will have any trouble further south." He pointed to the
trooper whose horse had been wounded. "If you call at the farm of
Decurion Princeps Metellus, his wife will let you have a replacement.
She is good with horses and his mount will benefit."

"Thank you, sir." He reached into his pocket for the money from the
bet.

Rufius laughed and shook his head, "No Chosen Man, I shall not take
your money. You will learn not to make such bets in the future."

Gaius was sorry to see the Explorate leave. He had more skills than
the Chosen Man could dream of.

Roman Wall

Rufius kicked on. He knew the trail to Ailis' farm as well as he knew
the back of his horse's head. He was still alert as he rode down the tree
lined trail. He knew that the farm was the most secure place in the world
apart from a Roman fort. Marcus' father, Gaius Aurelius, had made
strong walls and deep ditches to protect it. Marcus' brother, Decius, now
ran the farm and he maintained the high standards. Marcus' wife, Frann
and his children lived there in safety. Ailis, their mother, had been a
slave and neither of the brothers would countenance owning a slave;
instead they paid men to work their land and to guard their property. All
of Marcus' pay went into the upkeep of the homestead.

The trees were well cut back on the approach to the very Roman gate.
A sentry appeared from behind the gate. Rufius smiled; his approach had
been watched from a distance. He was, of course, recognised and waved
through. Marcus' Horse had been instrumental in saving the farm on
many occasions and he relaxed for he knew he was amongst friends.

A stable boy raced to hold his horse. Rufius noticed the eager look on
the boy's face. He would, no doubt, yearn to be a horseman like Rufius.
It was Ailis herself who came to greet Rufius. The Decurion had no idea
of her age but knew that it had been over thirty years since she had been
rescued. Yet, apart from the grey hair, she still looked as bright and alert
as ever.

She greeted Rufius as though he were her son. "Welcome Decurion.
How is my son?"

"As ever, domina, he is well and sends his love and felicitations." He
turned and went to his saddlebags. "I have letters for you and his lady."

She took them; gratitude written all over her face. She was nothing if
not astute. "But Prefect Livius did not send a decurion all the way here
with just a message, did he?"

Rufius shook his head. Ailis was said to be an acolyte of the Mother
and had second sight. She was certainly sharp for her age. "Can we
talk?"

"Come to my garden."

She linked Rufius' arm and led him through a narrow gate into a
walled garden. It was still filled with late summer flowers. The fruit trees
were laden with apples, pears and plums. There was a carved seat next to

the wall. This was obviously a favoured spot. She smiled as Rufius sat next to her. "I like to come here. It makes me closer to Gaius somehow and dear Uncle Gaelwyn. You can speak openly here for no one can hear."

"I have been tasked by your son with two missions. I am to return north with Felix and Wolf." She nodded. "And, first, I am to find out what is in the hearts of the Brigante. They have been quiet of late."

She frowned briefly and then gripped Rufius' arm tightly. "I believe my son has the second sight as I used to have. There is something brewing amongst the Brigante. Marcus is correct. No-one is speaking of war and yet warriors are practising the art of war. Many young warriors were missing from the villages for most of the summer. I believe they were being initiated."

"It is as we feared."

"Is that enough? Can you return with just the information of an old woman?"

Rufius laughed and kissed her on the top of her head. "You will never be old, domina. But I will have to go into the camps of these Brigante warriors. We need to know more of their plans."

"It is dangerous." She patted his hand and then said, "Take Felix and Wolf. The boy has grown much and reminds me of you when you were first a trooper."

"I had intended to. Where would you suggest I begin?"

"Not at Stanwyck that is for sure. That is visited by the patrols from Morbium and Cataractonium on a regular basis. They are greeted as friends and yet I know that the villagers there loathe the Romans. You were better to head west towards the land above Lavatris."

"We have a fort there also."

"It contains but half a century now and they maintain the road only. The peace has meant that the rest of the garrison was sent further north." She chuckled, "I suspect they have an easy time and they bother no-one. Most of them have been in the province for some time and many are due to retire."

Rufius laughed, "You would make a good frumentari."

She feigned outrage, "You think I am a spy?"

31

"No, domina but you give better intelligence than I could receive in Eboracum." He looked up at the darkening sky. "I had better leave if I am to find Felix."

"You will not stay with us?"

"I mean no disrespect, domina, but I have my duty."

"I understand. Call on the way back but, please, take one of our horses. Yours is clearly Roman. There is no point telling the Brigante who you are."

As she led him to the stables Rufius could not help reflecting on this remarkable woman who had survived slavery amongst the Picts, fought off raiders and rebels and yet was still able to function with such clarity of thought.

Ailis insisted that he use one of their saddles and she took his spatha from him and gave him another. "This was Uncle Gaelwyn's. It is a Brigante blade and it will arouse no suspicion."

"Thank you, domina." He mounted the horse which was really a large pony. "Does Drugi still live by the water?"

She nodded, "He does but they will see you long before you see them. Take care, Rufius and may the Allfather watch over you."

Chapter 4

Drugi had been a slave in the lands far to the west and he had helped to rescue both Marcus and his wife Frann. He was devoted to the family but preferred a lonely existence as a hunter. Rufius had thought himself a good scout and tracker until he met Drugi. The big man could disappear in an instant and was as silent as the night. The decurion knew that as soon as he was within four hundred paces of the house he would be under observation.

The house was where it had always been although Rufius noticed that it had been extended a little. That was probably to accommodate Felix. He reined in and tied his horse to the willow which overhung the stream. As he took the saddle off he heard a slight noise, "You are slipping Drugi; I heard that."

The ex-slave chuckled, "I made the noise so as not to startle you, Roman. I know how nervous Roman soldiers can be when they are in the woods."

Rufius turned and embraced the giant who came from a land far to the east where the winters lasted most of the year. Drugi never changed. His shaven head and face meant that you could not tell his age anyway. He was enormous but had no fat upon him. He was like a beast of the forest.

"Where is Felix?"

"He is hunting. Come inside he will return soon."

The hut was basic. There was a crudely made table and two chairs. The bed was a mattress filled with duck and goose feathers and the walls held an array of weapons. A small fire burned in the middle of the roundhouse and the smoke drifted up through a hole in the middle. Haunches of venison and wild boar were hung from the roof and were gently smoking.

Drugi found a place for the saddle and gestured for Rufius to sit. He took two carved wooden beakers and lifted an amphora. "Let us drink. Felix is too young to appreciate this."

Rufius knew what was coming. It was a potent brew distilled from plum wine made by Drugi. It was a reminder of his home in the east.

Rufius braced himself for the shock of the fiery drink. Drugi downed his in one, smacked his lips and poured himself a second.

"So what brings you here, Decurion?"

Rufius repeated his story and Drugi nodded. "The Lady Ailis is right. They have a camp well to the north of Lavatris close to the roaring waters. They keep good guards there." He shrugged, "If I could be bothered I would have investigated. I think they just play at being warriors." He drained his second beaker. "I can find out what they are up to if you like."

"I appreciate the offer, Drugi but I have been given the mission and I must do it alone."

He chuckled again and the deep rolling noise was somehow reassuring, "Except that you will take the boy and the dog."

Rufius nodded, "I will take the boy and the dog."

There was a growling outside and Rufius heard, "Wolf! Friend."

The door opened and Felix stood there with his sheepdog Wolf. They were inseparable and Wolf was as protective of his owner as any mother. Rufius held out his hand and Wolf sniffed it. Seemingly satisfied it went to the corner and curled up although its golden eyes never left Rufius.

"It is good to see you Decurion. Are the horse warriors returning here?"

"No, Felix. The sword needs you in the north. Will you and Wolf come to aid us?"

He looked at Drugi who nodded, "I will."

"You do not need to do this, Felix. If you wish to stay here with Drugi then we would understand."

Felix was a Brigante orphan and his allegiance was to Drugi, the Sword of Cartimandua and Marcus in that order. "If the sword needs us then we will come."

"But before we return north I would find out what the Brigante are up to. We will leave in the morning for the roaring waters."

"Good." He looked at Drugi. "It was a good hunt; the meat is outside."

Even as Rufius was enjoying the fruits of the hunt Scanlan was scrambling up the path which climbed alongside the waterfall known as Roaring Waters. He had run almost the whole way. His only worry had been when he had crossed the roads but there were no Roman patrols. He remained unseen. He crossed the river by the stepping stones and headed across the trail towards the distant camp. There was no wall around the camp; that would have alerted the Romans. Instead there were crude shelters dotting the flat areas and guards hid and observed all who approached. The spear in his back told Scanlan that he had been seen.

"So you return with your tail between your legs. Where is the whelp Carac?"

"If you do not take that spear from my back you will find yourself growing another apology for your manhood, Aed the Lame." He whipped around and knocked the spear to the ground. The guard was well known to Scanlan. He had been crippled by a Roman gladius and was now fit only for guard duty. "Where is Briac?"

The surly Aed pointed with his arm. "He is over there."

Scanlan followed the line of Aed's arm and saw a huddle of warriors seated on some rocks. He strode off towards them. He frowned as he approached. He could see a Roman with them. What was the wily Briac up to? As he walked across the open ground he could sense the hostility from some of the warriors. Aed the Lame was not alone. Briac's face appeared to be without expression.

He laid down his shield and his sword and dropped to one knee. "I beg your forgiveness, Chief Briac." He looked up into the face of his leader. "I made a mistake and I am here to atone for that error of judgement."

Briac nodded. "It is the mark of a warrior that he can admit when he makes a mistake. You are welcome." He stood and raised his voice. "Scanlan son of Tadgh is welcome here in our camp. Let no man offend him." He smiled at Scanlan. Scanlan, for his part, was studying the Roman who was sharpening his gladius. Briac noticed the attention. "This is someone who will help us to defeat the Romans." Scanlan nodded. "But tell me, Scanlan, where are Carac and the other warriors?"

Roman Wall

A small crowd had gathered. Scanlan stood. This was a tale which needed telling carefully. "Carac decided to attack a wagon on the road to the east. There were just fifteen soldiers guarding it."

The Roman looked interest and spoke for the first time. His Brigante was awkward and halting. "Horse warriors or men on foot?"

"Marcus' Horse."

There was a gasp from the warriors. Briac shook his head. "Carac was reckless but even he should have known better than to take on such warriors. How many died?"

"Carac and the rest."

The Roman spoke again. "And yet you survived."

Scanlan's hand went to the hilt of his sword. Carac and the others were already dead when I left. I did not leave the field of battle whilst any lived." There was a challenge in his voice and the Roman shrugged.

"I mean no disrespect. I have not heard of such a thing before. The horse warriors either kill all or take prisoners."

Briac put his hand out to calm Scanlan. "Scanlan is one of the best warriors we have. Look at the warrior bands on his sword. No man has killed more in single combat than he has."

The Roman nodded. "How did this Carac attack?"

"We hid on each side of the road and he and his men charged the wagons."

"But you did not?"

"I had bowmen and I used them."

"Good." The Roman gestured to Scanlan. "This man shows he has a mind."

Briac smiled. "And how many did our warriors kill?"

The silence hung in the air like a sword about to behead a prisoner. "None. We wounded a couple and a horse but that was all."

Scanlan expected censure but Briac stood and shouted to all who could hear. "Now you see why we need to think like the Romans. It is the only way we will defeat them. That is why the Romans are here. Heed their words and take what they teach." He stepped down from the rock and put his arm around Scanlan. "Your journey and the sacrifice of Carac and his men was not a waste. We can learn from this."

36

Rufius and Felix did not leave the next morning as planned. Drugi was not happy about Felix's appearance. "You still look and smell too Roman." The ex-slave spent most of the morning rubbing plant extracts on Rufius' face, hands and hair. He could not see the effect but Felix told him that he looked more like the Brigante and his beard and hair appeared less Roman. He also smelled less Roman.

It was not until early afternoon that they left. Rufius was not worried. He knew that they could easily reach Roaring Waters in a few hours. His anxiety was fuelled by the fact that there appeared to be something happening and it was occurring in the worst part of the land of the Brigante; in the centre. It had the least roads and the fewest garrisons.

As they headed north-west Rufius began to assess the number of Roman soldiers who might be available. By his count, there were just two centuries guarding the east-west road. A further century was based at Cataractonium. When the legion came south to Eboracum there would be nothing to stop the Brigante from flooding north and attacking the wall from the south. It was, potentially, a disaster. The forces on the wall were thinly spread out.

Felix had spurned the offer of a horse. He had grown somewhat since Rufius had last seen him but he appeared to be able to keep up with the decurion. Wolf ranged far ahead. He would be their early warning of an enemy. They did not speak much as they travelled but when they did it was in Brigante. The sun began to set ahead of them and they heard the roar of the waterfall.

Although Rufius had been travelling for almost two days he knew that they had to strike while the iron was hot. They tied the pony to a tree and, with Wolf ahead of them, began to ascend the narrow path leading to the top of the waterfall. Had Rufius commanded the Brigante he would have had a sentry perched there to watch for spies such as him. As he peered over the top he saw that there was none. They moved forward cautiously. The swiftly flowing Dunum was quite intimidating in the dark. Rufius had been there before and knew that if he went upstream he would find some stepping stones.

Felix had his bow and for that reason Rufius kept his sword sheathed. Felix would be in a better position to notch an arrow and silence an enemy than would Rufius. An excellent archer himself Rufius cursed his decision to leave his bow back at the fort. He could see, in the distance, fires burning. The lack of a wall and stockade did not surprise him but he knew that they would have some defences around. He paused and took in the whole area. Wolf and Felix were as still as the statues in Eboracum. He kept his head in one place as he rested on one knee and used his eyes to scan the camp for sentries. He was patient and his patience was rewarded when the hidden sentry stood and stretched. Having identified one it was child's play to work out where the others would be. He scanned the horizon and spotted them all.

He pointed to a gap. Then he waved for Felix and Wolf to guard his escape. He crept forward. Now that he knew where the sentries were patrolling he could plot and plan his route. It took him over rough ground and he had to carefully place his feet as he did so. It took him some time but soon he was on the edge of the camp. He crouched next to a shelter. There was silence from within; it was empty. He ensured that he did not look at the fires; that would destroy his night vision. He closed his eyes and sniffed the air. The smell of wood smoke could not disguise the familiar smell of horses; there was a herd close by. That in itself was important intelligence; the Brigante had not had large numbers of horses since the time of Venutius. He saw and heard a large number of warriors who were gathered close to a large fire. Taking a deep breath, he stood and began to move through the camp as though he had every right to do so.

Two warriors emerged from a shelter to his right and Rufius froze. He could smell the drink on them. They had been imbibing beer and were the worse for wear. When one of them stumbled and pulled the other to the floor Rufius gambled. He went over to them.

"Watch yourselves." He reached down and offered his arm to one of them. "Here let me help you."

A slightly slurred voice said, "Thank you, brother! Garth here can't hold his drink. Daft bugger pulled me over."

As he helped him up Rufius pointed to the unsheathed dagger stuck carelessly in his belt. "If you had fallen on this then you would have saved the Romans a job."

"Pah! Romans! I spit on them. Here let's get Garth to his feet."

Between them, they pulled the half-drunk warrior to his feet. "Come on, let me help you. Where are you going?"

The warrior pointed a wavering finger at the fire. "Over there. Briac might tell us when we are finally going to slit some Roman throats."

The two of them held the drunken Garth and stumbled their way across. The dark and Garth's hair hid Rufius from curious eyes. They reached the rear of the warriors who were seated by the fire and the three of them slumped down. Rufius played the part of someone who had been imbibing too. Garth's head lolled next to that of Rufius and he fell asleep. It completed the disguise. The warriors in front looked around and snorted their disgust at Garth's condition. The other warrior shrugged apologetically. Rufius kept his head down and listened.

"We know you are right to train us, Chief Briac, but while we are here our lands and animals are not being tended. When do we strike?"

"Your lands could be tended, Morgan, but you would end up paying taxes to the Romans. Better that your lands and animals suffer a little and we rid the land of the Brigante of Romans forever."

Another voice shouted, "We have heard this since before your grandfather led the tribe. Why will this time be any different?"

"Because we will have weapons which are as good as the Romans and we will know the secret of the Roman way of fighting. Be patient. I promise you that by the time of the first lambs the Romans will know that there are Brigante who will fight for their land!"

The fact that he had said a time and the optimistic tone he adopted, made everyone stand and cheer. Poor Garth was allowed to drop to the hard earth when Rufius jumped up and joined in the cheering. His new-found companion grabbed him by the arms. "Briac will make a difference! He will be his grandfather Venutius, reborn. We will finally drive the Romans back to their homes across the sea, brother!"

"This is a glorious day!" Rufius had heard enough and he feigned needing to relieve himself. "Got to pee."

39

His drunken companion waved a hand, "Help yourself!" He promptly fell asleep over the unconscious Garth.

He moved away from the light and headed for the shadows. There was so much noise and pandemonium that he was able to do so easily. When he drew close to the sentries he moved more slowly although they were not hidden from the camp side and were easily spotted. When he reached Felix, he gestured for him to follow. He was exhausted when they reached the bottom of the falls and the horse which was still peacefully grazing.

"We go back now?"

"No, Felix. I want to watch them in daylight and ascertain numbers."

Felix shook his head. "We cannot do it from here. They will see us. We must travel around to the high ground in the north. There is cover there and we cannot be easily approached."

The value of someone with so much local knowledge was invaluable and, tired though he was, Rufius complied. By the time Felix found a vantage point which satisfied him it was but two hours until dawn. The Brigante scout took off the horse's saddle. "I will watch while you sleep. You can relieve me."

Rufius was too tired to argue and was asleep on the hard ground as soon as his head met the turf.

Felix awoke him just after dawn. The young scout yawned and stretched, "They are not awake yet." He pointed to a stone which was covered with fruits. "I picked some berries from the bushes. The water skins are full."

"It is time for you to watch and I will get some sleep."

He nodded, lay down and curled up. Wolf sniffed Rufius and then he too curled up in the small of Felix's stomach. They both appeared to be asleep instantly.

Rufius ate and drank some water. After he had relieved himself he checked on the horse. It appeared content. He bellied up to the rise which overlooked the camp. The spot they had chosen was about a mile from the Brigante camp but, as the sun rose higher and the mist dissipated he could see more. The camp was bigger than he had thought. Briac and the Roman meant business. There was little movement and he could not ascertain true numbers but there appeared to be more shelters than he had seen the previous night. The sound of the horse neighing in the distance alerted him to the position of the herd. He located it and counted as the mist was burned off. There had to be two hundred ponies; that was the largest number of enemy horses Rufius had ever seen.

He slid down and rolled on to his back. He risked observation from the sentries if he remained on the skyline for too long. The Brigante had come here to escape the notice of the two half centuries at the closest forts. Had Drugi and Felix not been aware of the location of the camp then it would have remained hidden. From the Brigante chief's words he knew that the attack would not come until the following year. Rufius knew that he should return to the north and give the legate this information. The VIth could march south and quash this rebellion before it started. The officer in Rufius knew that he had to get as much information as he could. He needed numbers.

He slid to the ridge but moved ten paces to the right so that he was hidden by a solitary gorse bush. He was able to peer beneath it and observe the camp which was now coming awake. He worked methodically and counted from the east. He used a tally stick on which to mark the tens of men he counted. When the numbers milling around made it too hard to see new warriors, he laid it down. He would use it to check numbers later.

He saw the chief he had heard named Briac. A shiver ran down his spine. The man was wearing mail. He looked more carefully and saw another six warriors also had mail. They wore torcs which made then either chiefs or nobles. Now that the light was better he also noticed that there were new spears and swords in evidence. Even worse they looked to be Roman. This was not the normal hotchpotch of weapons the Brigante usually fielded. Then another shiver ran down his spine as a Roman soldier emerged from a shelter. Rufius saw the clean-shaven face and close-cropped hair before the Roman helmet was donned. Another four or five Roman soldiers joined him and they marched towards Briac.

This intelligence was probably the most frightening of all. The marching gait told him that these men were there as Romans. A Roman adviser meant that the Brigante would know how the Romans fought.

Roman Wall

Rufius remembered when Livius' brother had led an army of deserters who had joined the tribes. They had almost defeated the Romans. Had there not been two legions in the north it might have succeeded. Now there were even less Romans in the north. This revolt needed quashing before it grew.

Chapter 5

Rufius allowed Felix to sleep a little longer. He took the opportunity to check his counting. According to his tally stick there were over a thousand men. He wondered if there were other camps and then he looked again at the warriors. Most were of the same age as the two men he had encountered the night before. They were young warriors. These were being trained. The older ones were still on their farms and in their villages. Rufius mentally doubled the figure. Two and a half thousand men could devastate this region. If units were withdrawn from the wall then the Selgovae and Votadini would take the opportunity to flood across. He shook Felix awake. "It is time to go."

They saddled the horse and then headed north to a place they could cross the Dunum away from any of the Brigante. They moved slowly for sudden movement might alert any scouts the Brigante who were seeking them. Rufius doubted that they would; they looked to be preparing for war and their isolation would make them feel safer. The problem they had was that they were travelling across open ground. The source of the Dunum was to the north-west and was not much higher than they were. It meant that there was no place to hide.

The sound of hooves behind them told Rufius that they had been seen. He glanced over his shoulder and saw twenty horsemen on the ponies he had spotted earlier. The Parcae had been cruel. They had brought the horsemen to a place where Rufius could be seen. A shout went up confirming that they had been seen.

"Felix, run, across the river. Get to Drugi. There are over a thousand Brigante with horses!"

"But what of you, Decurion?"

"I am mounted. I will lead them away." Felix and Wolf were hidden by Rufius' mount. Felix nodded and he and Wolf took off with the easy ground eating lope he always used. The river was just half a mile away. He would soon reach it. Rufius jerked his horse's head around. He would head for the stepping stones. It would draw the Brigante towards him.

They would be able to close with him but he would be able to cross the river away from Felix.

"Right boy, let's see how good a horse you are."

He did not make the mistake of looking over his shoulder. You could easily cause your horse to stumble on this treacherous rock-strewn land. He lowered his shoulders so that his head was almost touching his horse's mane. He had learned he went faster riding like this. He concentrated on finding the safest line. He was hoping that the riders behind would not be as experienced and they might make a mistake. He just needed the numbers thinning out. If he could get their numbers down to five or six then he was confident that he could defeat them.

He heard the roaring of the falls in the distance and risked a glance under his arm. The leading riders had gained but he could see that they were now strung out and the two empty saddles told him that a couple of the warriors had not been attentive enough. He began to believe that he might escape. The river loomed up just forty paces away and he headed towards it. To his horror he saw twenty Brigante crossing the very stepping stones he intended to use. They turned and saw him. Their hesitation saved him. His appearance and disguise had worked. They were not certain if he was one of their warriors or not and it allowed Rufius to jerk the head of his horse around and ride parallel to the river. The problem Rufius had was that there was no place to go. He was stranded. He could not cross the river; the horses were behind him and to his right lay the Brigante camp. He was trapped.

The decurion had been well trained. He had been taught not to panic. He had only one alternative and, although it seemed impossible, he would have to try it. He jerked his horse's head around and rode towards the water. He would try to swim across the swiftly moving Dunum. Once on the other side, he had no idea how he would get the horse down the steep slope but he would deal with that problem when it arose. The warriors on the stones shouted their insults at him but the river was moving too quickly for them to risk it. Rufius' nearest pursuers were the horsemen.

He plunged into the icy waters. It was treacherous. Rocks abounded and the river went from shallow to deep in paces. He pulled the reins around and headed east. Lying along the horse's back he began to hope that he would make it when the current began to take both him and his horse towards the edge of the falls. The horse fought valiantly to counter the current but it was in vain. As it jerked its head around the slippery reins were torn from Rufius' hand and they were separated. Rufius tried to swim but he was hampered by his sword. He loosened the belt and managed to drop the sword to the bottom of the river. As he struggled to remove his cloak his head struck a rock. He was briefly rendered unconscious and then he was swept, along with his horse over the falls.

Felix had watched all of this from the safety of the eastern shore. He had seen the warriors in the water and wondered if he ought to risk loosing arrows at them. He had a wise head on his young shoulders and knew that would end in disaster. When he saw first the horse and then the decurion plunge over Roaring Water, his heart sank with them. He watched as the Brigante halted on the bank. One of them dismounted and walked gingerly towards the edge. He peered over and, when he returned to his companions, he drew a hand across his throat. The gesture was clear. The decurion was dead.

Felix waited until the Brigante had left and then descended the path. At the bottom he was about to head east to give Drugi the dire news when he thought about the horse. The decurion was dead but the horse might just be injured. Drugi had brought Felix up to respect all animal life. He could not allow an animal to suffer. He turned and waved to Wolf, "Find the horse."

The dog leapt off and disappeared before Felix had finished the command. Wolf waited at the foot of the falls. There, with its neck broken lay the horse. It had died instantly and Felix closed his eyes and asked Icaunus, the god of the river, to watch over the dead beast in the Otherworld. He saw the cloak the decurion had been wearing. It fluttered, like a banner, from one of the trees which had managed to grow from the rocks. The Roman would lie beneath the waters.

He was about to turn east and head home when Wolf darted away. Felix frowned. He did not shout. They were too close to the Brigante yet, for that. However, he was curious; Wolf rarely disobeyed. He loped off along the path. There was a pool at the bottom of the falls where the water eddied in a lazy circle. Wolf was in the water and swimming towards Rufius. He was lying with his arm trapped in a fallen tree branch. The Allfather had to have been watching over him for the branch had stopped him from drowning. Pausing only to lay down his weapons Felix leapt into the water to join the dog which was tugging at Rufius' free arm. Felix reached the unconscious Roman and put his hand to his throat. There was a pulse. Against the odds the decurion was alive.

The water was icy and Rufius knew he had little time to waste if he was to save the life of the decurion. He swam behind the Roman and supported his body with his left arm. He unhooked the right arm from the branch and then swam backwards across the eddy pool. Wolf tugged on the free arm. When Felix's feet found purchase on the bottom he stood and dragged the Roman from the water.

He laid him on his side and made sure that he was breathing. He said to Wolf, "Stay! Protect!" The dog lay over the prostrate body of Rufius and Felix left. No one would touch the Roman now.

He ran back up the trail and clambered up the tree to retrieve the cloak. He dropped it on the bank and then jumped from rock to rock until he reached the horse. The animal's dead eyes seemed to stare at the water. Felix loosened the leather straps holding the blanket to the saddle. He stuffed the leather straps into his tunic and carried the precious blanket to safety. He had contemplated removing the sheepskin from beneath the dead horse but he knew that would be too great a task. He ran back to the decurion who lay where Felix had left him. The cloak was almost dry and Felix spread it over the Roman. He hung the blanket to dry. He took his leather satchel from his shoulder. He examined the food they had left. There were a few pieces of dried meat and four apples. His water skin was still full but the river could be used for drink before they left this place.

He examined the decurion for a wound. He saw a gash on the Roman's forehead. The water had washed it clean and there appeared to be no bleeding. He could not see bone. It looked as though he had just suffered a shallow cut. He would leave that alone. How would he get the unconscious Roman back to Drugi? He could walk it in a day but not carrying the decurion. He spied some ash saplings. Taking his knife he cut four of them. Using the blanket and the leather straps he fashioned a stretcher. He laid it next to the Roman and carefully rolled him onto it ensuring that he lay face down. Then he stood between the shafts and lifted. He held the weight. Pointing down the trail he said, "Scout!" The dog ran off and Felix began to walk down the trail running alongside the river. He was fortunate that the first part was smooth and a little downhill. He soon got into a rhythm. He counted each step to help him gauge the distance. When he reached a thousand he stopped and lowered his burden. His shoulders burned with the effort.

He whistled for Wolf. The loyal sheepdog appeared instantly next to him. He broke off a piece of dried meat and gave it to the dog. He put another piece in his mouth and sucked on it. It would put off the hunger pangs. He had to keep enough food for the Roman. When the dog had eaten it ran to the river and gulped down the water. Felix pointed back up the trail and said, "Scout!"

The dog ran off. Felix did not think that they were being pursued but it paid to be careful. When his shoulders no longer burned he whistled and Wolf appeared. He shouldered his burden and they began their march again. Felix had counted a thousand five times by the time the sun was high in the sky and Felix was suffering. He decided to take a longer break. He found an overhanging tree and dragged the decurion there. After checking that he was still breathing he drank the contents of the water skin and went to the river to refill it. He had just turned when he saw the three magpies suddenly take flight. He had seen them four hundred steps along the trail and they had done the same when he had passed. There were humans somewhere along the trail. They would be Brigante and they would be hunting him.

He ran back to the decurion and picked up his bow and quiver. "Stay! Guard!"

He was glad that he had taken the Roman away from the river. He made his way silently through the undergrowth. He could now smell the Brigante. He halted and he heard them. There appeared to be three of them. He saw an old gnarled oak with a climbable branch and he swiftly ascended so that he could look down on the path. He still could not see them but he could hear them.

"I still don't know what is making these two lines on the trail."

"Neither do I but they make tracking easier. That Roman was right. There were at least two of them."

Felix cursed his mistake. He should have travelled over the rocks where he would not have left a trail. Nocking an arrow, he sighted along the path. He held another arrow in his teeth and a third in his left hand. The three men were staring down at the trail and ahead. They were not looking up. He allowed the first two to pass and then let his arrow fly into the throat of the third warrior who was but twenty paces from him. He nocked and loosed a second arrow at the middle Brigante who turned when he heard the body strike the ground. He died instantly. The last warrior had a shield and he turned with it held up to protect him from the hidden bowman. Felix's arrow thudded into the shield. As Felix drew another arrow the Brigante raced towards Felix. He almost flew over the ground. Felix was only saved by the fact that his branch was higher than the man and he was able to notch and loose quicker than any man alive. The warrior was so close that the arrow struck his forehead and half of its length emerged from the back of his skull.

He jumped down and examined their bodies. These were poor warriors and had little of value. He took the two best knives and threw the other weapons in the river. Although he knew it would be better if he got rid of the bodies he was racing against time. These three would be missed and there might be other searchers too. He ran back to the decurion. Wolf still guarded his unconscious body.

He picked up his burden again and looked for a path which would not be seen by trackers. He headed towards the river. There was a rock shelf just below the surface and he stepped into the icy waters. As the stretcher bumped down Felix heard a grunt and a moan. He turned his head and saw the decurion staring up at him.

"What happened, Felix?"

"The Allfather was not ready for you. You banged your head and a dead branch saved you." He smiled, "Wolf helped too."

"Here help me up."

Felix gave his arm to the decurion who stood, somewhat awkwardly. Felix looked down the trail apologetically. "Please Decurion, we must hurry. I killed three trackers up the path. There may be more."

"Right. Cut one of these saplings for a staff." He grabbed the water skin and drank. Felix handed him the staff and rolled up the blanket. He tied it about his body and then offered some dried meat. "No thanks. It was just the water I needed. Lead on."

Felix and Wolf left the path and headed first along the shelf beneath the river for forty paces. Then he led them across stones into the undergrowth. Now that the decurion could walk Felix could find a way to avoid their pursuers.

As he led the injured Roman he kept glancing back to see if he was coping with the journey. He appeared to be but Felix was not the healer that both Ailis and Drugi were. He was tempted to find a village and ask for help but he was an astute youth and knew that he could trust no one this close to the Brigante camp.

Rufius was feeling the effects of the fall. He vaguely remembered striking the rump of his horse before hitting the water. Felix was right; the Allfather had saved him. He had sacrificed the horse for the rider. When he had time Rufius would make an offering. He was determined to keep up with the Brigante scout despite the buzzing in his head and his desire for sleep.

Once again Felix took them for five thousand steps before he halted. He forced the decurion to drink and to chew some dried meat. "You will need the food inside you." He looked to the west. "There is a village close to the river and on a cliff. I think we should avoid it."

Rufius nodded, "You are in charge."

"It will mean a longer journey and we will not reach the farm before dark."

Rufius was suddenly aware that they had crossed the river. When he had woken it had been on his right. "But we can reach Morbium and that is as good."

Felix smiled for the first time since the fall. "Then the gods do smile on us. Wolf, scout!"

Severus and Briac stared at the three bodies. There was an accusatory tone in Severus' voice. "Had your men searched the land below the falls rather than returning to the camp to gloat these men might be alive and we would have prisoners to interrogate."

"Who knew that someone could survive that fall? I still cannot believe it."

Severus waved his hand at the three bodies. "Tell that to these men."

"We can still catch them."

"How? The trail stops just ahead and they could be anywhere. No, Chief Briac we have to assume that they have escaped and they are either Romans or Roman spies. Either way, we will have to send the men back to their farms."

"But the training?"

"The training is almost done and we need secrecy. Send your men back and tell them to hide their weapons. You and your oathsworn will come with me to Manavia."

"You are giving commands now?"

The Roman shrugged, "No, merely suggestions, but if you stay I expect to see your crucified body when I next return. They will know your name. They will know the numbers of warriors."

"But they only know of those at the camp and not the others."

Severus sighed with impatience. The man was a fool. "They will send soldiers as soon as they can and they will come here. They will search until they find you. If you are in Manavia for the winter then you cannot be found."

Briac was convinced. "We can still win?"

Severus grinned, "Oh we can still win. Had we not found these bodies and assumed the Romans were dead then we would have lost but the gods are helping us. We will win."

The centurion on duty at Morbium recognised Rufius. The lateness of the hour had made him suspicious. He admitted them both. The capsarius looked at Rufius while he hurriedly wrote a message for the commander at Eboracum. "Have you a spare horse?"

The centurion shook his head, "They decided we did not need any despatch riders. Your message will have to go by foot."

Rufius shook his head and regretted it immediately, "No, this is urgent. Felix, go to Ailis' farm. Bring my horse, one for you and a third one for the fort. Warn Ailis and Drugi of the danger they are in."

As Felix ran across the bridge over the Dunum with Wolf scouting ahead the centurion asked, "Are you sure about this threat?"

Rufius said, bluntly, "Centurion last night I saw over a thousand Brigante armed with new weapons and wearing mail, they were training for war and they were being advised by a Roman. They were just twenty miles from here. So, what do you think of the threat?"

In answer the centurion shouted, "Double the guards!"

Chapter 6

Decurion Princeps Metellus was not worried when four days had passed since Rufius had left. After all the Quartermaster and Gaius were not back yet, but the hairs on the back of his neck were prickling and that was a sure sign that all was not well with the world. He heard hooves as a horseman clattered up Via Trajanus. The fort had a clear view for half a mile and he saw that it was not Rufius. He walked to the gate. "A rider approaching. Better warn the Prefect. It may be a messenger from Eboracum."

The sentries acknowledged the command and stood in the middle of the gateway. During the hours of daylight, the southern gate was always left open, guarded but open. The rider halted and shouted, "Messenger for Prefect Sallustius, from the Governor."

As he was waved through Metellus wondered at that. The Governor normally communicated directly with the Legate Demetrius. He was intrigued. Nanna, his wife, would have said he was being plain nosey. He wandered down to be on hand when the missive was handed over. Julius Demetrius had joined the Prefect, no doubt also intrigued by the message's origin.

"Sir, the Governor said it is a personal matter for you. There is a box too." He unstrapped a box which had been hidden by the rider's cloak. Metellus hid a smile. He could see that the matter must have preyed on the rider's mind all the way from the far south of the Province.

"Thank you Trooper. Stable your horse. It is too late to venture forth tonight."

There was palpable relief on the rider's face. Since Eboracum, he had feared for his life. This was the wild frontier. He was used to the fortress with vaguely civilised people. Here the barbarians still went around half-naked! "Thank you, sir."

Metellus and Julius looked over the Prefect's shoulder, both were equally interested. Livius gave them a wry look. "Come along then. We will go to my rooms and examine this mystery."

Julius demurred, "No, no, Prefect. It is a private matter, after all."

Livius laughed. "No Legate, I insist."

Once in his room, the slave poured three goblets of wine and disappeared. Livius unrolled the papyrus. That in itself was unusual. Papyrus was expensive and messages were normally entrusted to wax; a more fragile but a cheaper medium.

Hail Prefect Sallustius,

The box which accompanies this letter was found secreted in the Governor's palace in Camulodunum which I am having refurbished. It was with some items belonging to your uncle. I knew him, albeit briefly and, for my part, he was my friend. Out of respect for a former Governor, I have not opened the box but I must tell you that there was a fragment of papyrus found with it which suggested that it was of some importance.

If I can be of any assistance do not hesitate to contact me.

Trebonius Germanus

By Order of Emperor Hadrian

Governor of Britannia

"Interesting."

Livius nodded, "I can see that he would have to be circumspect given the manner of my uncle's death. This is even more intriguing now." Livius' uncle had been executed for treason. It was an unfounded accusation but one could see how the new Governor would wish to distance himself from any hint of disloyalty.

The air of anticipation filled the room. Metellus nervously licked his lips whilst Livius drank his wine to give him thinking time.

Livius lifted the small chest on to the table. It was remarkably light, "Not filled with gold then?"

Julius looked at the workmanship of the box. "This is a well-made box and whatever is within it, your uncle would have deemed valuable. Be careful when you open it."

There was a knock on the door and Metellus looked up irritably. He glowered at the trooper when he opened it. "This had better be important trooper."

"It is sir, Decurion Atrebeus and the Brigante scout are approaching the gate, sir."

Livius looked up and waved a hand. "You had better go, Decurion Princeps. We will not be long." Metellus left and Livius slowly opened the lid. Disappointingly there appeared to be just a letter but, when Livius lifted it out he saw a ring with the image of a boar upon it.

While he read the letter aloud Julius examined the ring.

"*To those who follow me,*

If you are reading this letter then something has gone awry with my plans and those of my dear friend King Prasutagus."

Julius looked up, "Prasutagus, he was the husband of Boudicca. I didn't know he knew your uncle."

Livius shrugged, "They were both members of royal families so it is, perhaps, not really surprising that they were friends."

He continued to read, "*He has entrusted this ring to my care. It is to be used by whoever finds this box. I hope it is someone from my family for this is a matter of family honour but it may well be some official of Rome. In either case it is a most delicate matter.*

The king sent his royal regalia and the money he was given by Rome to his cousin, Ban in the land of the Votadini. The enclosed ring will identify the bearer as coming from King Prasutagus. He hoped that it would help his daughters for he had a premonition of evil. Sadly, I had never the opportunity to honour my promise. The king fell ill and he died leaving his wife to revolt against Rome. In that time it was impossible for me to travel north for those were dangerous times. Once the family were dead there appeared to be little urgency and I put it off.

My honour demands that I fulfil my promise. I hope to make the journey soon, especially as I am now Governor of Britannia. However, affairs of state may prevent my doing so.

I owe it to my friend to return the regalia and the money to the Iceni for they have been badly used by corrupt officials.

Lucullus Sallustius

Governor of Britannia by the will of Emperor Domitian."

Julius took the letter and examined the seal. "It looks authentic enough to me. This is where we could do with old Julius. He has an eye for this sort of thing."

"It leaves me in a dilemma though. The Votadini are hostile and they are north of the wall."

"But it is a matter of honour, Livius. I know that you feel a sense of duty towards your uncle. This will require some thought."

There was a sharp rap on the door and Julius put the letter and the ring back in the box. "We had better keep this between ourselves, Livius." He closed the lid. "Come!"

Metellus and Rufius entered. Rufius looked the worse for wear. His face was now blackened from his fall and he had ridden nonstop from Morbium.

"Sit down, Decurion. You look ready to drop."

"I am tired, Legate, but I bring dire news." He briefly told them what had occurred, minimising his own misfortunes and travails and concentrating on the key factors.

"You have done well, Decurion Atrebeus. It is all that we expected. Well, Prefect, can you put this putative rebellion down with ten turmae? It is all that we can spare."

"Then we will have to do so. Decurion Princeps, have the ala ready to ride first thing in the morning. We will leave four turmae here."

Rufius tried to rise. Julius put his hand on his shoulder. "Where do you think you are going?"

"I need to prepare for the morrow sir."

"No, Decurion. You will be staying here and resting; for a day or two at least. You have done more than enough."

After they had gone Livius picked up the box. "This will have to wait."

"Perhaps not old friend. We both know the power of the name of the Sword of Cartimandua. The royal regalia of the Iceni will be equally powerful."

"I am not sure about that. Since the revolt, they have been a subjugated tribe."

"We have a new governor. If he has any sense he will make moves to bring the Iceni into the fold as allies rather than a subjugated people. The return of the regalia costs us nothing and yet it might make that part of Britannia safe."

"You are the politician, Julius and not me."

He shrugged. "We will talk more when you return. Make sure that you take the ala along the valley of the Dunum. There may be other parts which are rebellious but we know that there is a faction there now."

"You do not expect them to be at their camp do you, Legate?"

"If they are then they are fools for they have kept this hidden from us so far. Let us assume they know what they are doing. Your patrol in strength is to let them know that we know. Meanwhile, I will arrange for the VIth Victrix to winter at Luguvalium. We may need them in the spring. I will write to the Governor and to the commander at Eboracum. They were due there in the spring anyway." He stared hard at Livius. "Show them that we are in control. Your ala has a reputation in that part of the world. Let us use it."

When the ala left the next morning poor Rufius felt as though he was letting down his comrades. His turma was left with the other turmae to patrol the wall and that would be a hard enough task. Rufius, however, did not like leaving a job half done. He and Felix stood on the gate tower and watched as the column of men headed south. They would reach the site of the camp by late afternoon. If the rebels were still there then they were in for rude surprise.

"I never thanked you for saving my life, Felix."

The youth grinned, "It was Wolf who found you and he swam to save you. Besides I could not let one of Marcus' Horse die. You are the oathsworn of the Sword."

Rufius heard the tinge of sadness in the youth's voice. "You would like to be with the sword, wouldn't you?"

"It will return and I will be happy."

Marcus and his turma were sent ahead of the main column to scout out the camp spotted by Rufius. He split them in two and approached from the north and the east. He was taking no chances. It was obvious that there had been a camp there but equally obvious that it had been moved for at least a day and probably more.

Titus picked up a piece of burned firewood and threw it. "It looks like we are too late sir. This is stone cold."

"I think they left as soon as they were seen by Decurion Atrebeus. He was lucky to escape with his life. We will take no chances. Put a skirmish line out while we wait for the Prefect. "

While Titus organised the men, Marcus dismounted and led his horse as he examined the ground. Although not as good a tracker as either Felix or Rufius, Marcus had been an Explorate and trained by both Gaelwyn and Rufius. He saw the unmistakable tracks of a pair, at least, of caligae. There had been a Roman in the camp. That did not bode well. He would mention it to Livius as soon as he arrived. It confirmed Rufius' report. The tracks showed that the caligae were kept in good repair. These were the shoes of a soldier and not a deserter.

The small ship had left the mainland for Manavia the previous day. As Briac and Severus stepped ashore they were greeted by Caronwyn who had been watching their approach. There was no hint of a frown as they abased themselves before her and Briac stuttered, "We were discovered and Severus thought it best if I returned here."

She lightly laughed, "You worry too much Prince Briac. Severus is right." She waved at the skies. "Soon it will be autumn and the men will be needed for the harvests. The Mother watches over us still. The Romans are suspicious but they will find nothing."

Briac looked in surprise. "How can you know that?"

"Your problem is that you do not believe deeply enough. I am a daughter of the Mother Earth and I see things hidden from mere men. You are our tools to mould events into the shape we wish. All will turn out well. Come and we will see Severus' mistress."

Severus was not certain he liked being called a slave however prettily it was dressed but he had to admit, as they trudged towards the large roundhouse, that the two women had both more sense and more ability than any officer he had known before.

Caronwyn seemed to notice the mail for the first time. "The weapons and the armour were well received?"

"They were. My men now have the heart to believe we can meet the Romans equally. But why did the Lady Flavia invest so much of her money in the weapons? She can never recover their value even when we win." He had been about to say if rather than when but he was learning how to speak to this most powerful of Druids.

"Like me, revenge burns fiercely in her heart but, fear not, the Lady Flavia will be rich when we reconquer our land. The Roman settlers have many treasures and they like to bury their gold beneath their homes. When they are sacrificed to the Mother and we have ripped their stone abominations from the ground then we will reap the harvest of Roman gold. We have learned that this love of gold can be put to good use."

The Lady Flavia beamed when she saw Briac. He felt a surge through his body. She was a beautiful woman and he realised that he desired her. That was impossible he knew. She was far above him. He knew he was a rough and ready warrior and she was a powerful woman but he could dream.

As he sat between the two women and drank the strange brew concocted by Caronwyn and her acolytes, Briac found himself both relaxing and feeling more powerful and potent. Their words, and perhaps the drink, were transforming him. Caronwyn, in particular, seemed to be able to mesmerize with her words.

"You must put yourself in our hands, Briac, Prince of the Brigante. Let us plan and think for you. You and your men just need to fight."

Part of Briac's brain still remained his own. "But we still need more men."

"And you shall have them. Even now I have my Druids casting through the tribes and sowing the seeds of rebellion and revolt. The tribes in the south will not fight but they do not like the taxes they pay to a government far away. There will be many instances of minor disobedience. The Roman grip is looser in the land they think they have conquered. That is in no small part due to you for your control over your men has lulled the Romans into a stupor. When the Romans are hunkered in their forts and their homes over winter then another enemy will attack them from within their own homes. We have those who prepare their food and watch over them. They are loyal to our cause and willing to die for it. There will be knives in the night and death at the table. All of this has been planned and foretold."

Roman Wall

Lady Flavia stroked his head. Her perfume and gentle touch intoxicated Briac almost as much as the powerful drink he was imbibing. "And I have placed servants and slaves in the homes of the Roman families who rule the land around the wall." Her voice became briefly hoarse with emotion. "I learned how such devices can be very effective."

"So you see Briac, you need to prepare this winter for a Brigante Spring. Put yourself in our hands completely."

Briac was suddenly aware that Caronwyn was now naked and she and Lady Flavia were undressing him. Lady Flavia leant down and kissed him lightly on the lips. "And tonight, we join the tribes and the priests under one roof. Tomorrow begins the dynasty which will rule this land."

Briac finally succumbed to the brew and to the innate power of the two women. That night he too became a follower of the Cult of the Mother.

Chapter 7

Rufius was summoned by the Legate two days after the ala had departed. "How are you healing, Decurion Atrebeus?"

"I am well recovered, Legate. I led my patrol this morning and there are no ill effects."

"Good. Good." Rufius wondered at the Legate's demeanour. He had known Julius Demetrius since he had led the ala. The Legate had no need to be delicate in his approach. The Legate seemed to read his mind for he smiled, "I know, Rufius that we go back a long way but I need to ask you something which requires an honest answer."

"I believe I have always spoken the truth to you, sir."

"Ah, but you may give me the answer you think I wish to have rather than the answer in your heart."

Rufius laughed, "I think your time in Rome made you forget that the men of Marcus' Horse were trained to give the honest answer to every question."

Julius seemed relieved. "That is what I wanted to hear. The Prefect received a letter from his past just before you returned." Rufius nodded. Metellus had been intrigued by the box and the message and mentioned it to Rufius. "There is something in the land of the Votadini which could be used by Rome's enemies. You are an Atrebate and you know the power of torcs and symbols." He lowered his voice, even though there was no-one to hear, "The regalia of the Iceni lie in the land of the Votadini."

"And you would like me to get them back for you?"

Julius laughed, "I sometimes forget how quick the minds of the officers of this ala are. No, for that matter will need greater planning and must wait until the Prefect returns. What I would ask you and Felix to do would be to find out if there is a family of a warrior or prince called Ban in the land of the Votadini."

"That is all?"

"It is a delicate matter and needs an Explorate to carry it out. We have no idea where this man lived. It is over sixty years since he received the box and I cannot believe that he will still be alive. He was an important noble. Someone may remember the family. But before I risk upsetting the Votadini with a military invasion I would know if the box still exists before I risk troopers."

"Perhaps the Votadini use the regalia themselves. They might harness its power."

"If that was true then I believe that we would have heard rumours. The fact that neither the Prefect nor I had heard of this means that the treasure is still hidden."

"It may be that it is lost."

"Then you will discover that and we will be able to forget the matter but if it exists then we require it to be south of the wall. The last thing we need is for a magnet to draw rebels north of the wall."

Rufius was an Atrebate and understood the significance of the regalia but he was also an intelligent officer. "Perhaps, sir, if it is still hidden we should leave it that way."

"Had the Brigante not shown that they had a revolt planned then I might have agreed but this rebellion has the hand of the spawn of Morwenna guiding it."

"I thought the witch and her daughter were dead?"

"We know not how many daughters she had. Julius Longinus had studied the cult and knew that the priestesses of the cult liked to have many daughters. He even told me that they strangled any boys who were born to them so that they could keep their purity. The Brigante had ever been ill served by the cult."

"Then why do we not wipe it out?"

"That is harder than you might think. When the sacred groves on Mona were destroyed we thought we had scotched the snake but it re-emerged on Manavia. It is like the Hydra and has many heads. When you cut off one head another appears." He spread his arms. "Will you accept the commission? I do not order, I ask. There will be no shame in a refusal."

Rufius considered. As an Atrebate, he knew the significance of such royal accoutrements. It would do much to bring the southern tribes more firmly into the Roman fold. If the north revolted then the south might become restless too. He had not been back to his village and his family for years but he knew that they embraced the Roman way of life and a revolt would end in tears for them.

"I will do this. All I need to do is to find where the family of Ban live?"

"That is all."

He nodded. "Who is the king of the Votadini now?"

He spread his hands, "We do not know. Since Lugubelenus was killed and Radha, his queen, disappeared we have heard little from them. It seems they have hidden away their new royal family. Their king lives in the far north of the land at an oppidum called Traprain Law. He may be descended from a relative of Ban, we simply do not know. Since we abandoned Alavna we have little intelligence from the region." His face showed the disappointment he felt in his own actions. "The Votadini have been more peaceful than the Selgovae and I have not paid them as much attention as I ought."

Rufius studied the map on the Legate's wall and began to work out the best way to complete his mission. He had neither shaved nor cut his hair since his mission and he looked less like a Roman soldier. He just needed a story for his presence north of the wall. He realised the Legate was watching him with amusement. "I am sorry Legate. I was working out how best to do this."

"There is a convoy of merchants who are travelling through Votadini country to trade with them."

"Have the Votadini anything worth trading?"

"They have some fine sheepskins and they smoke fish. With winter approaching the merchants are keen to get some stock while they can. They are being escorted by some mercenaries. You could accompany them."

Rufius nodded, "That would help me. Tell me, Legate, is there any of the black stone from the south, the jet in the fort?" Sometimes the soldiers confiscated goods in lieu of taxes. He knew that some had been taken earlier that month.

"I believe there is some. Why?"

"The Votadini and the other northern tribes revere it. I could go as a jet trader."

"I will get some. There is a small box of it in Julius' office. The convoy leaves in the morning."

Rufius left to plan his trip. He would not risk Felix and Wolf. There was no need. Besides he owed a life already to the young Brigante. Honour demanded that he repay the Brigante before becoming indebted a second time.

Livius gathered the decurions around him. "The Legate wishes us to make our presence felt across the valley. In a perfect world we would travel south too but, with autumn approaching, I deem it prudent to let the Brigante know we are close. Each turma will be allocated a patrol area." He smiled, "Decurion Princeps, you can have the area to the east of Via Trajanus and that way your turma can enjoy the comforts of your home for a night or two."

Metellus showed his relief with a huge smile. "Thank you, Prefect."

"Marcus, you know the area around Stanwyck better than any and, I dare say that Drugi can be of some assistance to you. As for the rest, you will be spread out from Metellus west in turma order. I will accompany our newest Decurion, Sextus Decimus."

Marcus was happy that he would see his family again but he knew that he would not allow it to interfere with his work. Of all the warriors in Marcus' Horse, the burden of duty sat heaviest on the young man's shoulders. It was not just the sword but his adopted brother who rode beside him. His new troopers always asked why he kept looking in the air when there were birds around. They were told that the spirit of his step brother lived in a hawk. To those born in the land of the Brigante that made perfect sense. The world of animals and man was intertwined; any fool knew that.

Marcus forced himself to visit with Drugi first. He would not lay himself open to a criticism that he saw his family first. Even though the troopers were watching for the hunter he surprised them all when he appeared from the undergrowth. He bowed, "It is good to see you, lord."

Marcus leapt from his mount and embraced his companion. "Old friend, having escaped from slavery there is no lord between us. I am Marcus still and you are Drugi."

He nodded, "What brings you here?"

"Rufius' news of the training camp has meant that we need to find the weapons they are hiding. What have you heard?"

"Stanwyck is quiet and that is wrong. I have lived here long enough to know that it holds a place in every Brigante heart."

"You think that they are pretending?"

"They are not what they seem."

"Then I will visit there first. Would you come with us tomorrow when we see other places where they may have hidden weapons?"

"As ever, I serve you." He waved at them and then disappeared in an instant. Chosen Man Gnaeus chuckled, "How someone his size does that is beyond me."

"He is part of the forest as much as the boar, the wolf or the bear. He is a truly special person."

"We are going to Stanwyck, sir, but Drugi said we would find nothing."

"And that is why we must go there. If we do not, it will look suspicious. Besides, Drugi is correct, it does hold a special place and those elders there will be part of Briac's plan."

"I thought we had finished with him when he revolted the last time."

Marcus' voice was cold. "The only way you finish a warrior's desire to fight is to kill him. Briac is a noble of the Brigante or the Carvetii and he will only stop fighting when he is dead. Remember that, Gnaeus."

Gnaeus shivered, his Decurion had become harder since his step brother had been poisoned. He had heard that some of the priestesses of the Mother cult had survived. If they fell into Marcus' hands it would go ill for them. There would be no mercy.

Although the defences of Stanwyck had been destroyed many years earlier, the ramparts and the ditches remained. It would have taken too long for the legions to destroy them. The villagers still lived in the roundhouses as they had in the time of Cartimandua although her hall had been destroyed during the fighting. The ramparts and ditches provided some protection from the elements and wild animals.

Roman Wall

Elidr was the headman of the settlement. He was a cousin of Briac and was devoted to the fight against the Romans. He had fought against the Romans and the long scar down both his cheek and his chest were testament to his courage. He had been the only man Briac could trust to oversee Stanwyck. He was privy to all parts of Briac's plan and had even helped to transport the weapons from Eboracum. When the rebellion came he would command a five hundred. He pretended that he was an ally of Rome and the local Roman garrisons sang his praises. The villagers knew the truth and knew just how ruthless he could be. Any sign of deviation from the plan resulted in pain or death for the offender. Two youths now lay at the bottom of the sacrificial pond.

When Elidr was told of the arrival of the horsemen he was neither worried nor surprised. The discovery of the training camp was the cause. He did not panic, nor did he bother to tell his people how to behave. They knew. He strapped on his old sword. It was part of the disguise. He was a warrior and had the battle rings as evidence. It would look wrong if he did not. There were, however, few weapons in the old fort. They were buried some way away beneath the remains of an old settlement, long abandoned. When the time came he and his warriors would join his cousin in the uprising and then the Romans would see the real Elidr.

Marcus did not take anything for granted as he led his men through what had been the main gate when there had been wooden walls on the ramparts. He ignored the smiles and the waves; they were merely for effect. It looked to be a prosperous settlement which surprised Marcus. He had not seen animals in the fields nor had he seen the signs of crops. It begged the question; what did these people do to survive?

The headman who strode down to meet them from the largest roundhouse was obviously a powerful warrior. He had a sword and he had battle scars but Marcus noticed his physique. This warrior trained still. He had not hung up his sword.

"I am Elidr, leader of these people. How can we serve the Emperor?"

"We have heard that some Brigante have been practising with weapons and heard rumours that an uprising is being planned."

Elidr smiled, "We have old weapons and we love Rome. We have heard of small groups of young men who are anxious to prove themselves in war but they are a handful only."

Marcus smiled his own false smile. "Then I am pleased that we have such a friend as you Elidr." He scanned the huts. "To satisfy my Prefect's curiosity would it be possible to search the huts? I believe you when you say there are no weapons but if I return without examining your huts I would be in trouble." Marcus said it with a smile and saw the smile on Elidr's face.

"Of course."

Marcus turned, "Chosen Man, search the huts but be careful and try not to disturb too much."

As the turma dismounted so did Marcus.

Elidr's eyes suddenly widened involuntarily when he spied the hilt of the sword. "Is that the mystical Sword of Cartimandua I see; the sword of the Brigante?"

"It is, Elidr, and it protects the people still." Marcus noticed the avarice in the headman's eyes.

Gnaeus and the troopers soon emerged from the huts. He shook his head to indicate that they had found nothing worthy of mention. They remounted and sat in a column of twos behind the decurion.

"Farewell." Marcus led the turma all the way through the fort to emerge at the far gate. He wanted them all to see Marcus' Horse.

As they headed back to Drugi's Gnaeus said, "Did you notice the strange thing about the villager sir?"

Marcus had been too busy with the headman to notice anything. "Not really."

"There were no men at all in the village save the headman and four or five old men. There were only boys there and I mean very young boys."

Marcus frowned. Boys meant they were not yet seven summers. Every man and youth over the age of seven was missing. That was sinister.

They headed for Drugi's and found him waiting on the road to Ailis' farm. "I thought you and your men would like a comfortable night at your mother's." He smiled, "And of course, Frann."

Marcus blushed a little. It had been some months since he had seen his wife and he missed her. He would feel guilty knowing that he had home comforts while his troopers did not but he also knew they would not begrudge him a night in his own bed. Ailis greeted all of them as though they were her sons. She had been rescued by Marcus' Horse over thirty years ago and she thanked them every day.

For their part, the troopers enjoyed the food and the comfort of the farm. Drugi was a fine hunter and they would all enjoy meat, something which the Roman soldier was largely denied in his daily diet.

The following morning Drugi led them some way away from the hill fort and the farm. The trail they followed was familiar to Marcus. He, Decius and Macro had used it to hunt hares and game birds when they were growing up. He struggled to remember where it led. The entrance to the old abandoned village was somewhat overgrown but the path was well-trodden.

"I know you have not brought us here just to give us exercise."

"No, Roman, although I think some of your men need the exercise after the meat they ate last night. I brought you here because I found many recent tracks leading from Stanwyck to this old village."

Marcus dismounted. "Gnaeus, put five men to watch the trail. The rest of you come with me." Drugi led them to the centre of the five crumbling roundhouses. "What did you find?"

Drugi shrugged, "I found tracks and disturbed earth. Drugi is a hunter; he does not dig!"

Marcus laughed, "Does he tell us where to dig then?"

Drugi pointed to the largest hut. "In there."

"Gnaeus, see what you can find in the deserted hut." As his men entered the decrepit and ruined hut Marcus asked. "Are there any more places like this?"

"Not close but there were mules using the old paths to the west." Marcus did not ask how he knew they were mules. Drugi knew the spoor and track of every animal that walked, crawled or slithered.

Gnaeus emerged. He held in his arms six spears. Titus followed with six swords and finally, Decius carried the mail shirt. Gnaeus shook his head. "These are ours, sir. These are quality weapons."

"Right. Give the spears to the first six troopers. The Prefect wants us issued with them so we can be the start. Let another six of our men see if these swords are better than theirs."

"And the mail shirt sir?"

"I think the Prefect should see that, don't you Chosen Man?"

Rufius did not like the merchant who organised the convoy. His name was Manius Postumus. He affected a Roman style of dress and speech but he was a Brigante trying to impress the Romans. He had tried to charge Rufius for his participation. "After all we have paid for these soldiers to escort us."

Rufius had cast his eye over the ten so-called warriors. They were all tribesmen who had no other function. They had a variety of arms and helmets and none of them looked at all military.

"If you have paid these then you have been robbed." He had drawn his own sword which was obviously better than those of the guards. "I will rely on my own weapon. When the Votadini have picked over your carcasses I will let your families know."

"Do not be hasty. We are, after all, Romans. You may join us."

Rufius had laughed, "Very generous of you I am sure."

That had been the previous night and now, just after noon the thirty mules, ten guards and six merchants trudged up the half-built Roman road. It had been started to provide communication with Alavna. The Roman fort had long been abandoned and the road was little better than a cleared trail but it was largely flat and even. The auxiliaries who had begun the road had cleared the sides of undergrowth which made ambush unlikely. Despite his words to Manius, Rufius was not worried about a Votadini attack. They had been quiet longer than the Brigante. They were a poor people with few resources. In the past they had been victims of attacks from the Selgovae, Carvetii and even the Brigante. Even so he watched every blade of grass, rock and bush for possible enemies.

Ernan, the son of Annis, was a Selgovae warrior. He had long ago learned that attacking Romans did not pay but the Votadini were a different matter. They provided a constant source of slaves. Slaves meant trade and provided the Selgovae with weapons and wine. He had led his fifteen men through the forests of the high country and now they waited close to the old Roman road and the village of Am Beal. They had spied the mules and the merchants long ago. Despite the fact that the merchants and guards outnumbered the Selgovae, Ernan was convinced they could overcome them. This would be a greater haul than just slaves. The mules looked laden with trade goods. They probably carried the fine pots and jugs the Romans made.

Ernan made his plans. He had six men on each side taking whatever cover they could find. He and the other five waited in the middle of the road. The road rose to the south and they would be hidden until the convoy crested the rise.

Rufius rode at the rear of the column. The mules made it the most pungent place to ride but he wanted to watch the others. He had learned that riding at the back could have advantages. You saw how men rode, walked, talked and sometime, fought. Only one of the hired guards looked to have anything about him. His weapons were well cared for and he had an alert look about him. The others looked more likely to rob than to protect.

Suddenly Rufius heard a shout from the front of the column. One of the guards ran back towards the wall. The merchants each grabbed the nearest mule as though it might afford some protection. Rufius kicked his horse on and rode to the top of the rise. There he saw fifteen well-armed Selgovae warriors. They were spread out in a half-circle across the road. Only Rufius who had the best horse would have been able to escape. The rest would have been caught had they tried to run.

Manius addressed the guards. "Defend us! It is your duty! We have paid you!"

The leader of the mercenaries, an overweight warrior of the Carvetii called Senlan, spat on the ground and snarled. "They outnumber us. If we negotiate they won't take all of our goods."

Manius looked desperately at the others for help. The rest of the merchants feared for their lives and the hired swords began to back away. The Selgovae leader, confident now, strode forward. He grinned insolently, "It looks as though the warriors you hired are not willing to die. We will allow you to live. Just leave us your mules, weapons and your goods. You may return to the wall."

Rufius nudged his horse forward. "You will take nothing of mine, Selgovae. Take what you will from these sheep but I pass."

Ernan frowned. He had not expected resistance. He had correctly assessed the quality, or lack of it, of the hired men but he had not seen this warrior on a horse. His men looked at him. This was a challenge and Ernan had to meet it. He looked at the warrior. He looked handy but he only had a sword. Ernan had a shield, a long spear and a long sword. He could defeat him.

"Will your actions match your words? Will you dispute the road with me?"

"If it gets me to a bed for the night quicker then yes, I will." He dismounted and handed the reins to the warrior who had the weapons which looked to be the best cared for. "Watch the horse for me. I will not be long." He dropped his cloak and drew his sword. He put his hand around the back and ensured that his dagger was still in his belt. The Selgovae had warrior bands on his sword and his arms. He had killed men in battle. However, he had never met an Explorate before and Rufius noted that the warrior was both short and stocky. Rufius had the advantage to height and he had a longer sword. The barbarian had leather armour and no helmet. As he approached him, Rufius noted that the shield had neither metal nor leather protecting the wood. It was not a good shield.

"What is your name, Selgovae?"

"Ernan. And yours, Roman?"

"Rufius."

"You have more balls than these others but it will avail you naught. Today you die and go to the Otherworld."

Rufius nodded, "If that is to be then I am ready but when you die your men will leave."

It was an imperative rather than a question and Rufius noted that the Selgovae warriors looked at each other nervously. They had not encountered anyone who challenged Ernan, yet.

Ernan nodded. "They will."

Rufius' words must have made the warrior nervous, for he thrust his spear forwards trying to catch Rufius unawares. Rufius spun around and brought his sword hard against the Selgovae shield. The chips of wood which flew from it were testament to its poor quality. Ernan could see that he was facing a warrior and he regretted making the challenge. They should have killed them. As he raised his spear, ready for a second thrust, he knew that he would have lost men but this way he could lose his life.

 Ernan edged forward. He had the advantage of length with his spear and he decided to use it. He jabbed at the warrior's head whilst stepping forward to punch with his shield. He expected Rufius to step backwards and he hoped that his opponent would trip up. Instead, Rufius grabbed the spear just behind the head and then swung his sword at Ernan's head. It was unexpected and Ernan barely had time to raise his shield. The blade dug into the unprotected edge of the wooden shield and a huge split appeared. Rufius twisted his sword to retrieve it whilst pulling the spear from the grasp of the Selgovae.

There was a cheer from behind Rufius and a groan of dismay from the Selgovae. Ernan stepped back and hurriedly drew his sword. Rufius grinned and Ernan saw not a warrior but a wolf. "Lay down your sword and return to your home with your warriors."

Ernan could not do that. He would have no respect if he did so. He roared and swung his sword overhead as he attempted to split Rufius' skull in two. Rufius had fast feet and he sidestepped the blow and swung away from Ernan's wild charge. He continued his swing and his sword sliced through the backbone of the Selgovae. He died with a surprised expression on his face.

The merchants and the guards all cheered. Rufius looked at the Selgovae. "Take your leader and go home."

They looked at each other and nodded. Manius Postumus said, "No! We should take them prisoner and deliver them to the Votadini!"

Rufius spun around and had the tip of his sword at the merchant's throat. "Had you fought the Selgovae then you could have made that decision. They may take the body of this brave but foolish warrior home."

He nodded to the Selgovae who picked up the body of their leader and his weapons. One of them said, "You have honour. I would follow you."

"Thank you but that is not my path. Become a warrior my friend. There is no honour in banditry."

He nodded and the Selgovae left. Rufius returned to his horse and mounted. "Come. We are burning daylight."

Chapter 8

When Julius Longinus and the Quartermaster returned from Eboracum they brought not only new weapons and supplies but ill news. Tribes in the heartland of Britannia were restless. It seemed that more of the formerly docile people now resented the Roman taxes. Pax Britannica was coming at too high a price. There were stories of Roman settlers being murdered. Rich merchants were discovered with knives in their backs. Bodyguards now demanded a high price. Although the perpetrators had been caught and dealt with this was something new. This was the behaviour of the frontier tribes not those who lived far better than their ancestors had.

The Legate listened to Julius Longinus and nodded. "When you have rested you had better send a message to the Tribunes of the VIth Victrix. Put them and the auxiliaries on alert. They must move to Eboracum before winter to prevent insurrection."

Julius shook his head, "I thought, like you, Legate, that the wall would bring peace. It seems the Emperor's plan for peace has gone awry."

The Legate frowned. It did not do to criticise the Emperor, even this far from Rome. "We just need time for the wall to become established. We have yet to control the movements of the tribes. When that is done we shall have peace."

As the clerk bumbled off to write the order Julius Demetrius reflected that Rufius' mission was even more vital now. The Iceni were not far south of Eboracum. If they rose then the north would be cut off.

The merchants begged Rufius to lead the caravan of mules. They had all been shaken to the core by the attack. Violence was not part of their world. The making of money was.

Am Beal was built on an estuary. It had a wooden wall and was also protected by the sea. It was the largest place they had seen since leaving the wall. The gates were not barred but a couple of warriors lounged by the gate. Rufius noted that their weapons were neglected and they did not look as though they could stop even the hired men that they had brought with them.

Manius stepped forward. "I am Manius Postumus and I am here to trade, as requested by your king."

Rufius' ears pricked up. The man whose relatives he sought, Ban, had been related to the Royal family. He dismounted and edged his way closer to the merchant.

A villager wandered up. He was flanked by two other prosperous-looking men. He smiled, "I am Angus and you are welcome, Manius Postumus. King Ardal warned me of your coming and we have gathered some fine trade goods."

Manius looked relieved. "Have you somewhere for us to keep the goods safe until the trade."

Angus pointed to a long building close to the gate. "If you use the warrior hall then your goods will be safe. There are no warriors using it at the moment."

Rufius took in that intelligence without a blink. This might be a warning that the King of the Votadini was also preparing for war despite this apparent peaceful meeting.

"Leave your mules outside the walls please."

"Of course." Manius had had enough of the smell of Mules and their droppings to last a lifetime.

Rufius spoke. "Have you a stable for my horse?"

The headman took in this powerful looking warrior whose sword looked well used. "Are you a merchant?"

Manius spoke up. "He is but he is also a warrior and he defeated some Selgovae bandits who tried to rob us."

The headman smiled at that. "Then there is stabling for those Selgovae robbers have plagued us. Did you kill them all?"

Rufius just shook his head, "Just the leader and the rest I sent back to their own lands."

"Then you are welcome indeed and I look forward to hearing your story this evening. It will enliven the meal."

After the goods had been taken from the mules and the gates shut Rufius felt relieved. The first part of his task had been completed; he was inside a Votadini settlement. Now he had to do the more difficult part; he had to discover where the relatives of Ban lived and that would be a much more difficult task.

It was too late for trading and the merchants were still agitated following the attack by the Selgovae. The headman, Angus, had arranged for food. Rufius had no doubt that the cost would be added to the price of the trade goods. As the merchants had doubled their prices anyway everyone was cheating everyone else.

The hired hands were left to guard the trade goods. Manius was less than happy with them. Rufius happened to be there when they were berated by the diminutive figure. He jabbed a podgy finger at the leader of the men, "You, Senlan, son of Fenlan have to do much to regain my favour. You were willing to abandon us. The man who fled was your choice and he will not be paid. All of you have half of your money yet to come. Unless I see more from you that amount will be halved." Senlan's face darkened and his hand went to his sword. Perhaps Manius was emboldened by Rufius' presence for he stood up to him. "Do not think for one moment that you can frighten me. I have seen how you face up to a real warrior. You have a decision to make. Do you obey orders or leave now and I will appoint this Brigante, Pedair, to command? He, at least, did not look afeared by the Selgovae."

Senlan nodded, "We will obey you but you will pay us the agreed amount when we return to the wall."

"Perhaps."

Rufius left. Senlan was a fool. He would only be given half the agreed amount. Manius would have the protection of the garrison once he reached the wall. He could almost see Manius calculating his increased profit.

The feast was not the best which Rufius had attended. It appeared to consist of herrings in various forms: smoked, soaked in vinegar and cooked over an open fire. The porridge they served was familiar although it was richly flavoured with autumn raspberries and brambles. The beer was drinkable but Rufius drank sparingly. Although seated opposite Angus, he had little opportunity to ask his questions before the entertainment.

The entertainment consisted of a one-armed warrior who had a fine voice. He told the tales of the Votadini. His own tribe had similar stories. He heard the story of Lugubelenus and the revolt which almost killed Marcus and decimated the Ninth. He heard the stories almost dispassionately for he knew the other side of the events. The fiction in the warrior's words was understandable.

When he finished his tale, there was much banging of beakers on the table. Angus gestured to Rufius. "And now, would you tell us the tale of the encounter with the killers of babies, the Selgovae."

Rufius was not known for his public speaking. He was normally a taciturn and thoughtful man but he was an Explorate and he played the part well. He stood and told the story. He did not use the hyperbole normally associated with a single combat but he did make it graphic for he knew they would expect that. Manius nodded his approval. The audience appreciated it and he received a standing ovation. Angus took the opportunity of coming to him and putting an arm around his shoulders, as men took the lull as a chance to relieve themselves outside and merchants began to haggle with prospective customers.

"You are an interesting merchant, Rufius. That is a Roman name, is it not, and yet you are not Roman."

"I am Atrebate but I served with the Thracians. They gave me that name." He shrugged, "South of the wall is a Roman world."

"And I can see that you handle yourself well. I am intrigued. What brings you here? What do you have to trade?"

Rufius had prepared well. He reached into his leather purse and pulled out a fine piece of jet. "I came into a quantity of this. South of the wall, it has little value but I heard that the Votadini use it."

Angus rolled the black stone around in his rough red hands. "You are right and you will make a tidy profit." He chuckled, "If you like fish or sheepskins."

Rufius smiled back, "I will see what kind of profit I can make. As you realise I am new to this. I have only recently left the Thracians."

"You could earn a living working for King Ardal. He is a young king and he seeks good warriors. He and our army are teaching the Venicone a lesson."

Rufius rubbed his unshaven cheeks as though contemplating the idea. "I have not heard of your king. The last king I heard of was King Lugubelenus."

"Ah, he was a good king but led astray by his wife. She fled to the west somewhere. King Ardal is descended from the sister of Prince Ban who lived long ago."

"Ban? I had heard he was king." Rufius knew how to fish and he dangled the false information before the headman.

"No, he was the king's younger brother. I can understand why you might think that for we heard that he spent some time in the south of the land close to the land of the Iceni. When his brother died fighting the Selgovae another family became kings and they ruled until Lugubelenus."

"Ah so King Ardal is the direct descendant of Ban and that is how he came to be king."

"Not quite. He married the young daughter of King Lugubelenus."

"I may visit with this king then and offer him my sword."

That seemed to please Angus. "Good. King Ardal will be a good king. His family lived on the island of Mercaut just along the coast from here. His uncle and his cousin still live at the family home there. It is easily defended and they enjoy the bounty of the seals."

"Seals?"

"Aye, they live in the waters there and give both good food and oil. It is why the family is so rich although there were rumours that they found treasure on the island. Of course, that is nonsense."

"I would like to see these creatures."

"If you visit our king then you will do so for it is on the road to Traprain Law. It is a good day's ride north of here."

"Thank you, headman, you have been most kind." Rufius took a smaller piece of jet than the one he had previously shown and he handed it to the headman. "This is for your kindness."

"Thank you."

The next day Rufius had to go through the tedious process of haggling when all he really wanted to do was ride north and spy out the land. Perhaps his disinterest helped him for he found he was given high value goods for his jet rather than the fish and sheepskins Manius and the others were receiving. He was traded some fine bone arrow heads as well as horn combs, drinking vessels and a hood made from sealskin.

Angus joined him when all the jet had gone. "The hood is a fine item. It will keep you dry. They have cloaks made of such things at Mercaut and they are wonderfully warm and dry in the wet. Here, this is for you. It is a token which might prevent my fellows from dealing harshly with you, although I think that your sword is all the protection you need." He handed Rufius a piece of carved bone on a leather thong. There was a thistle carved upon it. The carving was accurate and detailed.

"Thank you, headman, I may see you upon my return." Of course, Rufius had no intention of returning to the village. Once he left he would disappear.

As he headed north one pair of eyes watched him; Pedair the Brigante was not what he seemed. He was one of Briac's nephews and he had been sent to find out the mood of the tribes north of the wall. He could now return and suggest an alliance with the Selgovae but the warrior with the sword had intrigued him. He was a warrior and not a merchant and now he was going north. Pedair wondered why. Like Rufius he was keen to return to his own land and report his good news.

Briac was enjoying a very pleasant life. He was treated like a prince, quite literally and he could not believe his change in fortune. Despite its outward appearance the island of Manavia was a comfortable, almost luxurious place. They had weekly visits from ships bringing fine foods and the houses were well furnished and decorated. It was like being in a fine Roman villa.

Severus and the Lady Flavia's guards provided Briac with the opportunity to train and he and his oathsworn soon impressed the Roman with their skills. "I am more hopeful now. If you can control your warrior's tendency to charge at anything Roman we might just succeed."

"That is the way of my warriors I am afraid."

"Then they will suffer the same fate. I am a Roman and we know how to win. Your warriors are brave but they fight for themselves. The Romans fight for each other. Yet I spy a kind of hope. Your weapons are now the equal of the Romans and we can use the extra length of your swords and height of your warriors to our advantage."

"How?"

"The legions like to close and fight toe to toe. They form a solid line of warriors. Your men can use the full swing of their swords and not come close to the gladii. We will show you. They move slower than your men do. We can use your skills to your advantage. Your people have been fighting the Romans the Roman way. All of the tribes can benefit from my ideas."

"And why do you do this? Why do you betray your people?"

"For the money!"

And so Briac learned how to fight the Romans. He would have to impose his will on his warriors but, like Severus, he saw hope where there was despair.

By riding hard Rufius made the island shortly before dark. Close by was an oppidum but it looked to be uninhabited. It had such a strong location that Rufius wondered why it had no garrison. He would investigate that after he had visited the island.

He tied his horse in a stand of trees and made his way to the sand dunes. It was still light enough to see the island. He saw a knoll with a wooden stockade at the top of it. A path ran circuitously around the slope. It would be a hard place to attack. He could not see any of the local tribes managing it. Having seen the buildings, he concentrated on identifying the people. He did not see any armed sentries but he was below the level of the walls. He counted four women and seven men. By then it became too dark to see.

He returned to his horse and faced a dilemma. Where would he spend the night? He looked down the coast and saw that the oppidum was still in darkness. He mounted and rode south. He would investigate the fort and, perhaps, spend the night there. There was no moon but the trail he had followed was obstacle-free. He dismounted some two hundred paces from the fort. He could see that it was like the one at Mercaut; it was sited on a natural feature. There was a wooden stockade but he could see that the sea protected three sides and the fourth had a twisting path leading to it. Drawing his sword, he made his way across the damp sand. He could not smell wood smoke nor could he detect the smell of man. All that filled his nostrils was the smell of the sea and seaweed.

He moved through the dark like a fox. When he reached the causeway, he paused to listen for any sounds. The only thing he heard was the sound of the sea sloshing on the rocks. He darted through the open gate; that, in itself, told him that it was empty. A cursory examination confirmed it and he returned to bring his horse.

He found a well and a water trough filled with rainwater. Once he and his horse had drunk their fill he allowed his horse to graze on the grass in the middle of the huts. The length of grass told him no one had been here for some time. The roofs of the huts were all sound and he made himself comfortable and, after eating some apples, he fell asleep.

The screaming which awoke him was that of birds and not danger. His horse, well-trained beast that it was, still nibbled the grass. Rufius threw some water on his face and ate the last of his apples. He climbed the wooden ladder to the top of the guard tower and looked north towards Mercaut. To his amazement he saw a causeway linking it to the land. That explained the defences. It was too far away to be able to make out the people but he decided to trust to the thistle token and the headman. He would pretend to be on his way north and seek food. It would be no lie for he was hungry enough to eat seaweed.

He rode along the beach rather than the road. His horse was able to open his legs and gallop through the surf. Cato, who had been the horse master of the ala, had sworn that running in seawater strengthened a horse's legs. He slowed down as he approached the causeway. He could see that the tide was coming in and soon the causeway would be sea once more. He rode to the edge and was debating what to do when a woman of eighteen or so appeared at the island end of the causeway.

"Can we help you, sir?"

"I have ridden far and seek food and shelter." He held up his purse, "I can pay."

"Come then but come quickly or you will be swimming."

Rufius urged his horse into the water. The gallop through the surf had freed him from fear and he plunged up to his haunches. By the time he was half way across Rufius was afraid that he would, indeed, have to swim but then the ground began to shelve and the water remained around his waist.

The woman laughed as he dismounted. His lower half was soaking wet. "You barely made it, sir. I am Mavourna and my father is lord of this island."

"I am Rufius and I am travelling to meet King Ardal."

A frown passed across her face briefly. Then she smiled. "Do you know the king?"

He shook my head, "No, but the headman at Am Beal thought he might have employment for me."

He led his horse towards the cluster of buildings which nestled at the foot of the knoll. She looked at this ruggedly handsome man. She had few opportunities to see anyone who did not have a greybeard. "You are a warrior then?"

"I have been a warrior but now I am a trader in jet."

Her eyes lit up. "Have you some with you? I am sure we could trade."

Rufius was glad that he had retained a purse of the precious black gold. "I have."

They were a hundred paces from the huts and a cluster of men had emerged. "I have to tell you, sir, that my father does not take kindly to strangers. Be patient and leave your sword sheathed. It would be best for all."

"I will, I promise, and if this will cause trouble then I will return to the mainland."

She laughed, "Then I hope that you and your horse are good swimmers." She pointed behind and they were an island again.

An old man came towards them. He had white hair and a white beard, his back was crooked and yet there was a defiant look in his eyes. "Who is this intruder?"

Mavourna sighed, "He is no intruder, father. I invited him over. He is a jet trader and he will pay for his food." Her eyes implored compliance and I nodded.

"Aye well we have little enough but if you were invited then I reckon I will make you welcome. I am Ban son of Ban who was the last true king of the Votadini."

Rufius nodded although his mind was a maelstrom of thoughts. "And I am Rufius of the Atrebate."

"They are a tribe from the south eh? And you have a Roman name."

Both were jabbed at Rufius in an accusatory tone. "Er yes sir, the Atrebate people live in the land close to Camulodunum and I was given a Roman name when I served with the Roman auxiliaries."

The answers seemed to satisfy the old man. "You can leave your horse here," he chuckled, "he canna go anywhere until the tide goes out."

They climbed the twisting path. Despite his age and obvious infirmity, the old man climbed it unaided. The rest of the inhabitants all went about their jobs. There was a large hall within the walls of the fort. It was rectangular rather than round. They entered and Ban son of Ban slumped down in a chair. "Mead!"

A slave, identified by a yoke, rushed in and gave him a horn of the honeyed drink popular in the area. He swallowed it down, wiped his mouth with the back of his hand and said, "Sit down. Sit down. Well, what have you to trade for your food?"

Rufius noticed that the horn Ban used was well worn. He reached into his satchel and took out a pair of the horns he had traded for at Am Beal. "Will these do sir?"

Before he could answer the woman grabbed them. "These are more than enough payment." Her tone and her look shamed the old man into nodding his agreement.

Rufius then took out a particularly fine piece of jet and proffered it to her. "And this is for you, my lady, for your kindness." He had no idea what had prompted his action but he was pleased he had for she beamed, kissed his hand and fled with the jet.

Ban smiled for the first time, "That was kind, sir, and you must forgive my bad temper. Put it down to aching bones and a wish to be young again." He gestured to the door through which his daughter had gone. "We do not get many visitors here and I forget that she might be lonely."

Rufius nodded, "Was not, Ban, a king in this land at the time of the invasion by the Romans?"

"Mead!"

The question appeared to have angered the old man. The slave scurried in, refilled the horn and fled in fear. "Aye, but that was before my father's time. My father should have been king but that usurper Lugubelenus stole the throne from him and now Ardal has stolen it from me." His sharp eyes suddenly stared at Rufius. "How do you know of Ban the old king?"

Rufius smiled, "My grandfather met a Ban who was at the court of King Prasutagus. He told me the story although the way he told it the Ban who visited King Prasutagus was a king."

Ban's face relaxed, "Ah, King Prasutagus. He was kinsman to my father. Had he not died and his tribe not revolted who knows what might have been different."

The mood was lightened and the evening proved to be a pleasant one. Rufius was convinced that he had found the right place. He had no idea if the treasure was still here but he could return to the Legate with more information than he could have expected. The Ban he sought had been this man's father.

Chapter 9

Livius and the ala did not reach Cilurnum until the first, early snows had fallen. They were weary and their horses were exhausted. Whilst the troopers stabled their horses Livius reported to the Legate.

"We visited every settlement along the Dunum and all the way to the west coast. We found some arms, not many but enough to suggest that someone is supplying the Brigante with high quality weapons."

"That is disturbing news. Would you say you discouraged them from rebelling?"

Livius shook his head. He knew the Legate too well to give a flattering lie. "No, Legate, short of digging up every village and hanging a few headmen it is hard to see what else could have been done. Their hearts and minds have been won already. We are the enemy. Even Marcus and the Sword of Cartimandua appeared to have little effect."

Julius Demetrius suddenly looked his age. "Would that I had some good news to impart to you but I fear there is precious little. The VIth has finally departed for Eboracum. That should mean that the land south of the Dunum is safe but we are now in greater danger. The little good news is that we have two new auxiliary units on the wall. The 1st Aelia Dacorum, a double strength cohort, has arrived and is now stationed at Vercovicium and the 1st Batavorum cohort is to be based at Luguvalium. They are a mixed cohort. We have more cavalry now."

"Well that is a relief. We will need remounts from Nanna soon. I would not like to send the ala out on patrol any time soon."

"And the Quartermaster acquired those spears you wanted. Training can begin straight away."

"Well that is good news." Livius stretched. "It will be good to sleep in my own bed again. If that is all, sir?" He stood.

"Yes, Livius you and the ala have done well. Rest."

As he turned to go Livius said, "And I will give some thought to that box from my uncle. I confess it has preyed upon my mind."

Julius guiltily looked down. "Er, Livius, I er, well the fact of the matter is that I took it upon myself to investigate the matter."

A brief flash of anger appeared on the Prefect's face before he composed himself. "Sir?"

"Sit down, please." As Livius seated himself Julius began. "I sent Rufius to find out if he could find this Ban. He found his son and he believes that the treasure is on an island called Mercaut about two or three days' ride north of here."

Livius felt a mixture of relief and apprehension. "I think I hoped that it had disappeared. I worry that we are opening Pandora's box. We know not what the consequences might be."

"True but if we hold the box then at least we are in control."

"You wish me to retrieve the treasure then?"

Julius sighed, command was never easy and he knew he was going to upset his old friend. "I wish your men to retrieve the treasure."

"But sir!"

The Legate held up his hand. "You and the Decurion Princeps will be needed here to train the men with the new spears and to prepare for what I believe will be a bloody spring. I want you to send Rufius and Marcus north to this island. Rufius has already made contact with Ban's son and I believe he will be able to successfully complete the task."

Livius could not fault the Legate's argument but this had been a family matter. He wondered how it might have turned out if he had not opened the letter in the Legate's office. "Why two turmae? Marcus and his men have just had a gruelling few weeks away."

"I know. Give them a few days and they will recover enough. I am sending two because I want to give them a cover. This will look as though we are probing north. I have no doubt that there are Brigante spies all around us. It will allay the fears of the Brigante. I do not want them to know that we are aware of their plans. I want them to believe that their apparent innocence has fooled us."

"Have you informed the Governor?"

"I have but he is new and he is too busy making his palace more comfortable. Besides his intelligence reports suggest that the Brigante are pacified. Even your evidence of a few swords and spears will not convince him. I fear the frontier forces are on their own. The VIth has been ordered to stay in Eboracum. By the time we can deploy them the rebellion will have started. At least they will be in a position to prevent it."

Livius had forgotten the box already; it was a minor consideration. "And how will we deal with the threat?"

"I intend to call a meeting of the Prefects of the auxiliary units along the wall. Now that we have two more I hope we can field two thousand men to meet this threat."

"But the barbarians will have more men than that."

"I know. And that is another reason why you need to stay here. Your ala might be the difference between success and disaster."

Caronwyn was also gathering together an alliance of leaders. She had gathered the tribal representatives of many tribes. She had warriors and priests from the Selgovae, the Novontae, the Dumnonii and even a warrior from the Venicones. The only tribe she had invited who was missing was the Votadini. She was being shunned by King Ardal. It was a minor irritation. She suspected it was because she still harboured Radha on the island. Caronwyn had hoped that the former Queen of the Votadini might have been able to draw in the young king but her gamble had failed. She was philosophical about it. She still had enough warriors to flood the wall from both sides. When the leaders left her, she was confident that by the third moon after Yule the frontier would be in flames. Severus had told them all how to defeat the Romans and each leader had been given fine weapons,

There had been a couple of minor irritations which danced around the back of her mind like summer flies you hear but cannot see. Her Nemesis, Marcus' Horse, had swept through the heartland of the Brigante and found some of the weapons. She now wondered if she had a spy within her camp and Pedair Briac's cousin had reported the curious incident of the Roman north of the wall. It was a small thing but she could not understand its significance. What were Roman spies doing north of the wall? She knew that she would have to find out more before the fire could be ignited.

Roman Wall

Marcus, Metellus and Rufius were summoned to the Prefect's office a week after the return of the ala. Livius had insisted that the task of telling the young men what they were to do was his. The Legate ruled the wall but Livius was still the Prefect of Marcus' Horse.

When they were seated he began by telling them the story of the box. He told them of Rufius' work and the conclusions they had drawn. Marcus and Metellus were fascinated while Rufius just listened. He had not got the lovely Mavourna from his thoughts.

"I want two turmae to go to Mercaut and get the treasure. Rufius, you will need this." He handed him the ring. "This is the sign that you come from Prasutagus."

Rufius examined the beautifully made ring. Marcus asked, "Sir, why two turmae? It will draw attention to us. Surely it would be better for a couple of men to sneak into their land and retrieve the treasure."

"The Legate wants the Brigante to think that we are considering expansion north of the wall. We are not."

Rufius put the ring on the table, "Sir, what happens if the Votadini take exception to our presence? Do we fight?"

"No. We need no more enemies north of the wall. The Votadini are quiet let us leave them that way. You will negotiate or you will back off. Besides Traprain Law is far from Mercaut and with winter upon us the news would only reach King Ardal when you had completed the mission."

Rufius took a deep breath, "And suppose Ban does not wish to hand over the box? We have no idea where it is save that it is probably on the island somewhere."

There was a pause, "Persuade him." Rufius knew that he had to get the box at whatever cost.

In Traprain Law King Ardal was listening to his advisers. Some wished him to join the alliance led by the priestess of Manavia. Others wished him to consolidate the new gains made against the Venicones. His younger brother, Banquo, however, had other concerns. When the advisers and nobles had left them, the young man gave voice to his thoughts.

87

"It seems to me, brother, that none of those is our priority. We have held the crown for a short time. The evil Radha is hiding on Manavia and who knows what mischief she can cause. We should ask this Caronwyn to hand over Radha to us as payment for joining the rebellion. Then there is our uncle, Ban. He squats still on his island and we both know that he resents the fact that we have power."

King Ardal shook his head. His brother was the cleverest man he knew. Yet he could not believe that old Uncle Ban would cause trouble. "He has few men and he must be close to death."

"Perhaps we can make him even closer."

"I will not spill the blood of our family."

"Then at least allow me to get assurances from him that he will not oppose us. I will have him swear an oath."

King Ardal could not fault that. He had been mildly irritated that his uncle had not attended the coronation. Alone out of all the nobles, he had not sworn allegiance. "Very well, but no violence. Ban may be cantankerous but he is a loyal Votadini."

"And Radha?"

"I will consider your suggestion brother. It has merit." Ardal was pleased to have his belligerent and ambitious brother away from court. He offended too many people.

Banquo left, pleased that he had been tasked with something which suited his nature. Unlike his brother, Banquo was vindictive. Mavourna had humiliated him by rejecting his advances some years earlier. Now that he had the power he would make her rue her decision. He would also enjoy humbling his uncle who had ever disparaged the two of them. He and his oathsworn had spent many months preparing for war. This would be a chance to put some of those skills to the test.

The two turmae slipped across the bridge over the Tinea when the late autumn rains were slicing down. Almost all of the troopers had been born in Britannia and knew the vagaries of the weather but it was still a shock to the system. Marcus was amused when Rufius took out his hood and fastened it over his helmet.

"What in great Belenus' name is that?"

"I was given it by the Votadini. It keeps out the rain."

Marcus cocked his head to one side. "It does not look good Rufius."

He laughed, "When have I ever worried about how I look?"

"That is because you have no woman in your life. Frann would not let me wear such a thing."

"Perhaps that is one reason why I have never taken a wife."

"Or because you are too old and set in your ways."

"Now that is a good reason."

Marcus nodded up the road, beyond the horizon. "This is new land for us."

"Aye. You know the land to the west; it is where you and Marco defended the eagle but this coast has remained unknown to us all." He gestured towards the road where an unhappy Felix sat astride a pony with a suspicious Wolf trotting next to him. "I am hoping that Felix can become familiar with the land. I barely left the road when I headed north."

"Do we need to worry about attacks and ambushes?"

"I think not. I saw no sign of the Votadini and the last we heard they were busy with the Venicones. I feel we are too strong for the Selgovae bandits." As they rode in silence, however, Rufius was worried that they might not be as welcome as he had been when he had been Rufius the jet merchant. He would hate to have to show strength to Angus and those who had been kind to him.

They made better time than when Rufius had travelled with the merchants and they approached the town in late afternoon. As he had expected the gates were closed on their approach. Leaving the chosen men with the turmae, Marcus and Rufius rode up to the gates. The rain had abated somewhat and the hood was safely stowed.

Angus appeared on the gate and shouted, belligerently, "This is Votadini land. What are Romans doing here?"

Rufius took off his helmet and proffered the thistle token. "The last time I came here I came as a friend."

"You! Then you came under false pretences."

"No, I did not. I do trade in jet."

"And why are you here then. You are trading war now!"

Rufius shook his head. "No, we are not. Rome conquered all of this land in the time of Agricola. The rebellion of Lugubelenus does not change that. Rome is a forgiving mother. When I told my superiors of the bandits my Legate asked me to patrol the old Roman Road to Alavna for the protection of all. You have my word that we will not impose our will upon you. The wall is there as a frontier only. It is not a threat."

Angus seemed somewhat mollified but he added, "We will judge you when you return. If there are heads upon your saddles and slaves in your wake then we will know that you lie."

Rufius nodded, "Thank you, headman." They led the column north.

Marcus looked back, "That was quick thinking back there."

"You were an Explorate too. You know that it is always wise to have a story ready to hand." He waved Felix forward. "Felix, we will head towards Alavna. It is some miles to the northeast. See if it is safe."

Felix slipped his leg over the saddle and took off with Wolf like a startled hare. Marcus shook his head, "Why he prefers his own legs to a horse I will never know. Titus, come and get Felix's mount."

Alavna was on the Roman Road proper but it had long been abandoned. The Roman auxiliaries who had built and defended these forts now huddled in their mile castles on the wall. Whilst the defences had been rendered useless by the soldiers before they left, they would, at least, afford some shelter.

It was dark when they reached the fort. The glow of light showed them that Felix had examined the area and found it free from danger. There would be the possibility of hot food.

As they sat around the fires, drying out their cloaks and warming themselves, Marcus asked Rufius of their plan of action.

"We will head for the oppidum I found. We should reach it before dark and it will give us the opportunity to observe Mercaut. The headman may have sent word north about our presence and we will need to be careful."

Banquo and his twenty oathsworn were heading in the opposite direction to the Romans. He and his men were approaching the island. Banquo had not prepared well enough and the causeway was under water when they arrived. His first quest as a leader was not going well and they were forced to camp in the dunes. It was a cold and cheerless night. It did nothing to improve the young man's humour. He had forgotten about the tides.

The oathsworn of Banquo were all young men like himself. They styled themselves The Bears. Banquo had managed to get a set of bear claws and he wore them around his neck. He had not killed a bear but he had traded for them. All of them dreamt of hunting and then killing a bear. When they ate of its heart then its power would devolve to them. They would become warriors who could not be defeated. They wore painted markings upon their faces and they had the sign of the bear tattooed on their chests. They looked fierce and that was their intention. They were, however, not blooded. When Ardal had fought for the land Banquo had been with the rear-guard and they were not needed. He had hoped to find action against the Venicones but they had proved reluctant to fight. He and his oathsworn were frustrated. They were desperate for the chance to prove their courage.

As Banquo looked across the water he realised that this would not be a chance for glory but it would be an opportunity to show his men that he had power and he knew how to use it. It would be a chance for his men to flex their muscles. Ban still had warriors. They might be old but they would have to do. The Romans were too far away to fight.

Mavourna had seen the Votadini warriors arrive. Since the visit of the Atrebate she had taken to staring west in case he came again. There had been something in his eyes and his voice which she found appealing. When, however, she saw the warriors she became worried. There were too many for a social visit and they looked to be armed for war. The fact that they were all mounted told her much. She hurried to her father to tell him.

Her father was a deep man and a religious man. He had toyed with the idea of becoming a priest when he was younger for he had the ability to see into the future. His own father's death had put that idea from his mind but he still retained the ability to see beyond the obvious.

"This is the doing of my nephew, Ardal."

"How can you be sure? This did not look like a royal retinue."

Ban smiled at his daughter whom he loved dearly. She was the only child who had lived beyond childhood. When Ban went to the Otherworld his name would die unless she had issue. He did not fear his own death but he feared for his daughter and his line. "This may not be Ardal but it may well be someone sent on his behalf. You should leave. Take the boat and sail to the oppidum. You will be safe there. Go with the slave women."

She stood defiantly. "No! I will not! My place is at your side. Besides if this is an attack of some kind then you will need all the men you can muster."

They both knew, however, that the ten men who lived on the island were almost as old as Ban. Their days of defending the land were long gone. "In that case, we will let the seas and the lands defend us. Gather all the food and take it into the fort. We will wait out the storm."

That evening every animal and scrap of food was taken inside and as much water as they could collect was stored. There was no water on the island but they had huge stone tanks which collected the rainwater. If this had been summer then they might have been in danger of running out but at this time of year they had a surplus.

Finally Ban issued all the weapons he had. He looked sadly at them. They were all old and had seen better days. If this came to a fight then it would not be a long one but whoever came would know that they had fought a warrior and his friends.

When dawn came the tide was in once more. Banquo had missed his opportunity during the night. They had sat up until late drinking and had not set guards. He and his men had slept when they could have walked across the causeway. He rode to the edge of the sea and shouted across to the island. No-one was close and he could see figures standing behind the wooden walls. No one acknowledged him. It was frustrating. It was as though the sea was fighting him too. He wondered if he ought to have brought a slave to sacrifice; perhaps that would have turned the tide.

Inside the walls Mavourna recognised Banquo. He had been a nasty youth who had made a futile attempt to take her virginity when she was barely twelve summers old. She had never told her father but she was sure that her cousin still bore the marks of her nails. She told Ban what she had seen. His eyes could not see that far. "Then he has been sent by his brother. He is a young fool. We will see if he can shift us."

As the tide peaked so Banquo prepared his men. "We will give them the chance to allow us to enter the fort but if they resist then we will slaughter them all. The girl is not to be harmed. She is mine."

Even though his men knew the restrictions placed upon him by his brother they were oathsworn. Banquo would lead them to glory and they would do all that he asked.

Chapter 10

The two turmae reached the oppidum in the early afternoon. Whilst Felix and Wolf hunted, Marcus and Rufius climbed the tower. Rufius was just pointing out the island when he spotted the warriors. He frowned as he turned to Marcus. "I like this not. Leave your Chosen Man with your turma. They should prepare the defences of the oppidum."

"But Livius said that we were not to engage in warfare."

Rufius' eyes narrowed. I am the senior decurion and it is my responsibility." He softened his tone with a smile. "I have a feeling that we are doing the right thing. You can stay here with your men if you wish. I will understand."

Marcus nodded. "I will stand by you, Rufius, for I believe that you are doing the right thing too. We will face the Prefect's wrath together." He mounted his horse. "Gnaeus, we will ride to the aid of the island. Make the oppidum defensible."

"What if you do not return?"

Marcus smiled, "Then you will get a rapid promotion!"

Now that he was close to the island Banquo decided to wait until the causeway was shallow enough for them to cross. The water was a little rougher than he would have liked and, besides, his uncle and the bitch were going nowhere. When he could clearly see the rocks beneath the surface he led his men across the causeway to the island. They had to wade through the surf in places. As they approached the fort he could see that his uncle had armed his men. Had he had a warning of their visit?

He halted out of bow range. He did not know if they had such weapons but he was not willing to take a chance. He removed his helmet so that his uncle could see him.

"Uncle, it is your nephew Prince Banquo. This is not the welcome I expected."

He heard Ban's laugh. "So, you bring armed men to my home and expect a welcome. Be gone, whelp!"

"I can see how you are afraid of my men but we come in peace."

"Listen, puppy prince, I fear neither you nor those tattooed dogs with you. Say what you will and be gone."

A murmur of discontent arose from the oathsworn who did not like the way their leader was being spoken to. "I do not like your tone, uncle, and I will speak plainly. My brother has sent me here to demand that you swear allegiance to him and to me." Banquo knew that the last part was not his brother's words but he wanted the old man humiliating.

The answer came with a spear hurled by Ban. It struck Calum who was next to Banquo. The young warrior was hurled from his pony and died with a surprised expression on his face.

"There is my answer!"

"You will all die and that bitch of a cousin will beg for death before I have finished with her." He began to turn. The turn saved his life for Mavourna used her slingshot to send a large pebble in the direction of her cousin. It struck his pony rather than him. The animal reared and threw Banquo to the ground. He heard the laughter from the walls as he struggled to his feet.

His face was infused with embarrassment and anger. "No prisoners!"

Rufius led the troopers along the sand dunes. It meant he was hidden from view. He had no idea what was going on but the armed men had him worried. They could be Selgovae. He was not so arrogant as to believe that a word from him would stop Selgovae bandits. He had stopped one band only.

As he approached the island he slowed the troopers down and then led them to the top of the dune. He could see that the warriors were indeed attacking the fort. He could see at least one warrior lying on the ground. The attackers had dismounted and were now surrounding the fort. Rufius had seen the defenders and knew that they were not enough to defend all of the walls. Their defences would soon be breached.

He turned to the troopers. "This is an island. We have one chance to get across and help the people on the island. We ride as fast as we can before the tide comes in. I know not who those attackers are but we will destroy them." He raised his spear. "Marcus' Horse!"

The turma roared their war cry and galloped as fast as they could behind the two decurions. It was a reckless ride through the surf but each trooper was a master of his mount.

Banquo and his men had already sent arrows and javelins over the walls. Three defenders had fallen. Banquo thought that one of them was Ban. His attackers had not escaped unscathed. A second warrior had died and two more had been stunned by his cousin's sling. He was confident that they would take this place and then he would have it as his own. It would be called Din Banquo!

Marcus had not used one of the spears before but Livius and Metellus were keen for them to be the weapon of choice for the ala. In his heart Marcus would rather have used the Sword of Cartimandua but, as they raced across the flat land he could see the advantage. It extended his reach by half the length of his horse. He leaned forward with it as he pointed Raven at the warrior who was aiming a bow at the wooden tower. He pulled his arm back and then punched forward. Even as the tip speared the man in the back Marcus twisted and pulled so that the lifeless body fell to the ground and the weapon was ready once more.

The screams of the dying alerted Banquo to the fact that his men were being attacked. As he turned he saw, to his horror, that Roman cavalry were amongst his men and they were being slaughtered. He was pragmatic. He did not mind dying in battle but he wanted it to be seen by others. He yelled, "Bears! Fall back to the horses!"

Rufius and the others were already trying to turn. Marcus spun Raven around. A warrior's face appeared before him and Marcus whipped the spear across his face. He saw the edge rip a jagged line across the bearded warrior's forehead and then he was gone. He urged Raven on. The men on foot were fast. They reached their nimble ponies and then leapt into the waters which had risen alarmingly since the Romans had crossed.

Banquo and the handful of survivors plunged into the choppy grey water. If they crossed the causeway they might die. If they stayed on the island they would die.

Marcus reined in as he saw two ponies and their riders swept to their deaths. The other eight struggled as they half swam and half walked back to the mainland. Rufius halted next to Marcus. Marcus dug his spear into the ground to lean the blood. "It seems we are trapped here for the night."

"We are. Organise the men and I will go and speak with Ban."

Although they were not his turma the troopers were all known to Marcus. He dismounted and led Raven back towards the walls. Trooper Lepidus shouted, "Looks like you don't need your sword now sir. The spears are lethal."

He grinned, "Yes but I will not relinquish my blade just yet."

The wounded Votadini were despatched and the capsarius, Trooper Carpal, dealt with the few wounds suffered by the turma. He waved over Rufius' Chosen Man, "Better make a camp and get some food on the go. We will be stuck here for the night."

"But we left the food in the oppidum!"

"Then you had better forage or we will starve." He smiled, "We can always eat seaweed!"

"Very funny sir, I bet your lads love your sense of humour."

He put the spear into its leather bindings to free up his hand and walked over to the track leading to the gate. Rufius turned as he approached; he had taken off his helmet and was scratching his scalp. "I am not certain how many are left alive up there. I have shouted but no one has answered."

Just then Mavourna's face appeared and she looked distressed. When she recognised Rufius she looked surprised, "You I..." then she seemed to remember something more important. "My father is wounded."

"Capsarius! Follow me."

The three Romans entered through the gate. As they ran they saw that there were six bodies lying on the ground. The girl shouted, harshly, "They are dead but my father lives."

A wounded warrior was cradling the old man's head. It was a stomach wound. The capsarius glanced at Rufius and shook his head. "Now then sir, let us look at this."

The old man opened his eyes and smiled; a tendril of blood seeped out of the corner of his mouth. "I am for the Otherworld. See to my men they fought bravely."

97

The capsarius nodded, "You are a brave warrior. May the Allfather be with you." He turned his attentions to the warrior with the wounded arm.

The girl gave a slight sob and the wounded warrior placed her arm under her father's head. "It will comfort him child."

Ban looked up at Rufius. "I knew you were no jet merchant. You were not greedy enough. My daughter tells me you drove away the perfidious Banquo." Rufius nodded. "I am in your debt. Please care for my daughter. She is alone and she likes you."

"Father!"

"It is true and a dying man does not lie."

"I will." Rufius hesitated.

"Go on man. I cannot last much longer ask your question and be done with it."

Rufius took the ring from his tunic. "I believe this will allow me to have the box that King Prasutagus gave to your father for safekeeping."

Ban's eyes widened. "I knew the gods had kept me alive for a reason." His thin fingers grabbed hold of Rufius. "Promise me that you will care for Mavourna and I shall tell you all."

"I promised already but if you wish a sacred oath then I will give one. I swear to protect Mavourna with my life for as long as she needs my protection."

He sank back, seemingly satisfied. He spoke without opening his eyes, "The chest is hidden beneath my bed. There is the mark of a boar upon it." He winced and said, "I go to the…"

There was a last dying breath and he was gone. His daughter began to sob. The three soldiers and the warrior watched sadly. Rufius put his arm around her shoulders and raised her to her feet. She wiped the tears from her eyes. "You do not need to protect me, Roman, I absolve you of your oath. I can fend for myself."

Rufius smiled, "But I cannot absolve myself of my oath nor would I wish to. You shall come with me and I will look after you south of the wall."

She pulled away. "You want me to leave my home!"

The warrior's arm had been bandaged, "He is right my lady. You cannot stay here. Banquo will come back with more men."

She looked at the greybeard. "But what of you and the others?"

"We will follow you," he gave a wry smile and a shrug. "There are but four of us who remain and we will soon be following your father. While we live we will serve him." He looked up at Rufius. "We cannot bury him, Banquo will despoil his body."

Before Rufius could speak Mavourna said, "We will put him in our boat and burn it. He will be close to his home and his spirit will inhabit this island."

The warrior and Rufius nodded. They carried the body to the boat. Mavourna placed his helmet upon his head and his oathsworn placed his sword in his hands. The last retainers of Ban son of Ban held the boat against the wind while Mavourna kissed him. Then Rufius and Marcus dropped lighted torches into the small boat and the breeze took it out to see. Perhaps it was the vagaries of the sea or perhaps the spirit of Ban himself but the boat seemed to turn when just a few paces from shore. The flames engulfed the boat and the sail and the whole vessel hissed to the bottom of the sea just paces from where he had lived.

Rufius knew that he had to act swiftly. He went to the wounded warrior. "What is your name, warrior?"

"Scealis."

"Well, Scealis, help your mistress to gather all that she needs. There are eight ponies we can use to carry the six of you and your belongings."

"We have two horses too and a wagon."

Rufius shook his head. "The wagon will slow us down. We carry what will fit on the back of the horses and the ponies."

Scealis nodded, "I will see to it." He looked at Rufius. "What about the slaves?"

"We cannot take them. They could stay here."

Scealis seemed happy. "They know no other life. I will tell them." He paused, "You will get the box?"

"I will get the box."

He seemed satisfied, "The master was concerned about the debt his father owed the Iceni. It is good that it is paid. He will meet his father in the Otherworld and hold his head high."

Rufius waved Marcus over, "Let us get this box for the prefect or else I will have got into trouble for nothing."

Marcus laughed, "I do not think it was for nothing. You have managed to annoy the brother of the King of the Votadini. That is no small achievement, my friend."

They headed for Ban's room. It was something of an anti-climax to discover that the chest had merely been shoved under a bed. They pulled it out and saw that it did, indeed, bear the sign of Prasutagus. Marcus looked at Rufius, "Do we open it?"

The decurion shook his head. "We will leave that for the Prefect. Give this to Gaius and tell him to defend it with his life. I would hate to lose it now having caused so much trouble."

It took more time than Rufius would have liked to gather together all of Mavourna's possessions. The four warriors took just their weapons and clothes.

Scealis waved the decurion over. "The tide is beginning to turn. Soon we can leave."

Scealis and Mavourna addressed the slaves. There were just six of them. Mavourna smiled at them. She had known the older ones all of her life. They had been treated kindly and she hated to be leaving them but she knew it was an unavoidable decision. Banquo had seen to that. She hated her cousin. Putting his evil from her mind she spoke, "We are leaving here but we cannot take you with us. We give you your freedom."

One of the older women dropped to her knees. "Thank you, my lady, but we would serve you still."

Mavourna raised her to her feet, "That cannot be. We are going…" she noticed Scealis give a firm shake of the head. It would not do to give Banquo too much information. "We go far from here."

Scealis said, "You can stay here but I fear that Banquo will return and pay you back for our resistance. Take what you will and head west to make a new life. There are many fertile valleys where you can live in peace."

Rufius addressed the troopers. "We do not know if the men we defeated are waiting for us. Let us assume they are. When we reach the mainland, I want the whole turma in a defensive skirmish line until Decurion Aurelius has taken our guests to the oppidum."

Scealis nodded and they moved across the causeway. The water was still high but their horses moved through the swirling dark waters confidently. The troopers rode on either side of the young woman and the captured ponies with their precious cargo. When they reached solid ground Scealis turned and saluted the island with his good arm, "Lord Ban watches over us." On the island the slaves waved their goodbyes as they prepared to leave their home when the causeway was finally revealed.

The turma spread out while Rufius and Gaius led the others south along the dunes to the distant oppidum. Marcus waited with the turma, his sword drawn. They had neither seen nor smelled the Votadini who had fled but in the dark, they could be lurking.

One of the troopers shouted, "Over here sir."

When Marcus reached the man, he saw a dead warrior lying in the dunes. He lay with a savage cut to his stomach but Marcus could see that he had had his throat cut to send him to the Allfather. "It seems we did better than we thought." Convinced now that the others had fled Marcus led the turma down the beach towards the oppidum.

Felix and Wolf greeted Rufius as he approached the old fort. "What is amiss Felix? Why are you not in the oppidum?"

"We saw you leave the island and I came to see if you needed any aid." He pointed back to the walls, lined with Marcus' turma. "Chosen Man was worried."

"We are safe now."

Once inside the safety of the fort Rufius found that there was hot food prepared. While the horses were unsaddled and they waited for Marcus to arrive, the decurion ran through his plans in his mind. They needed rest. It would take them at least two days to reach the wall. He had to assume that Banquo would either go to his brother, in which case the pursuing Votadini would not catch them, or he would raise a warband and follow them immediately. Scealis had told him that there was another hill fort a half a day ride to the north. He decided to rest until an hour or so after dawn and then ride for Am Beal. He hoped that the presence of Mavourna and the others would persuade the headman that they were friends.

Far to the north an angry Banquo whipped his pony as he raced towards Traprain Law. His warriors were too frightened to approach him and tell him that they were killing their ponies. He had had to send his closest friend to the Allfather and that had just capped a disastrous day. In his warped mind it was Mavourna who was to blame for all of this. She became a witch who had summoned the Romans to their aid. How else could the sudden appearance of the horse warriors be explained? He was even angrier, for when he had asked the warriors of the hill fort to follow him south they had refused. What had promised to be his first glorious adventure was proving to be a nightmare of colossal proportions. Even as he rode north he began to plan the death of his cousin.

Chapter 11

A flurry of snow heralded the arrival at Cilurnum of the return of Rufius and his men. Livius had taken to watching each afternoon. He had felt guilty about his men risking their lives for what he believed was a family matter. Despite the Legate's words he had worried about the dangers they would face. When he saw the two turmae and the Votadini he was relieved and intrigued in equal measure.

The two decurions saluted as they passed through the gate and entered the fort. Livius counted the barbarians with them and was relieved that there were only five. They would be able to accommodate them. He had taken in that they were not bound and would be friendly. The vicus which had sprung up across the river had huts but nowhere for them to live.

"Chosen Man, give me the box." He took the precious box from his second in command. "Have the horses seen to and find somewhere for Mavourna and the others to stay." Rufius knew he had decisions to make about the future of his ward.

Marcus handed his reins to his Chosen Man. "Well Rufius, let us face the fury of the Legate and the Prefect eh?"

"I told you at Mercaut that I would bear the brunt of the punishment."

"It is not our way, brother. Come, this delay merely makes the punishment last longer."

Livius had sent for the Legate as soon as he had seen the approach of his men and they eagerly awaited them.

"Sir, we retrieved the box as ordered." Rufius placed it on the table.

"Did you open it?"

"No sir, that was not our job."

"Sit down both of you. You might as well be in on the grand opening." The Legate gestured to Livius. "It was your uncle's task Livius. Do the honours."

The box had not been opened since it had been sent north. The sea air had swollen the wood and the lid refused to budge. Livius took out his pugeo and ran it along the edge. A patina of dirt marked the shiny edge of the blade. He put the pugeo under again and gently levered the lid up. It suddenly popped up and seemed to sigh as it opened.

Unlike the small half-empty box Livius' uncle had sent to him this one was larger and packed to the top. The sight which greeted them was a torc and a small half crown. Both were made of gold. Both bore the mark of the boar. This was the regalia of Prasutagus. Livius reverently lifted them out and put them for the legate to examine. There was a necklace made of jet and precious jewels. Again, there was a boar carved from jet hanging from the middle of the golden chain. He removed the necklace and the handful of rings which were there.

"King Prasutagus must have been really worried to have sent this treasure north."

Marcus said, "Or he could have had second sight. That would have been what my mother said."

"You could be right." Livius then began to remove the heavy bags from the bottom. He opened one and spilled the golden and silver coins on to the table.

Julius picked one up and examined it. "This is Emperor Claudius. These must be the monies that were loaned to the king." He returned it to the pile. "We must now decide what to do with this but first, Decurion Atrebeus, give us your report."

"Sir, when we reached the island and the home of Ban son of Ban we saw that they were under attack. Even though we had orders not to fight it seemed to me that we ought to help."

"And me!"

Livius smiled at the loyal support given by Marcus.

"It was my decision that we aided the occupants of the fort. We drove away the attackers and spoke to Ban son of Ban just before he died. He told us where the treasure was and I promised to watch over his daughter. We brought them with us."

Julius Demetrius had a sharp mind. "A good report and I can find little fault with your actions. Yet it seems to me that there are some elements missing. Am I right?"

"Yes, sir although I had not finished my report. We discovered that the men we had driven off were Banquo, the brother of King Ardal of the

Votadini and his oathsworn. It is the reason we had to bring Mavourna with us. She is his cousin. I fear that we may have turned the Votadini into enemies."

"Did you have any trouble coming south through their land?"

"No sir. The headman at Am Beal seemed happy that we had rescued Mavourna. It seems that Ban son of Ban was highly thought of."

"You disobeyed orders, Decurion Atrebeus, and yet I cannot criticise you. It is what we would have done eh Livius?" Livius smiled and nodded. The two decurions before him were as near to sons as he would ever get. "And the decurion who first wielded the Sword of Cartimandua did much the same and was rewarded for his actions despite bringing the wrath of the Carvetii and the Brigante down on the frontier. I daresay King Ardal will now join with the Selgovae. Perhaps this will be a real test for the wall of our Emperor Hadrian." He replaced the regalia into the box. "We will need to send this to the Iceni. At least we can build bridges there."

Livius looked at Rufius, "And how will you care for this daughter of Ban?"

"I hadn't really thought, sir. Ban made it a condition of letting us have the box."

Marcus laughed, "Sir, as Drugi might have said, the daughter of Ban was making cow's eyes at Rufius." Livius looked confused. "She has set her heart on him. Even old Ban could see that. Decurion Atrebeus might not know it but it was obvious to everyone else. She wants to be his wife."

Rufius looked as though he might argue but he had no arguments left. Julius smiled, "It looks to be the way with the decurion of this ala. They save a young girl and end up with a wife. Perhaps you and I should try this eh Livius?"

"I think we are too old and set in our ways."

As they left Marcus grinned, "That wasn't as bad as it could have been."

"What was that about taking Mavourna as my wife? What makes you think that she wishes that?"

"You may be older than I am and a better warrior but you are a novice in the ways of women. Speak with her and ask her."

"She might say no."

Marcus laughed, "And you are afraid of such a short word? No means that you just need to find a place for her and her men to live. If she says yes then you have her for life. Think on it."

The wedding took place a month before Saturnalia. Mavourna still called it Yule but it mattered not. It was a cause for celebration in the cold of winter. Rufius had a roundhouse built in the vicus close to the fort. Scealis and the others were housed in their own roundhouse nearby. It was a happy arrangement for they could hunt, fish and repair armour for all of them had such skills. The year ended well at the fort despite what had been a potential disaster. The Votadini had not run amok and the frontier had an eerie silent quality. The white wall was shrouded in the white of winter. It was yet to be stained with the red blood of war.

Yule was also celebrated north of the wall. This time it had been organised by Caronwyn. Feanan, the king of the Novontae, had been persuaded to host a conclave of kings and would be kings. The Brigante, Novontae, Carvetii and Selgovae were all present as was King Ardal, the King of the Votadini. That had been the hardest negotiation that Caronwyn had had. The Selgovae and the Votadini had had a feud since the time of Lugubelenus and Radha. King Ardal agreed to a truce over Yule but he promised no more than that.

The hill fort overlooked the sheltered bay. The Novontae regarded it as a holy place for even in winter the waters were warmer than anywhere else on the west coast. Even more remarkable was the difference between high and low tides; it made it seem as though the gods had marked it as a special site. For this reason, the other kings, chiefs and princes were happy to be there. The Lady Flavia had sweetened the invitation by providing meats and delicacies from far away so that the Novontae would not have to use their own meagre resources.

Each tribe and faction had their own hut specially erected for the meeting. The wall and Rome were seen as common enemies. Despite the differences between the tribes they could unite in their hatred of all things Roman.

Caronwyn brought, not only her guards, but also her priests. There were many of them. Some were males but many were females. She had, hidden from public view and protected by her own bodyguards, Queen Radha of the Votadini. The high priestess of the Mother Cult had a master stroke to unite the tribes under her banner. She might not be a queen herself but she would lead these kings and direct their actions like a general.

The last to arrive, as she had expected was King Ardal and his retinue. He had brought the greatest number of warriors. That, too, was to be expected. Until recently he had been isolated from the other kings and had to cross through the land of his enemy the Selgovae. King Feanan made him welcome but Caronwyn saw the wary side of the young king when he ringed his hut with his armed warriors.

The other kings and princes sought Caronwyn's views on this matter. King Tole of the Selgovae had been a lover of her mother although he had not aged well since then. He was, however, a powerful king who wielded influence and power. It was he who led the deputation

"We thought we were coming here for peace and yet we see this upstart bringing heavily armed warriors and making his own fort here. This is not a good start to the alliance. If he cannot cooperate now then there will be no chance against the Romans."

Caronwyn smiled sweetly at the King of the Selgovae. "He is young and he knows none of us. Let me speak with him and see if I can change his mind. The conclave does not begin until the morrow. Give me until then."

Tole was not convinced. "Perhaps the gods do not smile upon this venture."

Her thin-lipped smile oozed venom as she hissed, "The Mother smiles upon it and tomorrow we will make a sacrifice which will guarantee success. That I promise you Tole, King of the Selgovae." Her power was such that he stepped back and clutched at his amulet of the god Belatucadros. This was not a woman to be crossed. He still remembered her mother who had brought him to power. He would trust the priestess yet.

The guards outside the roundhouse crossed their spears. "No-one enters without the king's permission."

She glowered at the man. "You know who I am?"

In truth the warrior did not and he looked into the cold green eyes. "I have my orders."

"And I take my orders from the Mother for I am Caronwyn the high priestess. Would you cross me?"

The man had heard of her now and he looked at his companion for help. He glanced at her and saw that she had no weapons and just wore the cloak of a wolf. "You are not armed. I will admit you. Allow me to introduce you." He entered the roundhouse and said loudly, "Caronwyn the High Priestess to speak with the king."

King Ardal looked at the woman who entered. She was the main reason he was here. He knew that the Mother cult was powerful and the powers of the Mother had kept the Romans from the island of Manavia. That, in itself, was no mean feat. Since his brother had told him of the incursion by the Roman horse warriors he had been worried. Although Banquo had made out that he had fought valiantly against them Ardal had questioned Banquo's oathsworn and discovered that the Romans had despatched his men with ease. It had enticed him into this nest of vipers.

She leaned forward to kiss him on the forehead, "Thank you for attending, King Ardal. We are pleased you have come."

She noticed the angry young man standing behind the king and realised that he must be the younger brother Banquo. He might be someone she could use.

"I came because I want to know how to defeat the Romans but I am not yet convinced that I need an alliance with these Selgovae dogs."

She put her fingers to his lips. "That is not the tone a king should adopt. At least not before he has discovered what we can offer." She waved a hand around the hut which was large enough to sleep twenty men easily. "You have no need to have your men surrounding you as though you expect to be murdered. This is a place of peace and I guarantee that no harm will come to any within this hut. Please, bring in most of your men. Leave a token guard without."

"Why should I?" he was aware that he sounded petulant. He could not think of a reason why he needed his men outside. He knew that one warrior lying across the door of the chamber would be an effective deterrent. He just did not like obeying someone else. He was, after all, king.

"Because I ask you. Tomorrow morning, we will make our sacrifice. If it does not please you then you can leave but I promise you that the sacrifice will make you want to stay and to join the alliance of the free people against Rome."

Her voice was calm and soothing and Ardal could not think of an argument. "Banquo, bring in all but two men." He opened his mouth as though he would argue but Ardal waved a dismissive hand.

"Good. Now we shall have a feast tomorrow evening when the ceremony of alliance is over. There we will show you the weapons we have which will defeat the Romans. Until then please think about the reasons we are here."

After she had gone and he and Banquo had time to talk he wondered at the power of this woman and her voice. He had heard that she was a witch and now he believed in the power of the woman. She had made him change his mind with just her presence.

"I do not know why you let her change your mind, brother."

"In the same way that I do not know why you disobeyed my orders and attacked Uncle Ban."

"He would not come from his fort."

"Then you should have waited until he did. Now we have many of those who live close to Mercaut and Am Beal resent us for he was a popular man. We will have to work hard to make them loyal again. It is why we need to be here for you have now made the Romans our enemies."

"They attacked me!"

His voice became harsh, "Remember I spoke with Angus of Am Beal. He spoke with the Romans and our cousin. I know that they came to the aid of Ban. It is you, my headstrong and wilful little brother, who have set us on this road to war so do not question my decisions."

The next morning as dawn broke over a misty bay the kings were met by one of the priestesses Caronwyn had brought with her. They were led up a gentle path to a small plateau above the fort. There was a small pond there and the ground around was boggy. Briac and his kin were the first to arrive and they noticed that Caronwyn was already present, shrouded in a white cloak with a hooded priestess next to her. King Feanan stood nearby with a mighty warrior who held a war hammer in his hand. A path of rushes had been laid across the boggy ground. Briac was intrigued. He knew that a sacrifice was to be made but he knew not what type. He looked around for the animal which was to be slaughtered but he saw none.

The next to arrive was his cousin, Tadgh, of the Carvetii. He and his men stood next to Briac. Soon they were joined by the rest of the Novontae and they were just awaiting the arrival of the two warring tribes, the Votadini and the Selgovae. Briac could not help admiring the way that Caronwyn had managed things for the two kings and their warriors arrived at exactly the same time from opposite directions. King Tole and his men stood to the left of Briac while King Ardal stood to the right of Feanan's men.

The mist still hung around giving the place an eerie and mystical atmosphere. Without a word being spoken all fell silent and Caronwyn threw off her cloak revealing that was naked beneath. In her hand she held a long and wicked looking blade. Briac could see that it had an engraved blade and that the hilt was covered in what looked to be bone and animal parts.

When Caronwyn spoke everyone jumped a little as her voice rang out across the misty bog. "We are gathered here today because the Mother has called us. She has been violated by the Roman wall which has cut her in two. We are here to join together to fight this insidious enemy and rid the land of this pernicious wall. We are here to join together the tribes who have fought against each other. The Mother knows that we must share our common blood. To do that blood must be shed and a sacrifice made."

There was silence and then the hooded priestess threw off her cloak and revealed her naked body. This time there was an audible gasp for it was Radha, the former Queen of the Votadini. She had an emaciated body and a skin so thin that the veins and the bones could be clearly seen through it. She walked forwards, albeit slowly, and stood at the edge of the rush walkway next to Caronwyn.

"Today we sacrifice a Queen and a priestess of the cult of the Mother. Do you give yourself to the Mother willingly?"

"I do. I go to the Mother with joy in my heart for with my death will come victory and I will watch the Romans fall and the wall crumble from the Otherworld."

Caronwyn kissed her and led her to the edge of the water. The warrior with the hammer followed her as did King Feanan. Caronwyn stepped back and said, "Go to the Mother and return to the earth."

The warrior hit Radha on the back of the head. She fell to the ground. The warrior picked her up and King Feanan put his hands around her neck and slowly began to strangle her. Finally, with the two Novontae supporting her, Caronwyn slit Radha's throat. The spurting blood told them all that she was still alive until that moment. The body was then lowered, reverently into the water. Almost as though it had been planned the mist evaporated and a weak sun appeared from the east. Caronwyn and the priestesses who stood around gave a joyful ululation which resounded around the hills.

Silence fell and Caronwyn said, "Radha's sacrifice has been made. King Tole and King Ardal will you join hands in friendship?" It was an imperative rather than a question.

The air was filled with tension. Briac had no idea if they would do as Caronwyn had said. The naked priestess stood there with her arms outstretched. Slowly the two kings walked forward and each took one of her hands. She moved the hands together until the two kings were palm to palm. She took the knife she had used to sacrifice Radha and, with the blood still dripping, she put a slice in the palm of each of the kings' hands. Pressing them together she said, "Now you are brothers. The feud is over and now we can go to war!"

Roman Wall

The whole of the hillside erupted in cheers as the kings embraced. The alliance had been forged in blood and blood would flow; Roman blood.

Chapter 12

The Tungrian detachment who occupied Glanibanta enjoyed their life on the lake. There were just a few people who lived close by and they had been more than friendly towards them. During the harsh winter they had just endured the local fishermen and sheep herders had brought supplies to them. Centurion Julius Decius Duocus could not believe his good fortune. Next year would see his twenty-five-year enlistment end and he would take his stipend and open a tavern close to the fort. It was the only thing missing. He would enjoy the peaceful life on the long lake.

The sentry had summoned him just after dawn. He went to the Porta Decumana. "What is it, soldier?"

The auxiliary pointed to the other side of the ditch. "It looks like the locals are feeding us again."

The centurion could not believe his eyes the locals were pushing carts and they looked to be laden with supplies. He frowned in suspicion. "What's this about? Winter is over and we aren't short of supplies."

The auxiliary had been born in Britannia; he was not a Tungrian. "It could be the feast of Eostre. It is the custom to give away some of your own food to celebrate the spring and to guarantee a good harvest." He shrugged, "They might get annoyed if we don't take it."

It made perfect sense to the centurion who looked down at the carcass of the freshly slaughtered lambs and anticipated the sweet succulent meat. As he descended the ladder he shouted. "Open the gate. Get the cooks out here."

He stood and watched as the gates were opened. To his horror he was not greeted by a friendly crowd of villagers with food, instead he was faced by a band of warriors who had grabbed the spears and swords hidden in the carts by the lambs. Even as he pulled out his gladius and shouted, "Stand to!" he knew he would never open a tavern.

He slashed his gladius across the throat of the warrior whose spear had glanced off the centurion's mail. His optio ran up with a maniple of men who had their shields all ready to protect their centurion. The ten men formed a line and began to move towards the advancing Brigante.

Roman Wall

Centurion Julius Decius saw warriors smashing the skulls of the
surprised auxiliaries they had surrounded. Already half of the eighty-man
garrison was dead or dying. The spears of the auxiliaries began to force
back the warriors. The centurion held out a kind of hope that they might
be able to drive them back to the gate. He grabbed the spearhead in his
left hand and ripped upwards with his gladius. The Brigante fell
screaming to the ground.

"Come on lads, keep pushing."

The auxiliaries were now rhythmically stabbing with their spears and
punching with their shields. Julius Decius began to believe that they had
a chance. They were just ten paces from the gates and the warriors were
not advancing as quickly as they had been. As the centurion looked he
saw that there were just six of them left. He had no doubt that there were
others behind him still fighting but he could not risk turning.

The Brigante had seen the danger of this handful of men. Four of
them roared their challenge and they recklessly charged the shieldless
centurion. Their long swords, made for Roman horsemen, had a longer
reach than the centurion's gladius. He blocked one with his sword and
tried to grab a second with his hand. It cost him three fingers. One of the
spathas slid through his mail links and scored a cut along his side. His
helmet took the force of the last sword. He punched his bloody and
maimed hand at the eyes of one warrior and ripped his gladius across his
stomach. He now had room to move and he pulled his sword back to kill
a third. As he did so the fourth warrior swung his spatha horizontally and
it sliced into the neck to the centurion. His head rolled along the ground
and his optio looked at his leader's body in horror. While he had lived
they had had a chance. Now they had none.

The last three Romans extracted a terrible price from the Brigante but
eventually, their hacked bodies showed that sheer numbers had won.
Glanibanta had fallen.

The same thing happened at all the forts to the west of the Roaring
Water. Roman power ceased for a large part of the frontier. The rebellion
had begun.

Roman Wall

The Camp Prefect at Eboracum was a gourmand. He enjoyed his food. When he had discovered the cook in the home of a Brigante noble he had moved heaven and earth to acquire his services. He knew that he had upset the noble when the man sold his home in Eboracum and moved west towards Mamucium. It did not worry the veteran. He had managed to acquire a fortune through lucrative deals and cheating local businessmen. He could afford the cook and, when his time was up and he retired to Gaul, then he would have the finest cook outside of the Emperor's Palace.

Gaius Metellus Portus was not a stingy man. He enjoyed having his friends around him. To celebrate the birthday of one of the Tribunes of the VIth he organised a fine feast. He had some wine from a particularly attractive female merchant, Flavia Gemellus. He had been amazed at the low price she had charged. He suspected that she was trying to bribe him. He cared not. He was open to bribes anyway. The wine he sampled was so rich and full of body that he knew he could cut it with half water and his guests would not know.

When the day of the feast arrived the only officers not invited were the centurions; the Prefect was with the Governor in Camulodunum but all the others were there. Gaius Metellus Portus did not mind the expense he would make far more from the charges he would levy. The VIth would pay for the feast but it would be the legionaries who would suffer and not their officers.

The head cook came in to watch them eat their first course. It was a dish of fresh oysters served with a snail sauce. The taste was divine. The whole room applauded the cook, who took a small bow. "I promise you masters that you will not forget your next course. I have stuffed a swan with a goose, with a duck with a hen and finally with a partridge."

The room erupted once more and Gaius Metellus Portus clapped his hands in glee. "I think, gentlemen, that now is the time for our first wine." A slave brought in the white wine. He had cut it by half.

The taste was divine. He knew that the red one was even better. That would be served after the swan course. They chatted amiably. The VIth were happy to be away from the frontier in the relatively civilised town of Eboracum. Although it had been the men who had had to build the wall they had lost a number of officers to Selgovae attacks. Here they could sleep knowing they would wake up! It was not so up on the frontier.

The cook, modestly, did not appear when the swan, looking as though alive, arrived. The slave carved choice portions for the officers and they waited until they had been served before, at a nod from Gaius Metellus Portus, they all tucked in. The taste was exquisite. Gaius had very refined taste buds and his tongue and mind struggled to identify the subtle under taste which lingered on his lips. He swallowed and took a sip of the wine. He picked up another morsel and felt a savage pain in his stomach. Had he eaten too quickly? The pain became even more intense. It felt as though someone had reached into his stomach and was squeezing the life out of his insides. He looked and saw that every other officer was suffering the same. As the pain became so intense that he began to black out he realised that they had all been poisoned.

The second stage of the insurrection had begun. The Brigante cook, placed there by the rebel Brigante, slipped out of the city and took a boat downstream. There he would rejoin his master and fight the Romans.

When First Spear, Quintus Licinius Brocchus, was summoned he could not take in the scene. Every senior officer save the Prefect and the Legate were dead. He watched as a feral cat slipped in and leapt to the table. A legionary went to move it but Decius Veridius waved his hand to stop him. The cat began to eat the flesh of the swan. After two mouthfuls it let out a squeal and began to tear at its own stomach. It died moments later.

First Spear nodded, "It looks like the food was poisoned. Find the cooks and interrogate them. Burn all this food."

The legionary looked sadly at the wine. "And the wine?"

"The stuff that has been opened, pour it away. We can't take the chance that it was poisoned too."

The legionary nodded and the centurion did not notice the sly look on his face. The man had seen two amphorae of red wine outside the dining room and they had not been opened. He and his barracks would enjoy that wine later. He would not be disobeying orders.

The cook was not found and despite the tortures inflicted on the rest of the kitchen staff no one could say where the cook had gone. Quintus Licinius Brocchus sent the messages first to the Legate on the wall and then to the Governor. The VIth was incapacitated.

The century managed to sneak the amphorae into their barracks unseen. It cost them a jug or two in bribes but it was worth it. They knew their limitations and they knew what they liked. They cut the wine two to one with water. It would last longer. Their actions saved many of them for the wine, too, had been poisoned. The backup plan in case the poisoned food did not work had succeeded. Stage three was in place and all over the northern half of the Roman Empire Flavia Gemellus' expensive wine claimed high ranking Romans and influential tribal leaders. The Celtic affection for their wine would cost them dear.

First Spear Broccus was exhausted by the time he went to bed. He had to write more reports and send more messages in one day than in the last month. He had checked the gates of the fort and no one could get in or out. The sentries had all been doubled and there was an armed guard on all of the food. He was taking no chances. All of the officers and senior officials might be dead but so long as he was in command then Eboracum would not fall. He had even taken the precaution of putting a sentry outside his quarters. He almost fell on to the bed and was asleep before his head hit the pillow.

Septimus Gaius Agrippa had ambitions. He would be an optio soon. The fact that First Spear had chosen him to guard his quarters was evidence of that. No Brigante warrior would get past him.

He heard First Spear snoring and smiled to himself. It sounded like a bull breaking wind. Suddenly he caught a whiff of perfume and his smile turned to a frown. One of the slaves appeared with a goblet of wine. She was a slave, that was clear but Septimus had never seen such an attractive one before. His eyes could not help but take in every uncia of her form.

He put his arm out. "Where do you think you are going?"

"It is for First Spear. He ordered it."

"Well, he is asleep so off you go."

She looked disappointed and her eyes widened. If you do not trust me then you can give it to him."

Septimus began to wonder if First Spear had ordered it. He did not wish to damage his chances by upsetting the centurion. "How do I know it isn't poisoned?"

She lifted it to her full red lips and she drank a mouthful. "See. Taste it yourself."

The legionary decided he would taste it and then, after he had sent her away, he would place it next to the sleeping centurion. That way he would have protected First Spear and yet not annoyed him. He took the goblet with his right hand. As he did so the razor-sharp dagger was ripped across his throat. It happened so quickly that he felt nothing. The last thing he saw was the blood spurting and the slave girl grabbing the goblet before it fell from his lifeless fingers.

She was stronger than she looked and she lowered the body to the ground. After placing the goblet next to the body, she slipped through the door as silently as a puff of wind. She saw the huge Roman lying on his back. He was snoring so loudly she could have marched in the room wearing caligae. She stepped closer. He had his left arm across his neck and appeared to be sleeping on his right. She could not cut his throat. She knew she had to kill him quickly and so she turned the blade and raised it. She would drive it through his eye and into his brain.

The very perfume, which had so captivated the dead legionary, woke the centurion. He was awake in an instant. He saw the dagger and swept his left arm to knock it away. The edge scored a deep cut along his arm. He whipped out the gladius which was in his right and drove it so hard that it entered her stomach and came out of her back.

He dropped the corpse to the floor. Although he had written many orders that day he would write one more. No slaves within the walls of the fortress!

When Julius Demetrius received the reports, he summoned his prefects. "We are under siege. The attacks have begun. We have the road to Eboracum which is open and that is all. The VIth cannot help us yet and I am convinced that we will be assailed from the north." He pointed to the map. "Prefect, I want your Thracians to keep the road open. I know that you are at half strength but if the road closes then we are doomed. Eventually the VIth will come to our aid but until then we are on our own."

The Thracian Prefect nodded. His ala had been badly handled the previous year and he only had ten turmae. None of them was at full strength. He just hoped that his men would cope.

"I intend to use the other auxiliaries to hold the wall. The Cohors Equitata from the 1st Batavorum will keep the Stanegate open. I want every mile castle double manned. They will attack the wall."

There was silence as the prefects realised that they were besieged in the largest fort in the world.

"And us sir?"

Julius looked sadly at Livius, "And you, Prefect, will be the force which takes the war to the enemy. You will not wait behind the wall you will attack the barbarians. I want your ala to keep the barbarians guessing."

The Batavian prefect was a horseman himself, "Sir, it is not cavalry country north of the wall. It is forest and thick forest at that. They will be slaughtered."

"No, Prefect, they will not. Besides we need the ala to cover all ninety miles of the frontier. Only cavalry can do that."

"What about the Classis Britannica sir? They could secure the two ends of the wall and supply us."

"I have sent a message to the Navarchus and I am sure that the Arbeia end will be secure. I am less certain about the other end of the wall. It will take ships some time to get there."

Livius had been studying the maps. "Sir, I think that when this is over we should do something about Manavia. All of our troubles emanate from there."

Julius laughed. "There you are, gentlemen, the prefect of the ala who is given the suicide mission is already planning what to do once we have defeated the enemy. Take that back to your men. This is a setback only! We will hold this wall for Emperor Hadrian but remember these rebels are armed as well as we are. I dare say they are already using the weapons they captured from our slaughtered garrisons. The difference will be that your men are disciplined and theirs are not. Make sure you have plenty of water and supplies laid in. I am not sure when we can be resupplied." He looked at the Thracian Prefect. "That all depends upon our Thracian friends."

"We will not let you down."

Livius did not relish the job he was giving his officers. They were like family to him and he knew that they would struggle to complete the mission. His comment to the Legate had not implied confidence in his own success and survival. He assumed that he and his men would die but he wanted the evil that was the Mother Cult wiping out. Their one avowed intent was to destroy the world of Rome. You could not argue with such an attitude. It had to be eradicated.

He and Metellus had already had a meeting and come up with a plan, of sorts.

"First I intend to take two men from each turma. They will form a reserve here, at Cilurnum, under my command. You will all have to function with just thirty men. We are luckier than the Thracians for we have a full muster. They have not. We will use the same method as we did when scouring the Dunum. Each turma will operate separately. We have two functions; one is to scout the enemy and the second is to disrupt and attack whenever possible. The auxiliary cohorts on the wall will be dug in. We will operate further from the wall. You will need to forage for yourselves. I know that we will become tired and so I intend for each turma to be out for just six days and then return. To ensure that we have constant patrols putting their spears into the enemy backs we will stagger the start of each patrol."

He glanced at Metellus who stood. "Rufius, Marcus and Marius will leave in the morning. They will head for the west and Luguvalium. They will only have four days on patrol for theirs is the furthest area. I will leave the day after with Lentius and Cassius. Julius Longinus here has the rest of your assignments. The other turmae will be on standby in case the enemy breaks through."

Cassius asked, "Sir, all the trouble has been in the south. What makes you think that they will attack from the north?"

"The reason is because they are attacking in the south. They want us to draw our forces south to counter these new attacks and allow the northern tribes to attack a weakened wall. The VIth are in the south. They can handle the Brigante revolt."

What they could not know was that the VIth had lost too many men and officers to be able to function immediately. Caronwyn had been crafty; they had negated the VIth to have a free rein in the east. The wall was almost cut off already.

Marcus looked over at Metellus. "Sir, our families are in the valley. What of them?"

Livius did not enjoy this. "The Thracians are guarding the Via Trajanus although I prefer the legionary name for it, Via Hades. I will ask their Prefect if he can watch over them." He shrugged, "It is the best I can do."

Marcus was not happy but he was an officer of Marcus' Horse and he would do his duty. They had warned Frann and his mother of the danger. Now it would be up to Drugi and the men of the farm. They would have to protect them as best they could. Sometimes Marcus cursed his sense of duty.

Rufius had less of a problem with his new wife. She and her men were close enough to the fort to seek shelter should events turn out badly. Even so, before he left he sought out Scealis, "The frontier is on fire. I go to fight the Selgovae. Watch over my wife for me." Scealis nodded although he had needed no urging from this Roman warrior to do so. He owed Lord Ban duty even though the old man was dead. "If you are attacked you can seek shelter in the fort." He saw the look on Scealis' face. "I know that you would fight these men but Mavourna…"

"We will protect her. You can trust us Roman. And, Roman, take care, you are a fine man and I would see your children when they are born."

Chapter 13

The three turmae left through the northern gate. Rufius wanted to get as far north as possible before they turned west. He guessed that the barbarians would be massing close by the wall. Felix and Wolf came with them. The scout and his dog had trotted silently into the forests before dawn. As Rufius led the three turmae up the road he saw Wolf and his master waiting patiently for them.

He reported quickly. "There is a band of warriors to the south of us. They are in a camp."

"How many are there?"

"They number an ala."

Rufius turned to Marcus, "That is over a thousand then. Are there any ponies?"

"A handful."

"Mount up, Felix." A trooper handed the reins of the pony they had brought for him. Rufius detailed a trooper to take the news of the band to the Prefect.

Rufius was the senior decurion and he took the decision. "We might as well begin our war here. We will attack them and then head west. They will expect us to return to the wall and we will confuse them." He looked at the two decurion. "We hit and run. We cannot afford to lose men but we must keep them off balance and looking over their shoulder."

Marcus nodded, "When we strike in the west they will think we have more men than we do have."

"That is what I am counting on. Lead on, Felix."

The ninety horse warriors plunged into the forest. It was not closely grown and they could manoeuvre their horses easily. There was new growth on all of the trees but it was not the dense canopy it would become in summer. Then this journey would be like a passage through the underworld.

Wolf's pricked ears told them when they were close to their prey. Felix slid from his pony. Rufius silently signalled the five archers to go with Felix. They knew their job without being told. They would silence any sentries.

Felix was completely silent as he stepped carefully through the trees. There were no broken branches on the trail to give him away. He spied the first of the sentries. He was leaning against the bole of a tree and staring up into the branches. Perhaps a bird had attracted his attention. Felix drew back his bow and his arrow pinned the neck of the dead Votadini to the tree. There were just three sentries on this northern edge of the camp and they all died just as quickly.

They quickly remounted. When the other troopers arrived, they edged forward towards the camp. It was still early and the Votadini were preparing for the day. They were all keen to attack the vaunted Romans. Banquo had promised them Roman heads and a chance of glory. The young brother of the king would have attacked already but King Ardal was cautious. He wanted Caronwyn's plan to have a chance to succeed. He had spies in the eaves of the forests watching the wall for the sign that they were sending troops south. Banquo had left the camp early that morning to watch for himself. He had a plan to send a report to his brother saying that the Romans had left. He would have his glory! The camp that Rufius and his men approached was leaderless.

The Votadini had cleared a large area for their camp. The warriors had used the branches they had cut to form crude shelters. Someone had wanted a sense of order and there were clear avenues between the shelters. Rufius halted the turmae and said quietly to Marcus and Marius, "We will attack in a column of twos. We sweep south and then I will head west and finally north. I will sound the buccina when we enter the camp. Marcus, your turma will take the rear. Felix, go and wait for the trooper we sent to the Prefect. Find us."

With their new spears in their hands, the three turmae swept into the camp. Rufius waited until he saw the first face before he sounded the buccina. Plunging his spear into the surprised warrior the troopers galloped south. The Votadini who were already outside their shelters tried to go back for their weapons. Some were speared as they attempted to do so. Even those who managed to grab a weapon had little chance. The long spears meant that they could not close with the Romans. The cavalry achieved complete and utter surprise. Their spears gave them a decided advantage and the speed of their horses meant that they flashed by the warriors who were still waking up.

Swinging west Rufius led the turmae through the part of the camp which had had more warning and they were being organised as the troopers smashed into hastily arranged shield walls. The horses broke them as they were a spider's web.

Marcus, at the rear of the attack was encountering more dead warriors than living. He knew that he would soon have to face more dangerous foes. The lack of Votadini leaders meant that the barbarians had no sense of order. Some ran to where Rufius and his men were charging whilst others ran to the end of the camp where the troopers had first attacked. The barbarian warband was in a state of confused chaos. The Romans, in contrast, rode in neat lines. The spears devastated both sides as they galloped through.

Suddenly five Votadini warriors burst out of a side trail. Their leader had a long sword which he swung doubled handed. The men with him had their spears ready to thrust into the horses when their leader killed Marcus. Marcus kept his eye on the warrior's head. He pulled back his spear and punched forward with it. He timed it so that the wicked looking sword was pulled back over the warrior's head as he prepared to strike. The spearhead ripped into the warrior's head. As the metal entered the brain the sword fell from the warrior's lifeless hands. His surprised followers fell to the spears of the troopers behind Marcus. It had been a warning, however. There was now some resistance. The enemy were awake.

As Marcus and his troopers swung west he saw the first dead trooper. It was one of Marius' men. He speared the warrior who was wastefully hacking at the dead trooper's head. As they thundered through the carnage of the camp Marcus heard the recall. He saw an avenue to his right. "Follow me!" He led his turma up an avenue which had seen no fighting. As they galloped towards the safety of the forest to the north they surprised warriors running from one side of the camp to the other. Many were still half asleep and none was prepared for battle. The Romans were and all they came across died. As Marcus and his men entered the woods he reined in Raven and began counting. All of his men had survived. He saw bloodied legs and arms showing where the Votadini had scored hits but all rode and grinned at him.

"Right. Let's find the others." Marcus led them west and they soon found Rufius and Marius. A sudden sound from the east made them grab their weapons but it was just Felix and the trooper who had delivered the message.

Rufius seemed satisfied. "A good start. We only lost two men."

Although he meant nothing by the comment Marcus saw the hurt in Marius' eyes. They had been his men and the newly promoted decurion was not sure that it had been a good start. He was learning the problems of command. He determined to make a better fist of it in the future. By late afternoon they had crossed through the forests and were just fifteen miles north of Luguvalium.

"Here is where we split up. You know your patrol routes. In five days' time we can head back through the fort at Luguvalium. Marcus, you take Felix. I know he likes to be close to the sword."

"Sir."

The three turmae disappeared into the land of the Selgovae as though they had never been there. Their war had begun.

Banquo was furious when he returned to his devastated camp. The dead and dying littered the ground like fallen autumn leaves. The two Romans' horses and dismembered troopers were the only sign that they had had any success. He had already sent the message to his brother, further north, that the Romans had begun to send troops south but now he had to send another to tell him that they had been attacked themselves.

"Burn our dead and then prepare the warriors. Tonight we pay back the Romans."

"But the king said…"

"The king is not here and besides the Romans will be back in their fort now feeling pleased with themselves. They will not expect an attack tonight. They will think that we have been weakened by this attack."

His men's confidence had been shattered. Even his oathsworn were beginning to question this young prince. The Roman horse warriors had met them twice and had had the better of them both times. The omens were not good. They wondered if it should have been a warrior who was sacrificed and not a withered old woman. Perhaps the gods were unhappy and were punishing them.

Briac and his men began their raid through the Dunum valley. Their training at the Roaring Waters had stood them in good stead. Elidr and his men joined their cousin. They had four warbands of five hundred men each. Their plan was simple; they would attack the small farms and settlements which had Roman sympathisers. They hoped to drive the refugees towards Morbium where the small fort would not be able to accommodate them. With two thousand warriors they would easily destroy all resistance and with Morbium in their hands then the wall would be isolated. It would slowly be strangled to death. The VIth was helpless inside Eboracum, still reeling from the many acts of sabotage and by the time they had recovered from the attacks within the fort the bridge over the Dunum would be destroyed. Caronwyn and the Roman Severus had come up with a good plan.

At the farm, Drugi and Marcus' brother Decius knew the danger they were in. Riders had warned them of the rising. Frann wanted to take her family into Morbium but Decius advised against it. "There are barely two hundred men in the fort. We will have almost half that number here when the Brigante begin their attacks."

Ailis agreed with her son. She knew the Frann was afraid but she also knew that their farm was well built and the equal of the fort at Morbium. Decius had taken his brother's advice and prepared great stocks of food. He knew the Brigante warrior; they would try to assault the farm but once they were repulsed they would find easier targets.

"Drugi, hunt as much food as you can. It will feed the people and you will have the first warning of an enemy."

As he left Drugi smiled at Frann. "Fear not, little one, Drugi will not let anything happen to you and the Roman warrior's children."

He took his bow and loped off through the woods. He headed west. There was a watering place the deer came to. He knew that the rut was over and he hoped to get a stag. He was too good a hunter to kill the does and the calves. They would be the food of the future. He made a kill before noon. He gutted the beast where it had fallen and left the entrails for the woods. The heart and liver he would save for himself. He hefted the carcass across his huge shoulders and made his way east towards his home and the farm.

He had gone but half a mile when he smelled something different in the air. He hung the stag's body from a branch and nocked an arrow. He retraced his steps. The smell grew stronger and he identified it quickly. It was the smell of warriors who had limed their hair. He could never understand that. Their hair would fall out before they were thirty.

He moved stealthily and began to hear them as they moved and spoke. They were the scouts of the Brigante warband. He found a tree with foliage and he climbed. Once he reached the upper branches he was able to see the Brigante descending from the higher ground of the hills. He estimated their numbers at more than three hundred. Descending carefully, he looked for the first scout. It was a young warrior who was peering through the undergrowth. He was little more than eighty paces from him. Drugi felt almost sorry for the youth. The eager young warrior had out run his companions. It was an easy kill for Drugi who moved his aim to the right. Another scout hove into view and Drugi's arrow struck him in the back. So far neither warrior had made a sound as they died.

He quickly ran to his left. There he saw two scouts. At the same time the body of the first scout he had killed was discovered. He loosed one arrow and, even as it was in the air, loosed a second. Both men screamed as they died and Drugi ran back to his deer. He could hear the pandemonium in the woods. The Brigante would be looking for multiple enemies and he would have the chance to escape. With the stag on his back he ran to the farm which was three miles away.

As he dropped the body of the stag he said simply, "They come!"

Decius nodded. All morning refugees had been arriving. Most had barely escaped with their lives. It was those who lived to the west and were absent who upset Decius. It meant they had not escaped and his friends lay dead. The walls were soon manned. Decius and Drugi looked down at the ditch and the stream which surrounded the walls of the farm.

Both had been sown with lillia and caltrops. Any Brigante foolish enough to try to cross them would get a shock. Some of Decius' men had replaced the bridges over the stream and the ditch with the two traps. They looked whole but any weight would result in them breaking. The real bridges were put in place behind the gate so that it made the entrance three layers thick.

Drugi heard them first. He pointed away to the west. "They are coming."

Decius had never served as a soldier but his father had been one of the finest and his brother had helped to train him. He had the mind of a soldier, defensively at least. "Everyone crouch down so that they see no one. I will tell you when to rise."

Half of the men worked on the farm and the others knew Decius well enough to obey his orders as though he was a soldier. Even Drugi crouched down. Decius hid his smile as the huge man tried to make himself as small as possible.

Briac and his men had moved cautiously once they had discovered the bodies of the four scouts. They had hoped to find this Roman farm with its gates opened so that they could race in and slaughter the well-known Roman sympathisers. When he saw the closed gates, he knew they were prepared.

He and Elidr stood behind a tree some hundred paces from the walls. They were within bow range and they knew that this farm would be defended. Caronwyn had been firm; they had to destroy the farm and kill those within before they moved on. She seemed to hate the family more than any other. They would do as the priestess commanded. So far, her decisions had been good ones.

A handful of the younger warriors seeing their leader sheltering behind a tree and observing no one on the ramparts took it upon themselves to charge the walls. They would gain the glory. Each had one of the spears Severus had brought, a small shield and, at their waist, a fine sword. They screamed their war cry and raced forward before Briac could restrain them. Boru and Anlan were the fastest and the most reckless. They struck the weakened bridge together. They fell into the stream. Boru looked down at the sharpened stake which came up through his leg. Anlan lay in the water; his fall had broken his ankle and he had fallen onto another of the deadly lillia. Anlan watched his lifeblood redden the stream as he began to die.

The others saw the trap and tried to leap the stream. Two of them made it. The others fell screaming on to the spikes which were hidden beneath the streams waters.

"Come and fight you Roman cowards. I, Tadge, son of Lugos challenge you to fight me." There was silence behind the wall and Tadge and his companion began to wonder if there was anyone within. They both ran over the second weakened bridge. Both were heavy warriors and it too collapsed beneath their weight. The fall was greater as the ditch was deeper than the top of the water. The cracks as their legs broke were followed by their screams as the lillia speared them.

Briac turned to his men and snarled, "That was a waste! We do not throw our lives away." The ones still alive in the stream and the ditch moaned as they found themselves unable to move.

"Shield wall." Briac was under no illusions; there were defenders within the walls despite the apparently empty walls. They would move forwards cautiously. "Elidr, make a fire. We will burn them out."

Briac put himself in the second rank of the shield wall. The road to the farm was thirty paces wide and they filled it. Ignoring the shouts from the stream and the ditch they moved forward. Briac expected a shower of arrows at any time but the silence was unnerving. He felt his men move more slowly. This was the unknown.

They reached the edge of the stream. The walls were just thirty paces away but it might as well have been thirty miles. They had to get over the two obstacles first. Briac turned and shouted, "Cut down some trees to make a bridge." Even as he spoke Drugi stood and loosed an arrow. It plunged into Briac's shoulder. The shields went up but Drugi had dropped back behind the wall.

Elidr raced up to his cousin. Briac stood still. He grimaced, "The mail saved me. Pull it out cousin."

Drugi had chosen this arrow well and it was barbed. Briac was lucky that it was not close to an artery for as Elidr pulled it out it ripped a piece of flesh the size of a thumb from his left shoulder. He screamed in pain.

Elidr shouted to Briac's oathsworn. "Take him to the healers." As they carried the white faced Briac from the shield wall Elidr said, "I will take charge until you return."

He looked for the men who were supposed to be cutting down trees. They were nowhere to be seen. "Where are the men with the axes?"

"There were no trees big enough close by. They have gone back into the woods."

Decius had ensured that no attacker would have a ready supply of wood. He grinned at Drugi. "Did you hit anyone?"

"Aye but he had a mail shirt on else he would be dead."

"How many are there?"

"They have a shield wall of, perhaps, two hundred men and there are more in the woods. They have fire."

Decius nodded. It was what they expected. The walls had been soaked with water that morning and they had pails with more. It would cost them lives to burn them out. He would not waste his arrows trying to hit men in a shield wall. He would wait until they were bridging the ditch and the stream. They could not bridge and hold a shield at the same time.

Elidr cursed the tardiness of his men. It was unreasonable of him. They needed trees which were, at least, six paces long. They needed trees which were straight. By the time they had cut them and carried them back to Elidr, Briac had been attended to. Despite his men's objections he had followed the tree trunks. His shoulder was heavily bandaged and Elidr could see the blood seeping from it.

"Did you not trust me, cousin?"

"I want to be here when we breach the walls and I will eat the heart of the archer who struck me."

Elidr nodded and shouted to the men with the tree trunks, "Carry them to the ditch and the stream."

The trunks were heavy and the defenders had plenty of time, having heard the orders to rise and aim at the men who carried the trees. They were cut down to a man. Briac cursed again. "This time I want a warrior with a shield to protect the man with the tree."

Pairs of men, eager to impress their leader, ran forward. As they knelt to lift the trees from the grasp of the dead men the archers were loosing arrows. Some of the shields afforded protection but others found their mark. It took some time for the trees to be carried and deposited over the stream. Those fallen within were silent. They had either died of their injuries or taken their own lives. What use was a warrior with broken legs?

It cost the Brigante another ten warriors to breach the ditch next to the wall. By this time the defenders were lining the walls. Slings used by the boys of the farm hurled stones to catch the unwary while the men threw large cobbles collected from the river at Morbium. Briac had been forced to rest by the tree he had sheltered against. He could still see the farm and yet he was not in danger for he was far away from the walls.

Drugi saw the wounded leader lying by the tree. The warriors below were all using their shields and there were no decent targets. They were putting kindling next to the gate as they attempted to burn it. He selected his best arrow and took aim at the leader. The warrior had taken off his helmet and his head made a good target. He pulled the bow back until his hand was next to his ear and took aim. Elidr's son, Cam, was watching the wall and he saw the huge archer aiming at Briac. He shouted a warning even as the arrow flew through the air. He dived and his body went between the arrow and its target. Drugi shook his head, sadly. The gods did not want him to kill this Brigante.

Elidr took his son's body in his arms. He had died without having the opportunity to kill his enemies. Elidr swore that he would more than make up for his son's death.

Briac pointed at Drugi, "I want that archer brought to me."

"It will not be long cousin, the fire is already lit. It will not take long."

Decius had anticipated the fire. The women had been heating up pig fat. His men brought up the steaming cauldron of molten fat. They carefully ascended to the wall and, at a nod from Decius, poured it upon the flames. It erupted and covered all the warriors in fire. Their shields burned, their hair burned and they could not get rid of the fire which insinuated itself beneath their clothes and burned them from within. They threw themselves on the ground. Some even threw themselves in the stream. All was in vain for the ones who took refuge in the stream were speared by the lillia and the ones who threw themselves on the ground could not douse the flames. The wooden bridges so carefully constructed began to burn too. As soon as it was obvious that the attackers were all dead Decius ordered his men to pour water on the burning gate. It was a thick and well-made gate. When the flames were doused the Brigante could see that the gate was merely blackened.

A few miles away Decurion Cassius Nubius of the Thracian Auxiliary Cavalry saw the smoke rising from the west. His Prefect had told him that there was a farm there which needed his protection. He led his turma to investigate. The road had had the undergrowth cleared from both sides and when Cassius saw the Brigante in the distance he ordered the buccina to be sounded.

Briac knew when to cut his losses. They would not take the farmhouse this day and he did not want a defeat to Roman cavalry. "Order the men to withdraw into the woods. We have been thwarted."

Elidr looked at the bodies which lay all around them. "What a waste!"

"It is a setback only."

By the time the Thracians reached the farm, the Brigante had melted into the woods. All that remained were the dead and the dying and the whole place reeked of burning flesh. The farm had held.

Decius and Drugi opened the gate. "Your arrival was timely my friend. We owe you much."

Decurion Lucius Spartacus Culpidius shook his head, "We fooled them into thinking that we had more men than we had. They may come back."

"And we will repulse them again." Decius pointed to the ditch and the stream. It is easy enough to put more spikes in the water."

Drugi chuckled, "And I can use the bodies to frighten them. It is a trick we use in my country." He would hang the bodies from the trees. If they returned they would, indeed, be terrified. It was like putting dead crows on a fence and it worked.

"I will have to report to Eboracum. There is too much here for one under strength ala. This needs the legion."

Decius nodded. "Fear not decurion we will be here when you return. We have weathered worse than this before now."

Chapter 14

Inside Cilurnum the Legate and Livius prepared their defences. Livius knew that his men outside the walls would attempt to disrupt the Votadini but with a mere ninety men, they could not do much. The reserve turma was sent to the walls along with the two centuries of Batavians and the rest of the ala which had not yet set out. It was not a huge number of men. Julius could have summoned more soldiers from the mile castles and turrets on either side but he did not want to risk a breach there. The fort was the strong point. They had both seen it built over the years; if it fell then they had built it badly.

"Make sure the men have eaten. I think this will be a long day and an even longer night."

Julius Longinus came in with some food. "Take your own advice gentlemen and eat too."

"I am surprised you returned with the Quartermaster from Eboracum when you had the chance to stay there."

The old clerk shook his head irritably. "It has taken me long enough to train the troopers and cooks here to my likes and dislikes. This will do for me."

Outside the walls, under the eaves of the trees Banquo had divided his remaining men into smaller parties. He would attack the wall at a number of places. The defenders would be forced to move men and he had a reserve of a hundred warriors who would exploit the weaknesses. He gave the task of attacking the fort to Demne. He had fought the Romans before and had been one of King Lugubelenus' most successful warriors. Although he knew that Banquo was not obeying his brother's orders he supported the young warrior. He wanted revenge for many of his family had died when they had fought the IXth.

"Demne do not take chances but I want the Romans to believe that our main attack is on their fort. I will take my warriors and attack the smaller mile castle to the west. Guthrie will take others and attack the

134

mile castle to the east. We will sound the carnyx when we are through. Your men can withdraw and join us."

Banquo joined his men. There were turrets every few hundred paces. He intended to attack one of the mile castle forts and the two turrets on either side. There had to be far fewer men in those than in the main fort by the bridge. He was convinced that his luck must change soon.

The two hundred men he had with him made their way silently towards the ditch. Banquo and his men had been scouting the ditch and the walls for a few days and knew that there were traps in the bottom of the ditches. They had counted the men on the walls and they knew that there would be ninety-six men at most to face them in the mile castle and two turrets. They would outnumber the defenders by two to one. Banquo hoped that some of the Romans would be asleep and perhaps the odds would be even more in their favour.

Two of his warriors slid down the bank while others watched for the sentries. The cloudy night meant that it was hard for them to see the patrolling Romans but they knew that it would be just as hard for them to be seen. There was a small groan of pain from one of the men in the ditch and everyone froze. There was no sound of alarm and Banquo peered down to see what the problem was. He saw one of his warriors clutching a bleeding leg. Banquo tapped another two men who slithered down into the bottom of the ditch. Their task was to eliminate the traps and clear a path for the rest to pass through.

It seemed to take forever although in reality it only took them a short time to clear a narrow path through which the barbarians could move. The waved signal came as a relief to the young leader. He and his men slid down the narrow cleared stretch of the ditch. Perhaps one of the warriors was too eager for he caught his foot on one of the cleared lillia. His sword clattered as it struck the spear of the man in front. The sentry hurled a javelin, probably at the sound but luck was with him and it struck the warrior.

They heard the shout, "Alarm!"

There was nothing else for it. They clambered up the bank. Banquo had both a helmet and a shield. It was fortunate for him as the javelin hurled by the second sentry clanged off it. Two of his men had reached the wall of the mile castle and they turned their backs to it and held their hands before them. Banquo sprang from the outstretched hand as though he was a hawk soaring into the sky. He managed to grab hold of the top of the wall and he hauled himself over the top. He landed on the wall at the side of the mile castle. The Batavian auxiliary who raced to meet him thrust his spear at Banquo's side and the Votadini just reacted. He grabbed the spearhead with his left arm. The sharpened blade bit into his palm but it pulled the auxiliary off balance and Banquo's sword hacked into his neck and he fell dead. Banquo felt elated. He had killed his first Roman. He turned and hefted his shield up to cover his body. He ignored the blood dripping from his hand. He was a warrior. He ran towards the door to the fort. The auxiliaries were pouring out. They were forced to use their spears as they had no room to swing their long swords. It gave Banquo an advantage. He blocked the spear as it came and then swung his sword at head height. The Batavian had nowhere to move for another was just behind him. As with the first Roman, Banquo's blade found the auxiliary's neck and bright blood sprayed from the ripped artery.

By now his men were pouring over the walls. The Batavian centurion had already lost a quarter of his men. He made a fateful decision. "Back inside the tower." He was counting on being able to pour javelins from the top of the tower while the door held. Although they managed to get inside the tower the Votadini had brought axes. They began to chip chunks from the thick, metal studded door. Banquo did not care if he blunted a few axes. He would have his first victory.

The centurion left ten men inside the tower and took the rest up the ladders to the top. They hurled javelins and spears down on the Votadini. Each weapon found its mark but more and more Votadini were pouring over the walls. The small turret close to the fort had also been taken and those warriors raced along the wall to reinforce Banquo. A huge warrior called Rogan took the place of the axe man who had just been slain by a javelin from above. Rogan wielded a war hammer. It was not a finely made weapon. It was a large piece of rough iron with a long ash handle. It was, however, heavy and Rogan was an immensely strong man. He swung it with all of his might at the hinges. His first blow shattered the top one and the second took out the bottom one. He pulled back and then smote a mighty blow at the middle of the door. With a crack which signalled the doom of the Batavians it crashed open and Rogan leapt in. He seemed impervious to the spears which darted ay him like the tongues of snakes. He swung his hammer around his head. It takes either a brave or a foolish warrior to face such a weapon. Rogan cleared the room by himself.

His companions leapt over the bleeding giant who lay slumped on the floor. Half of them raced up to the top of the tower while the other half flooded through the gates. They had breached the wall! As the warriors leapt up the ladder to deal with the last Romans above them Banquo ordered the horn to be sounded. He would soon have another two hundred men at his command. He had shown his brother. They could invade Britannia for no one stood in their way.

When Livius heard the horn sound he wondered what it meant. Metellus told him. "Prefect, they are pulling back."

Livius frowned. It made no sense. The attack on Cilurnum had been half hearted. They had seen a cautious approach and watched as the Votadini had tried to clear the ditch. When javelins and bolts fell amongst them they had fallen back. The horn had sounded from the west. "Metellus go and look west. See if the Batavians are still at the turret and the mile castle."

Julius had joined him. "That was too easy Livius."

"It isn't over, sir." He pointed north. "They lost barely forty men. When have the tribes ever withdrawn after such light losses?"

"You are right. I must be getting old."

Metellus ran up. "They have taken the turret and the mile castle to the west. They are flooding south towards the vallum and the Stanegate."

"Mount the ala." As Metellus ran down the stairs Livius said, "We can catch them now sir. They have forgotten the vallum."

The vallum was the last part of the defences and was not complete. It consisted of a raised pair of mounds and ditches. The only way to cross them was at the forts. The warriors racing south would find a new barrier in their way and it would slow them down.

"Very well. We will hold them here."

By the time Livius reached the southern gate the ala was ready. All ten turmae were armed and ready to go. "I fear the mile castle to the east has fallen too but we will deal with these first. Hopefully the vallum will slow them up but just in case send Decurion Lentius and his turma to the other side of the vallum. They can wait on the Stanegate for them."

The two hundred and seventy men clattered out of the fort and wheeled west. "Column of turmae!"

Within moments there were nine lines of thirty troopers and they rode west towards the unsuspecting Votadini.

Banquo had lost over a hundred men; not all were dead but if it was not for the reinforcements from the aborted attack on Cilurnum he would not have had enough men to continue his raid. This was the flaw in his plan. His brother had intended a number of strikes at the same time. Banquo was alone and isolated but all that he saw, as dawn began to break in the east, was the open lands before him. They would be able to strike at the soft underbelly of the rich farmland.

"On, my warriors. Rome is there for the plucking!"

The first men who had left the fort now ran back towards Banquo. "My lord. There are more defences south of us."

"Are they guarded?"

"No but they will be difficult to cross."

"Nevertheless, we will cross them! Are we women or are we warriors? My sword has tasted Roman blood and it wants more."

They were less than a hundred paces from the vallum when they heard the crash and thunder of hooves. They were coming from the fort to the east. Banquo could not believe his misfortune. It was the Roman horse warriors again!

"Shield wall!"

Even though many of his men had no shields they bravely turned to face the line of steel which charged towards them. Those who had thought to steal a Batavian shield were the lucky ones for they could protect most of their bodies. Banquo found himself in the fifth rank of the mass of men who faced the line of thirty horse men. Banquo felt his confidence return. They outnumbered these horse warriors.

As Metellus, Livius and the 1st Turma struck the Votadini warriors Banquo found how wrong he could be. The thirty-two spears all found a target. They were twisted tugged and they stabbed again. Before the Votadini could react the first line had wheeled away and a second line hurtled in. Meanwhile the first line had reformed to the south of the Votadini and their javelins were falling amongst them. They were preventing them from moving south and out flanking the warband. By the time the sixth turma has struck most of the Votadini had had enough and many began to run back to the wall. The trickle turned into a flood.

"My lord, we must leave or we will die here too!"

He did not wish to but he could see that he had been thwarted once again. His oathsworn formed a ring around the young warrior as they shepherded him back to the fort. Pausing only to loot the dead bodies of the auxiliaries in the mile castle the Votadini climbed the wall and returned to their camp. They were chastened. They had had a victory of sorts but it had cost them dear.

The Prefect had no time to pursue the defeated warriors. "Reform the ala. Sound the recall. We must get to the eastern mile castle."

There they found their task easier. Although breached some of the Batavians still held out in the tower and only thirty or so had managed to begin their southern journey. As the sun finally climbed over the eastern horizon, the last of the Votadini left the wall and retreated north. The wall had suffered its first breach but it had held.

Far to the south Briac and Elidr had joined the warriors surrounding Morbium. The plan had been for the Brigante to secure the valley and then seal it off. That would now have to wait. If they captured Morbium then they would control their own land for the first time in three generations.

Their only losses had been at the farm. Although personally grievous they had not diminished their fighting power. Severus waited with the rest of the Brigante and the well-armed gang of deserters he had gathered about him. Briac and his men had to ford the river to reach them on the northern bank.

Severus' face was non-committal as the wounded Briac approached him. "We did not take the farm. The horse warriors came to their aid."

Severus nodded. There was, perhaps, a malicious gleam in his eye but his voice was neutral. "The priestess will not be happy but when we have taken this fort then we can turn our attentions to this farm which seems to have such importance." The soldier in Severus could not understand why Flavia and Caronwyn wanted the farm so desperately destroyed. He wanted to eliminate the military targets and then they could pick off the civilians at their leisure.

Severus suddenly seemed to take in Briac's words. "You say it was the horse warriors?" Briac nodded. "Which ones?"

Briac could not remember what had been upon their shields and he looked at Elidr who was still brooding about his son. "Does it matter? They all look the same and fight the same way."

Severus laughed a cruel laugh, "That is where you are wrong and I can see now why you have been beaten so many times." He ignored the angry reaction of some of the Brigante. He spoke the truth. "If this is Marcus' Horse then it affects our plans. With those in the area we are in trouble. If, on the other hand, it is the Thracians, then we have little to fear. The Selgovae knocked them about a little last year."

The faces of the Brigante showed little comprehension. They had heard of Marcus' Horse; they were renowned but they had assumed that all Roman auxiliaries were the same.

"I know not who they were."

"No matter. Will you put your men under my command, Prince Briac?"

Briac's arm was aching and his confidence was shaken. Perhaps it would be better to allow a Roman to destroy a Roman fort. He nodded. "I will."

"Good." He looked at the mailed warriors standing around him. These were the leaders. "These are my orders. You will do all as I say. If you do so then we will win."

Centurion Vibius Marcus Coccius had seen the smoke rising from the south west. He had worried about the farm ever since dawn. The

Thracian patrol had spoken of bands of Brigante rampaging through the land. The decurion had told him that there were many burning farms both north and south of him. Since the extra century had been sent to the fort the Batavian centurion had been happier but now he realised that he could be the next target. The messenger from Eboracum had told of the disaster there and they had had no news from the north. The omens were not good. The wall was under attack too.

The sentry on the northern gate called to him, "Sir, soldiers coming from the north."

He moved eagerly to the gate. Perhaps the Legate had received the news of Eboracum and was reinforcing the forts. It was about time. He saw the column of forty men as they marched down the road towards the fort. He realised that they were legionaries. That was even better. He had thought that all of the VIth had left the wall long ago. This must have been a vexillation left there. He frowned when he saw that they had no signifer. That was unusual. Still, they were obviously the legion for they marched smartly in that easy rhythm of veterans. However, he had been on the frontier long enough not to take anything for granted. He looked up at the tower. "Can you see anyone else? Are there any further along the road?"

"No, Centurion Coccius."

"Right. Ready at the gate."

He descended the ladder. Perhaps this handful of reinforcements meant he could check on the farm. He owed Marcus' Horse many favours. He would hate to think of the family being in peril.

He did not recognise the centurion who marched in at the head of the men. That was not a surprise as the VIth was a full-strength legion. The vexillation stopped smartly on command. "Centurion Severus Catullus, second cohort, sixth century, reporting with a vexillation on route to Eboracum."

"Does the Legate know about Eboracum then?"

"I don't know, Centurion. I just follow orders."

Coccius did not like this arrogant centurion. He was like all of the regulars; he thought himself better than the auxiliaries. "Well, we have a spare barracks for the night. It is the one over there."

Even as he was pointing the sentry from the southern gate shouted. "Alarm! Brigante!"

The sentry on the northern gate shouted, "Brigante to the north!"

Centurion was about to order the gates to be closed when the gladius slid into his back. He looked in horror at the Roman centurion who had just stabbed him. Severus's men ran to the two gates. They killed the sentries there and held open the gates. The two testudoes they formed ensured that the Batavians would not be able to easily remove them.

Elidr led his warriors eager for revenge and they flooded through the two gates. The heavily outnumbered Batavians were slaughtered to a man. Their bolt throwers were ineffective and their centurions lay dead. A brave young optio and a few Batavians held the Praetorium for a few minutes longer than Severus would have liked but then they too were killed. Morbium fell and the Legate and the men on the wall were completely cut off.

Chapter 15

Marcus and his men had reached their patrol area. It was in the land of the Selgovae. They were just twenty miles north of the wall and close to an old deserted Roman fort from the time of Agricola. These wooden structures had been hurriedly built to protect the auxiliaries as they tamed the wild frontier. Although the walls had been destroyed and most of the buildings removed the ditches and a couple of roofless wooden rooms survived. Marcus used it for it was defensible and in a prime position. It would make a good base for the next four days.

They had not seen any signs of Selgovae but he had sent Felix and Wolf off to scout for any evidence further afield. They lit no fires and ate cold rations. They were hardy men and it was preferable to a fire and the attention of the barbarians.

Rufius had taken the land bordering the Novontae and Marius, as a newly promoted decurion, was between them. The three were close enough to each other for mutual support. With the horses taken care of and the food eaten Marcus began to sharpen his sword. It was a nightly activity. A blunt sword was like swinging an iron bar. Chosen Man Gnaeus and the signifer, Titus, joined him. They were the three officers from the turma and the troopers gave them space to talk.

Gnaeus had a piece of gristle from the cold meat he had just eaten stuck between his teeth. He picked at it with his pugeo. "With all due respect, sir, I am not sure that the Prefect has made the right decision. Wouldn't we be better behind the wall and hitting them when they cross? It's why the wall was built."

"And normally you would be right Gnaeus but with the Brigante on the loose we might be caught between two rocks. I know what you are saying; we are but thirty-one men and we are trying to stop hundreds of barbarians from getting over the wall but think of it from the viewpoint of a Selgovae. If you are attacking the wall then you assume your rear is safe. You have a safe way home. Suppose you are attacked? It doesn't matter how many men there are attacking you there will be a doubt when you race to the wall or when you fight the Batavian. Those hesitations can cost a man his life. We know that."

Titus nodded, "You could be right sir but this is not cavalry country is it; dense, bloody forests and steep valleys."

"Yes, you are right but there are just thirty-one of us. We can ride in a column of twos and escape through the woods if we need to."

One of the sentries suddenly shouted, "Who goes there?"

The growling of Wolf told Marcus who it was. "It is the scout. Let him pass."

Felix was grinning as he jogged past the sentry. Wolf kept a suspicious eye on him as he slouched after his master. "I am sorry sir. I made as much noise as I could so that the sentry would not be afraid but he only saw me when I was twenty paces from him."

Marcus had kept some rations for Felix and Wolf. "Here eat first and then make your report."

The three of them watched as Felix devoured his food. Wolf waited. As soon as Felix had finished he said, "Eat." The dog lived up to its name and wolfed it down.

Felix drank from his water skin. "The Selgovae are just along the valley. They have made a camp for the night." He pointed north. "If we had kept on to the west then we would have run into them."

"How many?"

"Two hundred. They have no horses but they have good weapons."

Marcus stood and looked towards the west where the sun was beginning to set. "We passed no Selgovae on our way here. They must be heading for Luguvalium." He closed his eyes as he tried to picture the map in the office of Julius Longinus. "There is a road we built from the heartland of the Selgovae. This joins on to it. They must be gathering for an attack on Luguvalium. We passed a camp a few miles down the road, Castra Exploratorum I think it was called. It is built where the road emerges from the valley. If they are heading for the fort then they will have to pass it. We will ambush them tomorrow." He smiled at Titus. "Then we won't be in your dense bloody forests and steep valleys, will we?"

Titus grinned. "No sir. I guess that is why you are the officer and I just carry the standard."

As Marcus rolled himself in his cloak he worked out his plans for the following day. Once they had made their ambush he would head west, towards Marius. It meant he would have support should things go awry. The other three turmae would only just be heading west. An easterly escape might cause them to be trapped between Selgovae and Votadini.

Felix and Wolf left even as the turma was saddling up. The men paraded before Marcus and Chosen Man. Gnaeus addressed "We are going just five miles down the road today my lads. The decurion is being nice to you; no forced march today. We are going to lay an ambush for a couple of hundred Selgovae who are coming down this road. Now half of you will be with me and the other half with the decurion. When Titus here sounds the charge then we throw two of our javelins and attack with our spears. Listen, boys, we want no heroes today! Kill them and do not let them get close to you! It gets right up my nose when I have to train new troopers so no dying! That is an order!" They all laughed dutifully. "When you hear the recall, the orders are to head west. The Selgovae are on foot and have no horses so we will reform. Is that clear?"

"Yes, Chosen Man!"

Marcus took out his sword. "Remember men, Gnaeus is right. You all swore an oath on this sword. You swore to protect it and the frontier. This day we will do both." They all took their oaths seriously. They would not let Marcus and his sword down.

The old fort had been perfectly positioned astride the road. The route from the north had to pass by it. In the forty years since the fort had been built and then abandoned the trees had grown back a little. As Marcus had expected the growth was more vigorous towards the edges and there were scrubby trees and hedges fighting for light. It made a good hiding place.

He took Titus and his half of the turma to the east of the road. "Felix, I want you to head west and find us a camp for tonight."

Nodding, Felix and the dog trotted off. Marcus smiled. He would guarantee that the young scout would find time to hunt. It was in his blood. If they were far enough from danger then Marcus might chance a fire.

"Stay here, Titus. I will ride down the road and see what the Selgovae will see."

He rode half a mile down the road. He saw that it dipped rose slightly before it dipped down the valley bottom. The road was not cobbled. It was just a cleared track with pounded rocks on it. If they had had time then the builders would have put in a gully and cleared the land back further. Agricola had thought he was conquering Britannia but a jealous Emperor had recalled him before he had finished.

As Marcus crested the rise his eye was drawn to Luguvalium some fifteen miles in the distance. That is what the Selgovae would see. The decurion was looking for his men but he could not see them. He rode to Gnaeus. "The men are well hidden. Have them dismount. I think we have an hour or two before they reach us."

He dismounted and gave Raven an old apple from his saddlebags. As his mount chewed contentedly Marcus took off his helmet. He let the cool air blow over his head. His men looked relaxed. He did not like the idea of using two of their three javelins in one fell swoop but he had to cause casualties and this was the only way he knew. He wished his men had bows too. However, if they carried everything that they needed the horses would be overloaded. They had to make do with what they had.

It was Raven who alerted them to the Selgovae. His ears pricked. The rise hid an approaching enemy. "Mount lads." Titus whistled and Marcus knew that Gnaeus would be mounting his men.

The scrubby undergrowth allowed them to see the warband as they trudged down the slope. As Marcus had expected they were cheered by the fact that the legionary fortress was in view. Warriors liked to fight, not march.

"Stand by Titus." Marcus balanced the javelin in his hand. The two halves of the turma were far enough apart so that they did not risk hitting each other. They could throw blind. They would be hitting a mass of unprepared men. With luck they would hit a large number of barbarians. Not all would die but the shock effect would be great. They would be disrupted and a charge with spears might just rout them.

His men had the advantage of seeing his actions and, as he drew back his arm, so did they. "Now, Titus!" The buccina sounded and sixteen javelins flew through the air. Marcus loosed his second and grabbed his spear. "Charge!"

They burst through the bushes. There were more warriors in the warband than Marcus had expected. Thirty or so had passed the ambush but the writhing bodies showed him that they had killed many. He wheeled left and his men followed. They fell upon the vanguard. The rest would have to negotiate the dead and the dying to reach them. Raven was the most powerful horse in the ala, never mind the turma, and Marcus raced ahead of his men. He aimed his spear at the warrior with the fine helmet who led the vanguard. The decurion took in the shield and the sword as he adjusted his spear. He pulled it back and, as the Selgovae chief raised his shield he punched forward at the man's middle. The shield protected his head but his mailed stomach was vulnerable. The spear head ripped through the links and then tore into the man's stomach. With a twist of the wrist, Marcus withdrew his spear. A string of wriggling guts looking like an enormous worm emerged with them.

He glanced around and saw Titus using the end of the standard to take out a Selgovae warrior's eye. A warrior dropped to the ground to avoid Marcus who stabbed down and pinned the man to the earth. He reined in Raven while he withdrew the spearhead. There was no immediate danger and he looked at the scene. The vanguard had been destroyed but the rest were now advancing in a solid line of shields and spears, "Sound the recall."

He watched as his well-drilled troopers thrust their spears one last time and then wheeled off. He was about to follow them when he saw a gaggle of Selgovae race recklessly towards Gaius and Lentius who were at the rear of the line. A warrior hurled his war axe and it struck Lentius' horse. It went down instantly as the axe embedded itself in its skull. The young trooper staggered to his feet, dazed and the Selgovae eagerly raced to finish him off. Gaius put his arm down to lift his friend on to his horse's rump. Marcus cursed. They would both die.

He kicked hard and Raven leapt forward. Lentius was too dazed to be able to grab the outstretched arm and a warrior speared him in the back as he stood trying to reach Gaius. The warrior screamed in triumph and he pulled back his spear to gut the helpless Gaius who just stared at his dying friend.

Yelling, "Trooper! Retreat!" Marcus hurled his spear. It was not meant for throwing but Marcus had hidden strength. It flew straight and true and embedded itself in the warrior's stomach before emerging from his back. Marcus drew his sword and galloped towards the charging Selgovae. He no longer had the advantage of length for the spear was gone and he used his speed of hand, eye and horse to charge at them smashing their weapons with his sword. They did not help themselves as they got in each other's way. Marcus kicked one warrior in the face as his sword tore across the throat of a second. He felt a spear slide across his left leg. He raised his shield and smashed the edge onto the skull of the warrior.

He had enough space to wheel Raven around and he took off after Gaius who had finally listened to his orders. Gnaeus had halted the men, again, against the decurion's orders, just four hundred paces from the ambush.

"Follow your orders and ride!"

He felt the blood flowing down his leg but he dared not stop. Had Gaius not disobeyed his orders they would have been well away from the Selgovae. As it was they had had time to catch up a little. Marcus knew that they would lose them eventually but he wanted to be able to escape detection at their new camp. In fact, they were four miles from their camp for the night at Blatobulgium before they gave up their chase.

Felix saw them and he and Wolf ran from the deserted fort to meet them. As he reined in Marcus felt light headed. Gnaeus grinned at him, "Well sir that was a little reckless wasn't..." he suddenly saw the blood. "Capsarius! The Decurion is wounded."

Titus was the closest and he managed to reach the decurion before he slid from his horse. They lowered him to the ground and the capsarius began to work on him. There was an anxious silence and even Wolf appeared worried as he licked the decurion's hand. After tearing open his breeches the capsarius reached into his bag and took out some vinegar which he poured over the wound. Taking out a needle and some gut he said, "Signifer hold the two sides of the wound together and try to keep pressure on the wound."

The blood continued to seep between Titus' fingers. He bit his lip. It would be ridiculous to lose the decurion to such a simple looking wound and yet Titus knew that Marcus could bleed to death. The capsarius worked quickly ignoring the blood. The stitches would be rough but they would hold the skin together.

"Just keep the pressure on for a few moments longer." The capsarius took out a bandage and wrapped it around the decurion's leg. He looked up at Gnaeus. "He should live but you can never tell. He really needs something hot inside him."

"Then he will have it. Felix, is the fort safe?"

"There are no warriors for two miles in any direction."

"Right you four troopers put two of your shields together as a stretcher and carry him to the fort."

Gnaeus and Titus rode at the rear of the turma with weapons drawn. "He nearly bought it then, Chosen Man."

"I know. His courage will get him killed one of these days."

This fort was similar to the one they had slept in the previous night. They found one wooden building with a roof of sorts and they placed the decurion within. "Right I want a small fire making. Just use old wood. I want no smoke."

Titus said, "Are you sure? You know it might draw the bastard barbarians on to us."

"He needs food and he needs to recover. Both need a fire. It's my shout." He looked at Felix. "Now I am hoping that you have some food." The scout grinned and held up two pigeons and a small hare. "You'll do for me son. Get a stew of some description on. I know that Drugi will have taught you."

He stood and addressed them all. "Listen; we are in the deep shit here, lads." He glared at Gaius and jabbed a finger at him. "And it is this useless bugger's fault. When we get back to Cilurnum you will be on horse shit duty for a month my son!"

"I'm sorry sir but Lentius was my friend."

"I don't care if he was your brother we all know the rules. You fall and no one comes back for you. You nearly got three men killed there, son, not just Lentius. Any man other than the Decurion and it would have been three. You owe him your life."

He looked at the determined faces. The turma felt that they were the elite. They served the sword. If the decurion needed fire then fire he would have.

"Half of you are on duty now. Spread yourselves out and listen for the Selgovae. This is their land." He nodded at Wolf. "And listen to the dog. If he growls then there is someone out there. We will swap over after dark." As the troopers arranged their duty partner Gnaeus said to Titus, "This will be a long night old son!"

The band of Selgovae ambushed by Marcus was not the only one moving south. King Tole was already watching the fortress of Luguvalium with five hundred of his warriors. By morning he would have well over a thousand. That would be more than enough to destroy the auxiliaries within. These were not the vaunted legion which had defeated the last rebellion of the Selgovae. These were the barely trained barbarians the Romans called auxiliaries and they would fall.

As his bands arrived he was disturbed to hear of Roman cavalry behind their lines. Already he was over a hundred warriors short of the number he had expected. Had it been just one incident then he would have put it from his mind but there appeared to be large numbers of them. The last band who came reported over sixty horse warriors. They had boasted of almost killing the officer but when they said they had only killed one man then he knew that they were fighting Marcus' Horse. One band of horse warriors would not stop the invasion but they might slow it down. He just waited for his brother Tiernan. He hoped that he would have avoided disaster.

The Allfather was watching over Marcus and the turma. He awoke a few hours after sunset. The capsarius called Gnaeus over. "You had us worried sir."

"Is that smoke I can smell?"

Guiltily Gnaeus said, "You needed hot food and we have kept a good watch. No-one came."

"Well put it out now. I am awake and I feel fine."

"Go on Titus, put it out."

The hissing from the fire told Marcus that his orders had been obeyed. "Anyone else wounded?"

"No sir, just you."

Marcus suddenly seemed to realise where they were. "I thought the other turma would have used this."

"He's a young decurion sir. Perhaps he didn't know about it."

"Perhaps. Tomorrow we will sweep north and then head east again. I would feel happier if we saw signs that the other turmae were around."

"Me too, sir. I don't know how you and the other Explorates ever did that job. This is bad enough but at least there are thirty odd of us. You did this in ones and twos."

Marcus smiled at the memory of those far off days. "You get used to it and it was easier than this. Here I worry about all of you. As an Explorate you just worried about yourself."

Marcus did not feel fully recovered as he mounted Raven the next day but he had his duty and besides, there was no alternative. In the ala you just got on with it.

"Felix, see what is ahead."

As they rode up the partly finished Roman Road Marcus wondered if they would ever recover the land they had lost. He had met Emperor Hadrian and, although a good Emperor, he seemed happy to settle for the frontier where it was. Marcus' father had told him how Agricola had almost conquered the whole of the Province. They had come so close it seemed a shame to settle for half of Britannia.

Now that he had used his spear and left it in a dead Selgovae Marcus would have to go back to relying on the Sword of Cartimandua. He did not mind. It had never let him down. He believed it was a good luck charm. The wound yesterday could have been worse if it had struck an artery. The sword would continue to protect him so long as he was true to his calling; he was a warrior.

151

Felix ran back down the road with Wolf in close attendance. He looked agitated, "Stand to and ready your weapons."

He looked genuinely upset. "Sir, I have found the other turma. They are on the other side of the woods."

Marcus asked no more questions for the look on Felix's face and the crows, magpies and ravens swirling in the sky bespoke their own story. As they crested the rise they saw thirty bodies impaled upon stakes. The heads were all missing.

The whole turma approached silently. There was no hurry. They were not recently killed. Marcus could smell the bodies. As he looked he realised that the one body which was missing was Marius'. He would ponder that later. "Chosen Man, get the bodies off the stakes."

"What do we do with them, sir?"

"We burn them!"

"But sir, the Selgovae will see the smoke."

Marcus' voice was as cold as his eyes as he said, "Burn them while I try to work out what happened here. Felix, come with me."

As an Explorate he had been taught to read signs and make inferences. He saw that at least half of the troopers had been dead before they had been impaled. It was obvious that some of the others had been impaled alive for there were huge puddles of blood and dark soil lying at the base of the stakes. Some of the turma must have surrendered or been overcome.

"Felix where did the ambush take place?"

He and Wolf trotted off in a large circle and Marcus watched as his men took the bodies off the stakes as carefully as if the troopers were still alive. These were their friends and they would honour them in death. Other troopers were gathering wood for the pyre.

Felix had disappeared. There was another rise ahead and the scout appeared there. Marcus mounted Raven and rode towards him. His leg was not strong enough for walking yet. When he reached the top of the rise he saw the ambush site. There were four dead and partly butchered horses lying between a stand of trees. There was a great deal of blood on the trees and the road.

Felix pointed as he spoke. "Many Selgovae hid behind these bushes. They had some sort of barricade here." He gestured to a track in the grass and the tree trunks which had been dragged away. "They did the same at the other end."

Marcus nodded. Poor Marius was inexperienced. You never took your men into a narrow gap. You scouted, you waited, you smelled, you took a different route; what you did not do was what he had done and ride between trees where you could be surrounded and slaughtered.

"Any sign of the decurion?"

Felix shook his head. "The horses and the warriors headed south."

As he returned to his men he knew that they had taken Marius with them to Luguvalium. He thought he knew why. He hoped his young friend was already dead but in his heart, he knew that he was not.

Gnaeus had waited for the decurion to return before burning the bodies. The stakes were laid alternatively to form a funeral pyre for the thirty warriors who had died. Marcus nodded and Gnaeus lit the fire. It seemed to take an age to get going and thick black smoke billowed up into the skies.

Titus shook his head, "We might as well tell them where we are. We will be joining these soon, Chosen Man."

Gnaeus shook his head, "You don't believe that. We have the best decurion in the ala. He wouldn't walk into a trap like these lads. We just have to keep him alive."

Chapter 16

Tiernan proudly paraded the bleeding and wounded decurion. He was tethered to his own horse and had been half dragged the fifteen miles from the ambush site. King Feanan and his Novontae took this as a good omen. They had a Roman officer. Although they had not brought the numbers the Selgovae had the king knew his warriors would relish the chance to do as Tiernan had done. This was a Roman from their horse warriors. They were a fierce foe. It was a sign that the gods were impressed. He wondered now at the wisdom of leaving a third of his forces to guard his homeland.

King Tole was impressed. "A fine prisoner, brother."

Tiernan nodded. "We killed all the others." He sneered at the chiefs who had lost men to these horse warriors. "I brought him here to guarantee victory. We will sacrifice him here in the river."

Although King Tole would have liked to make that decision he thought it a good one. "You are right brother and we will show the priestess that we too can make a sacrifice which will ensure victory."

Marius was stripped and his hands bound behind him. Tiernan and Tole themselves took him to the edge of the river across from the legionary fortress. He knew that the garrison was watching them which was why they had chosen this spot. Tiernan wielded the hammer. He struck Marius on the side of the head. For Marius, it was a mercy. If he could he would have ended his own life. He had been a fool and his men had paid for his mistake with their lives.

Tiernan held up the limp decurion while Tole slowly throttled him. He hoped he had not killed him for he wished the gods to reward them for this sacrifice. Finally, he took his knife and slashed the throat of the young officer. The blood spurted; it showed that he was still alive. The watching warriors screamed their joy. Tiernan threw the body into the water as Tole shouted, "Allfather, take this Roman as a sacrifice and grant us victory."

Even if the garrison did not see exactly what happened they saw the tribal tokens and the weapons waving in the late afternoon light. They heard the roar from the barbarians and prepared themselves for the worst. The Selgovae and the Novontae were coming. The mixed cohort readied themselves. They would be fighting for their lives soon.

With the bodies still burning Marcus led his troopers west. They had to find Rufius. He would assume that Marius was to the east of him. Marcus could not leave Rufius isolated. Felix ran, not along the rough tribal road, but through the trees. He was able to move as quickly as though on the road but he was hidden and that was important. Drugi had taught him well. He and Wolf were like two shadows that flickered through the trees.

The Romans had built few forts in the land of the Novontae and even fewer roads. It was a wild hilly country. As Felix ran through this new land he began to worry about the decurion and his men. The sight of the headless corpses had shaken the Brigante scout. That sort of thing did not happen to the horse warriors he served.

Suddenly Wolf stopped and his ears pricked. A low growl emanated from his throat. From the growl, Felix knew that it meant an enemy ahead. He unslung his bow and took out an arrow in the blink of an eye. He sniffed and then he peered. The rough road was thirty paces below him. It was fortunate he had avoided it for there were two warriors hiding in the trees with their own bows ready to ambush anyone loping along. Felix had a dilemma. He had been told to find the lost turma. If he returned now he might have to travel a long way to get around this obstacle. On the other hand, if he failed to kill them then they might summon others.

He nocked an arrow and slipped a little further west so that the barbarians' backs were towards him. They would not expect an attack from that direction. He breathed slowly. At thirty paces distance, he should not miss. The arrow thudded into the back of the first Novontae. The second hesitated as his companion fell next to him. The delay allowed Felix to notch another arrow and, as the warrior turned the arrow struck him in the throat.

Felix saw that they were dead and continued to head west. He had travelled no more than five hundred paces when he heard the sound of battle. He ran a little quicker. The ground began to fall away as the sounds grew louder. He stopped when he came to the edge of the road. There, on the hill opposite, was a deserted Roman fort. He could see the warriors attacking it. The standard which still stood amongst the defenders told him that they were Rufius and his men.

He turned and ran swiftly back through the forest. The trail ran in a circle around the base of this hill and he made good time. He saw the turma. They were on the road. He ran as fast as he could and slithered down the last slope to appear next to Marcus' horse.

"Sir, the decurion is being attacked. They are two miles away at a Roman fort."

"Good work, Felix. You wait here for us." Felix nodded and began to get his breath back. Wolf panted next to him. They had both run themselves to the point of exhaustion. They needed the rest.

Marcus urged Raven on and the turma galloped down the road. The decurion did not need to tell his men what they were about. The headless troopers and Felix's agitated state told them that their comrades were in trouble. Every trooper readied his spear and, as they rode along the rough road, slung his shield on to his shoulder.

Marcus' mind was working out the best approach. If he was able to then Rufius would have fled such a trap. That meant that he was surrounded. That helped Marcus to come up with a solution to the problem. The enemy would have to spread their numbers around a perimeter. Marcus would punch a hole in one side and provide an escape route for Rufius. He shouted as they rode. "Gnaeus I want a wedge when we near the enemy. We are going to clear the barbarians from one side of the fort."

He heard, "Sir!"

"Titus, have the horn ready, I will tell you when I want the charge sounding!"

"Sir!"

Even above the sound of the horses' hooves, they could hear the sound of battle. Marcus hoped that they were not too late. If Rufius and his men were dead by the time they arrived then his own turma could be in dire straits. The road bent around the hill and Marcus saw the beleaguered turma. They had a barricade before them. The old Roman ditches helped them and Marcus recognised Rufius as he jabbed down with his spear. Had the Novontae had arrows then this would be over but they had been forced to fight an enemy with height advantage. Marcus saw at least fifty warriors fighting on their side of the fort.

The ground flattened out. "Wedge!"

Gnaeus appeared on his right and Titus on his left. The barbarians were so intent on the fort that they did not hear the drumming of the hooves until the last minute. As the warriors at the bottom of the hill turned, Marcus shouted, "Sound the charge!"

The buccina's notes and the screams of the skewered warriors were almost simultaneous. Marcus had no spear and he leaned forward to slice his sword and split open the skull of the Novontae before him. He was the point of the arrow which was driving inexorably up the hill. Their momentum carried them half way up and then they started to slow.

In the fort a desperate Rufius had seen the attack and heard the buccina. He shouted, "Chosen Man, pull back those on the west of the hill and mount up. Help is at hand. It is the Sword of Cartimandua!" That magical name brought instant hope to the fifteen troopers who remained. Rufius jabbed his spear into the side of the warrior who made the mistake of half turning to see the danger below him.

"Get on your horses! Now!" Rufius swung his spear in a long arc. The Novontae recoiled and he ran to the picket line and leapt on to his horse. The remaining troopers had grabbed their horses and Rufius could see the barbarians flooding over the western wall. There were just fourteen troopers left.

"Charge!"

The ragged line leapt the ditch and the vengeful troopers hacked and stabbed at the shocked Novontae. Their horses had been rested and their leap struck and killed many warriors. Hooves killed as effectively as a spear sometimes. Suddenly there were no more Novontae. Marcus was there before him.

"Sir, head down the road. We will cover your withdrawal." Rufius nodded. "Javelins!" His turma had one javelin each left and they threw them at the Novontae who appeared at the fort's edge. The ones who were not struck took shelter. "Sound the recall, Titus!"

The buccina sounded. Marcus was proud of his troopers as they wheeled their mounts around and descended the steep slope. The infuriated warriors tried to purse them but the horses were more surefooted and they were able to leap the dead Novontae whilst the warriors tripped and fell. Gnaeus and Marcus rode at the rear of the column of troopers. They kept glancing behind them but the Novontae gradually stopped. He heard their cheers ringing at the top of the fort. They regarded this as a victory. Their enemy had fled. If so it had been a costly one. The bodies of their warriors lay in piles around the fort. Rufius' men had not died without a fight.

Rufius did not stop until he and his men reached Felix. They dismounted for there were wounded. "Marcus, we need your capsarius; mine was killed."

"Capsarius, see to the wounded. Gnaeus, put scouts out on the road. The Novontae may return. Felix, we will camp where we did last night. See if it is clear." The scout ran down the road

Rufius drank from his water skin. He wiped his mouth with the back of his hand. "That was a timely intervention but we were not expecting you. What made you leave your patrol?"

"Marius' turma were massacred. We didn't find his body. He may be a prisoner. You will see their remains at the camp. We had run in with a couple of Selgovae warbands. We lost one trooper and I picked up this." He pointed to his bandaged leg.

"You did better than us. We managed to hit a Selgovae warband but as we tried to leave the fort we found we were trapped between two bands of Novontae and the valley was too steep to escape. Had you not chanced upon us then I fear we would have been done for."

"All sorted sir." The capsarius lowered his voice. "There are a couple of deep wounds there sir. I have stitched them but they won't stand up to combat."

Rufius nodded, "Thank you." He mounted. "I think this curtails our patrol. It would be foolish to risk the rest of the troopers. We have done enough I think. We were due to return tomorrow in any case. The

Selgovae and the Novontae will be looking over their shoulders. We will cross the river and head for Luguvalium."

Blatobulgium was empty but an air of melancholy hung over it. The smoking pyre was a reminder of their dead comrades. "I would carry on to the fort now but my men need a rest. We will leave in the morning."

Marcus was pleased that there was someone else to shoulder the responsibility of command. "Right, sir. I'll get Felix to go hunting again."

Rufius shook his head. "No, I want him to scout out the fort."

"Right sir. I will go with him."

He shook his head. "You are wounded. I will go. You take charge here."

Rufius was not being heroic as he rode down the road behind the scout and his dog. He felt he had made a mistake by getting trapped. He had meant what he had said to Marcus. The Allfather watched over his young friend that was certain. The road suddenly opened up and Rufius heart sank. They need not go any further south. The fort was surrounded by Selgovae and Novontae warriors. Their escape route was barred.

Inside Luguvalium the Prefect was also surveying the scene. The Legate's warning had ensured that there were plenty of supplies in and they had prepared their defences. The bolt throwers and ballistae had carved bloody lines in the advancing barbarians. They would not attempt that again. They had made a classic barbarian attack in broad daylight and had not even come close to the ditches. They had lost no men and the bodies outside showed their success.

He had also sent his mounted troopers from the fort to harass and harry any barbarians not in a large warband. Horse warriors were of little use inside the fort and it was difficult finding feed for the horses. At least this way they could graze at will. They could use the Stanegate to find refuge in another fort along the wall if they wished. Despite his preparations, however, he wondered just how long the barbarians would wait outside his walls. He knew that they did not have the determination of the Romans and he hoped they would leave and find an easier target. Nagging at the back of his mind was the thought that they would simply attack the wall at a mile castle or a turret. If that was the case then they would be truly isolated.

That was, indeed, the debate between the Selgovae and Novontae kings. The glory of the slaughter of the turma had been tempered by the losses they had sustained attacking the fort. "Let us leave this edifice and attack an easier target."

Tiernan was there with his brother and he took offence at King Feanan's words. "We can take this fort!"

Feanan sighed, "You are right but it would cost us many warriors." He looked at Tole who appeared to be more reasonable than his fiery brother. "Remember the plan, King Tole. We are to join up with the Brigante. If the Romans remain in the fort, they will not be in a position to come to their comrades' aid, will they? My scouts have reported that the wall is lightly held further to the east. There are just turrets and small fortlets. The ground is also better for our warriors. It is twenty Roman miles to their next large fort."

It was a persuasive argument and King Tole made his decision. "We will do as you suggest King Feanan." He saw his brother redden. "You can lead the assault on the wall my brother and gain all the glory you wish. How is that?"

Mollified the warrior nodded, "And we will slaughter every Roman we find!"

The Roman troopers were relieved to leave the camp. They were all superstitious and the spirits of their dead comrades seemed to hang in the air. They headed west. Felix and Wolf, inevitably, ranged far ahead. The only crossings of the wall were at the forts. Men on foot could climb the turf and the stone wall but horses could not. They would have to ride to Banna. It was the newest fort on the wall and, as far as Rufius could remember, the garrison still lived in tents and the walls were wooden. If the Votadini and Selgovae scouts had been thorough they would have discovered that it was held by half a cohort of Tungrians and was the weakest part of the whole wall.

Roman Wall

They moved cautiously. There would be many bands of barbarians prowling in the vicinity of the wall. The last thing they needed, in their depleted state, was to run into a warband in this land without roads. The ground undulated giving tantalising glimpses of the wall. Felix and Wolf suddenly appeared as they crested a rise. The scout had seen something. "Decurion, the barbarians have left Luguvalium. I went to the high crag and I saw them. They are heading towards the wall."

"Damn!" Rufius looked west as though he could see them. When he and Felix had seen their camp, he had been appalled at the numbers. There were two huge warbands: one at each end of the wall. "This is a large warband, Marcus. There could be up to two thousand men. If they cross the Stanegate then we are in trouble. We need to ride as quickly as we can."

Banna was built where the crags started. It was a good site and, when it was finished, it would be almost impossible to take. The Tungrian sentry was surprised to see the troopers. The marks on the wall and the handful of bodies by the ditch showed that they had been attacked.

"Decurion Atrebeus and two turmae of Marcus' Horse requesting permission to enter the fort."

The centurion who allowed them to enter checked carefully to see that this was not a trap.

He pointed to the soldiers being tended by the capsarii. "As you can see we were attacked a day or so ago. We beat them off but…"

Rufius dismounted to speak with him. "I hate to be the bearer of more bad news but there are up to two thousand barbarians heading this way. They may attack you but I think it is more likely that they will attack your men in your mile castles and turrets. I don't want to tell you what to do but I would pull them inside the fort. The river at your front will give you a little extra protection."

"That is a good idea. We are undermanned here. Any chance of help from the Legate?"

Rufius shrugged, "I will send a rider along the Stanegate to tell the Legate but the Votadini attacked Cilurnum and the Brigante have revolted too."

"Thank you for the warning." As the turmae left the fort he heard the centurion ordering the signals which would bring his men from the isolated turrets and mile castles to the east and the west, into the safety of the fort. It would double his garrison.

As they headed for the Stanegate, Gnaeus asked, "Doesn't pulling them from their turrets defeat the point of the wall?"

"There are too many barbarians. They would die. This way the barbarians might get over the wall but they will be on foot."

They reached the Stanegate and Rufius summoned his Chosen Man. "I want you to take the other wounded troopers back to Cilurnum. Tell the Legate what has happened. I suspect he will pull the other turmae south of the wall. You had better tell the Prefect at Vercovicium too. Tell the Legate that I will try to harass the barbarians on the Stanegate but we need help."

Rufius could see that his Chosen Man wished to stay but he obeyed his orders and took the twelve wounded men back along the Stanegate. There were just twenty-four troopers left. Marcus realised that ninety-three had left Cilurnum. The ala had paid a high price already and the rebellion had barely started.

He watched Felix and Wolf as they darted in the distance. They were not looking for the barbarians; their numbers were so large that they would be easily seen. Felix was looking for a sign that the tribes had crossed the Stanegate. Rufius had contemplated sending the young scout back with the wounded but he was invaluable. The needs of the many outweighed the risks to the individual. The wall was clearly visible as they rode west along the Stanegate. In the distance, he could see the Tungrian auxiliaries running back along the wall to Banna. Rufius breathed a sigh of relief. They would have more chance of survival there.

Suddenly Felix disappeared. Rufius knew the young scout well enough to realise that something was amiss. "Stand to." Even though this was largely Marcus' turma, as senior decurion Rufius took charge. Like Marcus his spear had gone in the fight and, like Marcus, he drew his sword. He saw movement. There was a body of men coming along the road.

"Shall we recall Felix sir?"

"I think not. He has enough wit about him to evade whoever it is. We know that they have no horses south of the wall. Whoever it is we can out run them. Let us wait and see."

They all breathed a sigh of relief when they saw the Batavian standard and the horses. It was the cavalry from the mixed cohort. That meant there could be eight turmae ahead. The Cohors Equitata was not equipped as well as Marcus' Horse and they had less experience. Even so Rufius was happy to have them by his side.

They did not have a decurion princeps. The senior decurion was an older decurion who had served with the Cohors since its foundation twenty years earlier. He was a grizzled old veteran. As soon as he saw the turma his spirits lifted a little. He recognised the standard; this was Marcus' Horse. He had heard of them. On their patrol the Cohors Equitata had seen many barbarians and had chased the smaller bands away. The large warbands they had just seen climb over the wall had made Decurion Ulpius Marcus Albius decide to head for Vercovicium for orders. His own fort was surrounded.

The eight under strength turmae all halted. He saluted Rufius. "I am glad to see you. Where is the rest of your ala?"

"Where we were this morning, north of the wall."

Shock rippled down the troopers within earshot. "How, in the Allfather's name did you escape unscathed?"

"We didn't. There were ninety of us set out. The Legate's orders were to harass the barbarians. We did that but now they have spread across the wall."

"I know we just saw a huge band of them climbing over the wall."

One of the Batavians shouted, "Decurion look!" He pointed to the north-west where Felix and Wolf were racing towards them.

"Rest easy Decurion, he is our scout."

"We just passed that place and didn't see him."

"If Felix doesn't want you to see him then you don't."

Felix drew up next to the decurion. Wolf growled irritably at the strangers. "Selgovae and Novontae warriors, decurion and they are heading for the Stanegate."

The Batavian troopers looked over their shoulders nervously. The decurion said, "Perhaps we should head for the fort too."

Rufius shook his head. "We have orders from the Legate. We will follow them. Besides we are impotent behind walls we will use our advantage." He patted his mount, "Our horses and our speed."

"You can't be serious! We have less than two hundred and thirty men. If this is the same band that we saw then there will be more than a thousand of them."

Marcus said amiably, "More like two thousand actually."

"And you still want to harass them? That is suicide."

"No, decurion. They have no horses and few bowmen. Your men each have three javelins. Have they still got them?"

"Aye, we used our swords to despatch the barbarians we found."

"Good. My lads have their spears. All we have to do is to slow down their advance. Pick them off. We attack and run. I have sent a message to the legate. There will be reinforcements." Rufius was stretching the truth. At best there would be four turmae for the rest were north of the wall.

"Felix, did you see any warriors across the Stanegate?"

"No sir."

"There you are Decurion. You have fought barbarians before. Do they ever fight in solid lines?"

"No, they charge like mad buggers and every warrior tries to reach the enemy first."

"And that is how we will whittle them down. We show them one turma. They will charge to get to grips. The turma will release their javelins and retreat. The next turma will do the same."

"So that the barbarians will think that we have used all of our javelins."

"Exactly and we will be killing their best and bravest warriors. Eventually whoever leads them will make them halt and try to advance in a single line. I have another plan to deal with that."

Decurion Ulpius Marcus Albius thought it was a good plan. Then a sinister thought passed through his head. "And where will you and your lads be during all this? At the back watching my lads get killed?"

Rufius looked at him. "No, decurion, our turma will always be with those throwing the javelins. We will use our spears to protect your men and it will add to the illusion that it is the same men."

"I am sorry that I doubted your honour." He turned to his men. "First Turma to the fore."

While they arranged themselves in a straight line Rufius said to Felix. "Find the ala. You may have to walk all the way to Cilurnum but you need to let the Prefect know what we are doing." He pointed to the spare horses from the dead troopers. "Take a horse. You will be quicker."

He nodded and left.

As he rode away Marcus was happy. The scout would survive. He was not sure any of the rest would but that did not matter so long as they stopped the barbarians.

Chapter 17

Far to the west King Ardal was less than happy with his young brother. Despite his initial success they had had to withdraw back across the wall and he had lost too many men in the abortive and premature attack. King Ardal wished that his little brother had obeyed his orders. However, he had been led to believe that the Romans would withdraw their soldiers to face the threat from the south. Caronwyn and the Roman, Severus, had been confident that the Brigante attack in the south would draw Romans from the wall. There appeared to be as many Romans now on the wall as there had ever been. At the back of his mind was the impression that they had been duped. The Brigante were letting his warriors bleed so that they could attack when soldiers were sent north. This was his first test of leadership. He determined to make one more attack. If this failed then he would take it as a sign from the gods that they did not support this uprising.

After he had spoken to his leaders he watched their faces for any sign of dissension. There was none. His plan was the best that he could come up with and it met with the approval of those who would lead their men against the fort.

"Brother, let me lead the attack!" Banquo was desperate to make up for his failures a few days earlier.

Ardal's smile was without both humour and warmth. "Banquo, you have done more than enough. You have put your life in danger for our people. It is my turn to lead."

Ardal was already annoyed. He had promised the priestess and the other kings that he would attack when they did. Banquo's reckless assault had meant a delay. Even worse the Romans would be expecting the attack. They would have reinforced the walls. The mile castle and the turret they had taken would now be strengthened. Since he had been told of Banquo's actions the Votadini king had wracked his brain for a solution to his dilemma. Had he not promised his mother on her death bed to care for his little brother he would have had him executed out of hand.

He turned to his oathsworn. "Find men with axes. I want as many large trees cutting down as they can." He turned to his brother. "There is something you could do while we are making preparations. If, that is, you still wish to gain some honour."

"I do brother. Anything!"

"I want you to take your warband to the north-western wall of their fort. Go close to the northern gate but stay out of range of their bolt throwers. Challenge a Roman to single combat." He saw the look on Banquo's face. "Do not worry brother it will not be accepted. The Romans have no honour. I want you to keep their attention on you."

"I am happy to fight any Roman in single combat." King Ardal nodded. "And what will you do, brother?"

"I will attack the fort."

When his oathsworn returned just after noon he saw that they had managed to cut down twenty trees. "I want them tied together to make five rafts."

"You are going to attack the bridge!"

"I am going to use them to get a large number of men to the bridge so that we can pin down their men. There are neither towers nor turrets on the bridge. They have one tower at each end. My brother took one such tower easily. If we take the bridge then the fort is cut off."

The leader of his oathsworn, Barac, looked almost disappointed. "Then we do not attack their fort?"

"That would merely waste men. When night falls we will do as my brother tried to do and use cunning to breach the walls. My brother and his men can continue to distract the Romans."

Barac was much older than the young king but he saw in him a wise warrior. He would not throw lives away.

Livius and Julius looked over the wall at the Votadini. Banquo had disobeyed his brother's orders again and ridden to within a hundred paces of the Roman fort. He was doing so to show his men how brave he was. He enjoyed the adulation and attention he would receive. The six hundred men of his who remained were all out of range of the bolt throwers. Banquo could not know that they would not waste an arrow or a bolt on one man. He thought that they were afraid of him. He paraded up and down shouting out his challenge. At one point he turned his back on them and lowered his breeks to reveal his bare rear. His warband hooted and cheered their approval. He strutted like a young cockerel.

Livius and Julius were almost ignoring the young warrior who kept shouting insults. "The attack might have been repulsed but it has stopped us sending out the next three turmae."

"Yes Legate, but we now have more men within the fort."

"I would they were out there sowing the seeds of doubt in their mind. Besides, I hate to think of the three turmae we sent out isolated in the west. Poor Metellus is beside himself. He feels it should be him who is surrounded by barbarians and not those other decurions."

"The question is what is this all about? Why is the young man still parading around? It must be obvious that his challenge is not being accepted."

"They are planning something. We now have extra guards. I want a watch kept on all the walls but the southern wall."

Livius left to organise the extra sentries and Julius began to walk along the north wall. The defences had held. The casualties had been heavier than they had hoped but the Votadini had lost more. That did not help the Romans. The barbarians could be reinforced with an almost inexhaustible supply of men eager to fight. Julius could not even replace one man! The problem was that the Legate had not had any word from the south. He was blind. He knew that he should have arranged for vessels to be at Coriosopitum. They would have been able to travel to Eboracum and gather news. It would have been slow but he would not be in the dark.

Livius caught up with him. "I can see what they are up to. They have rafted men down to the bridge. They are attacking there."

"Reinforce the tower at the western end."

"I have done so but we do not have enough men on the bridge. They will be able to capture it. Our artillery is sited to cover the north. We have no weapons which can clear the bridge save the arrows of the archers and we have few of them."

Julius smiled, "You know this is very thoughtful of the barbarians. They are finding out all the flaws in the wall." He patted Livius' arm. "Come we will go to the east gate and put our minds to the problem."

Barac and King Ardal had managed to ferry a hundred warriors on their crude boats. Only three men had been lost before they reached the bridge. The Romans had been taken by surprise and they had managed to scale the bridge. The sentries had fought bravely but they were too few and they had fled to the two towers at either end of the bridge. The archers had killed three warriors before the Votadini withdrew to a safer range.

Barac signalled the waiting warriors. They were ready to move down the river bank and assault the tower. It was only made of wood and held but twenty men. He looked admiringly at King Ardal who hefted his shield around as he prepared to lead a wedge of warriors to attack the wooden gate in the tower. This was a good leader.

The king nodded to Barac who shouted at his men. "You men with the bows, I want the Roman archers' heads kept down! I'll take it out of your hides if their arrows strike the king."

The handful of archers had been chosen for their skill. They were all hunters and although they were not using war bows the arrows could still kill. The auxiliary archers were gradually whittled down. When King Ardal and his men reached the gate, they raised their shields while the two men with the axes began to hack a hole in the door. Stones were dropped on to the shield but King Ardal had anticipated that and the shields were angled out so that little damage was done.

One of the axe men died when his axe finally punched a hole in the door and he was speared as he barged in. King Ardal killed his killer and his sword sliced and hacked the auxiliaries who stood in his way.

The optio knew when he was beaten. "Back to the fort!" The ten survivors ran the hundred and ten paces back to the east gate and safety.

Livius and Julius had moved two bolt throwers to the ramparts above the gate and they were ready to clear the bridge but were puzzled when the Votadini made no attempt to follow the auxiliaries. Metellus had joined them and he pointed to the river. "Sir, they are reinforcing the bridge from the river."

"Very clever. The bank protects them and they have now cut the wall in two."

"They will attack tonight."

"Of course, Livius. I want your ala mounting just before dusk. Take them out by the southern gate. Just issue javelins; five for each trooper. We will attack the men on the river bank."

"What about those on the bridge sir?"

"We will use the bolt throwers and the ballistae. The tower should burn well."

Julius stayed there while the afternoon dragged on. He became alarmed when he saw the Votadini beginning to damage the piers on which the bridge stood. "That won't do." He turned to the crew of the bolt thrower. "Gentlemen I want you to stop them damaging my bridge. Take your time but I want the barbarians discouraged."

He watched as they carefully chose their bolt and then aimed the wooden and metal machine. Julius smiled. He could almost smell the tension. They were under the eyes of the legate. Normally it would just be the centurion who would watch them but they had the most senior officer north of Eboracum.

The Votadini obviously thought that they were safe. Six warriors formed a barrier with their shields whilst the other twelve worked with axes to scrape away the mortar. Decius and his bolt thrower crew had watched the bridge every day for the past month of their duty and they knew where the barbarians would be working. Even though their view was masked by the shields they were confident in their aim.

Decius nodded to his crew and then released the bolt. It made the reassuring crack followed by a whoosh as it sped towards its target. It went through the shield of the first warrior and the warrior himself. It did not stop there but plunged through the head of the next Votadini sending a bloody mass of bone, blood and brains over the warriors around. The last two men were pinned together in death. The bodies of the warriors who had been struck hit other warriors, knocking them into the river.

With just one strike twelve of the eighteen men who had been working at the bridge were either dead or incapacitated.

Julius Demetrius patted Decius on the back. "Excellent work soldier!"

Decius was also delighted. They were far closer to their targets than they normally were and even he had been astounded at the effect of their weapon. They reloaded as the Votadini tried to begin their work again.

Julius was confident that the Votadini would not be able to destroy the bridge; it was too well made. He wanted their attention on the gate and not on the open ground to the south. Julius could have sent the ala out by the lesser east gate but he wanted complete surprise. As the second bolt thundered towards the Votadini the Legate knew that they had succeeded for the barbarians all looked towards the fort and began to realign their warriors.

He walked over to the crew of the small onager which had just been moved into position between the two bolt throwers. "Now you see what your comrades have done?" The crew nodded. "Let us see if you can do as well. I want you to burn that tower."

They looked at the wooden tower which was less than a hundred and forty paces away. "It's a bit close for us sir."

"I know lads, just take your time but when it gets dark about two hundred of our hairy arsed friends will suddenly erupt from there and come across here to do fairly wicked things to us. I think it would be better if we stopped them before they got here eh?" Julius was used to talking to such men and his words had the right effect.

The optio grinned, "Will do, sir. Gaius, go and get the incendiary ammunition. You two bring that brazier over here but be careful. We don't want to burn the Legate, do we?"

"I'll get out of your way, optio."

Julius felt some sympathy for the crew. They were there to attack an enemy who was further away. They had not envisaged having to attack their own defences. The crew had had to swing the machine around as it normally defended the area to the north. All the time the crew were preparing their machine Julius could hear the regular crack of the bolt thrower. He glanced to the south. There was still no sign of the ala. He knew that Livius would want everything in place before he attacked.

171

"Ready sir."

"Very well, optio."

The optio released the machine which made a softer crack than the bolt thrower. The flaming ball flew high and over the tower to strike the bridge beyond. One poor warrior was struck by the missile and he and the ball of flame fell hissing into the Tinea. His companions immediately took shelter behind the tower. It was a mistake. The next missile was short and burned on the stones of the walkway but that seemed to please the optio. He made a slight adjustment to the mechanism and then rubbed his hands. "Right sir, the third time should do the trick."

This time the flaming missile hit the wooden tower halfway up and the wooden structure burst into flames. They loosed their missiles far quicker now that they had the range. Julius turned to the second bolt thrower crew. "Right boys. See what you can hit eh?"

The crew were eager to join their companions and they sent bolt after bolt into the fiery tower. Soon the onager crew had stopped wasting missiles for the tower was almost destroyed. The Votadini who had been within were either dead or hurling themselves from the bridge to the waters. Even King Ardal was forced to escape that way. The effect was to make every Votadini warrior stare in horror at the burning pyre.

When the buccina sounded, heralding the charge of the ala, there were no warriors facing south. Livius himself led the first turma along with Metellus. They galloped the hundred or so paces to the Votadini and hurled their javelins. Smartly wheeling to the west, they cleared the space for the second turma. By the time the fifth turma had thrown their missiles the Votadini were flooding north away from the disaster of the bridge. Soon the only Votadini who remained within sight of the wall was Banquo who could not believe the disaster which had unfolded almost before his eyes. He was the last warrior to leave the wall as the Votadini part of the rebellion ended in failure. He trudged off alone wondering where it had all gone wrong. The rest of the Votadini either floated down the river or lay in untidy and bloody heaps on the banks of the Tinea.

Once the bloodletting in Morbium had finished Briac gathered his leaders around him. They needed to plan their next moves. He looked around, irritably, for Severus. He was nowhere to be seen. Severus and his Romans had not participated. They were in this for the money. Whilst Briac and his men had butchered and dismembered the garrison, he and his men had found the Praetorium and removed the chest containing the auxiliaries' money and the next month's pay. It was a hefty chest. Severus, as leader, took the lion's share but all gained more money than they had been paid during their whole service to Rome. Between them they had decided to stay with the rebellion so long as there was money to be made but at the first sign of defeat then they would head for the boat they had bought. Even now it was lying moored off the coast. Their three crippled comrades were there to guard it. Severus kept their share for them.

When they emerged from the office, Briac said, "About time too! We have plans to make!"

Severus shrugged, "You and your warriors seemed happy to be torturing the Batavians. We did not wish to interrupt you and spoil your fun."

"We have finished now. I intend to sweep north and conquer the land up to Coriosopitum." He waved a hand towards the west. "The farm is a distraction. This is our business; destroying Roman garrisons! The Votadini and the Selgovae should have subdued the wall by now. We don't want them claiming too much Brigante land."

Despite all his training with the tribes and the new weapons, Severus doubted that the tribes would have succeeded. They would hurt the garrisons, of that he was certain but the barbarians were not equipped to take Roman forts. But for his trick, the fort at Morbium would still remain in Roman hands.

He nodded, "Then my men and I will guard this crossing for you."

"Surely that is unnecessary."

He laughed, "Now I know why you Brigante have failed in all your rebellions thus far. If you leave this fort then when the VIth come north, and believe me they will, then there will be nothing to stop them reinvesting it and then trapping you and your army between here and the wall!"

It was annoying but the Roman was right. "Very well. We will leave our wounded warriors with you as extra garrison."

Severus doubted that they would be of any use but, if the VIth came and he and his men had to flee then they would slow the pursuit up long enough for them to escape. "Thank you Briac."

Chapter 18

With Marcus at one end of the line of troopers, Rufius in the middle of the line and Decurion Ulpius Marcus Albius at the other the sixty warriors prepared to charge the Selgovae and the Novontae. Out of sight and hidden by a fold in the land were the rest of the Cohors Equitata. This was not the best country for a cavalry charge. It had bumps, rises and hollows all over but it also provided good cover to disguise numbers. Rufius gambled on the fact that the tribes would not be able to differentiate between one group of Romans and another. He hoped they would think it was just his turmae and the Selgovae had already tasted their blood; poor Marius and his dead turmae were testament to that.

The first warriors who had leapt the wall had halted to allow some of their fellows to join them. After having scaled the partly finished Vallum they had moved south for more glory. They had expected more Romans to be waiting for them to kill. Now that there were a hundred of them they felt emboldened enough to head south. As they crested the rise they saw the long line of horseman galloping at them. Some of the warriors were from Tiernan's band and they had already massacred one such troop. The rest were the Novontae who had chased Rufius from the fort. They had the option of standing and receiving the charge or charging themselves. They made a bad choice. They charged the horsemen swinging their newly acquired long swords above their heads and screaming their war cry.

"Javelins at the ready." Rufius did not need to issue orders to his own men. Their spears would be ready to repel any attack.

The barbarians were expecting the horsemen to charge into them and they were already selecting their targets. At thirty paces Rufius yelled, "Wheel! Release!"

The thirty javelins flew into the air. Half of them found targets and before the barbarians could even blink, the Romans had turned and fled. Angus son of Torin took this as a sign that they feared the barbarians. He looked and saw that the sixty or so horsemen had only caused eighteen or so casualties. It had been he who had captured the Roman officer with

175

the fine red horsehair plume. He had that now tucked in his belt. "They are afraid! After them!"

Rufius led the turmae back and he and his troopers took their place with the second turma while Decurion Ulpius Marcus Albius led his troop to the back of the line. Rufius had worked out that his horses could manage another two attacks before they needed a rest. They began to trot towards the enemy. They were more spread out now as the fitter, braver and keener warriors left their fellows behind.

Rufius had chosen the position of danger in the middle so that he could make instant decisions. "Halt! Aim and release!"

This time it was not a shower of javelins. The troopers chose their targets. Individual javelins were aimed at specific warriors. They were much more accurate. Angus deflected the javelin with his shield and then raced towards the line of warriors. Rufius saw him coming. He had his sword drawn already and he trotted forward swinging his sword. The Selgovae swung his weapon at the horse's head. It was how he had captured the other officer. When he killed this one he would have two red plumes.

Rufius wheeled his horse to the right and the sword smashed into his shield. Behind him he heard Marcus yell, "Release!" and a second flight of javelins fell amongst the barbarians.

Rufius suddenly jerked his reins to the right and the horse snapped at the Selgovae. He jerked his head out of the way of the teeth and Rufius slashed down at the exposed neck. The killer of officers died quickly.

"Withdraw!"

Marcus had been well trained and he knew when to issue such an order. Rufius soon caught up with the line of exultant troopers. Thirty-five barbarians now lay dead and the Romans had suffered not a casualty. Rufius glanced over his shoulder. The barbarians had halted. The death of their hero had unnerved them. The auxiliaries had some respite.

Banquo had had words with his brother. They had been in private but Banquo fumed that the Votadini had retreated north after an ignominious defeat.

"We can beat them, brother. We almost did so!"

"It is over. We have lost too many good men. The Venicones will see that we are weak and attack our heartland. The wall is too far to the south to be of concern to us. I can see that your hatred of Ban's daughter Mavourna has made you rash. It will take many days to reach Traprain Law. You will come to see that I am right."

The thought of a shameful return was too much for the young Votadini. "I will stay with my oathsworn and any others who will follow my banner."

The exasperated King now made a fateful decision. He had kept his promise to his mother. To continue to support Banquo might result not only in the loss of many fine warriors but in the crown itself. It was time to cut the young man adrift. "Then do not come back at all. Little brother, you are exiled."

Banquo's anger was quickly tempered by the realisation that he could create his own kingdom. This was freedom for Banquo. He would no longer be hampered by the decisions of others. His brother was correct, Traprain Law was far to the north but he could fortify Mercaut and rule the southern half of the land of the Votadini and then in the future… who knew?

"Then the next time I see you it will be war!"

"I hope not little brother for I would hate to kill you."

It did not take long for the Votadini to realise there was a rift between the brothers. Ardal was disappointed that many of the younger warriors sided with his younger brother. He knew that they still resented leaving the field with their tails between their legs. Banquo, for his part, was delighted. He had six hundred keen and loyal young warriors. They were well armed thanks to the priestess and the Votadini prince was ready to return to the wall. He had breached it once. He would do so again.

The Thracian turma reached Eboracum. Decurion Culpidius reined in outside the Praetorium. They had had to dodge bands of marauding Brigante and the journey had taken much longer than it ought. First Spear called him in directly. "We have seen the fires burning in the distance but we have heard nothing from the north for many days. Tell me the worst."

"The Brigante have revolted. Morbium has fallen and the whole of the Dunum valley is in their hands. When we left Coriosopitum Legate Demetrius told us that the tribes from the north of the wall had begun to attack."

"I thought when we had the treachery in the fort that it was something like this."

The decurion shuddered. They had seen the crucified bodies of the slaves outside the western gate. "Does the Governor know?"

"I sent half of my cavalry south with the message but..." he could see the exhaustion on the decurion's face. "Get some rest, decurion. I am afraid you and your men will be heading north tomorrow with the First Cohort. We will see if a little legionary steel can humble these rebels."

Caronwyn and Lady Flavia were less than happy when they arrived at Morbium and found just Severus and his handful of men. "Where is Briac?"

"He and his men have gone to devastate the land hereabouts. I waited here to protect the crossing."

Lady Flavia smiled, "There is no criticism of you, Severus. And the farm, it is destroyed too?"

He shook his head. He had been dreading this moment. "Briac could not take it." He was swift to shift any blame. "He was wounded in the attack and we lost many men. The auxiliary cavalry came to their aid."

Caronwyn put her arm around Flavia. "That is a minor consideration. The men who killed your brother and my mother are north of here close to the wall. Briac has done the right thing. He is taking the rebellion closer to those we wish to harm. With the Northern tribes attacking the wall we have our enemies between our claws." She turned to Severus. "Destroy the bridge. It will make the fort more secure and we do not need it now."

Severus nodded. "He was glad now that he had sent two of his men to bring their boat from the estuary. If things went awry he wanted an escape. He had more than enough money for a nice little place in Sicily. It was warm and filled with olive and lemon groves. He had had enough of cold Britannia.

The following morning a message came from Briac. He looked nervously at the witch and her priestesses. He did not know that she had arrived. "The message is for Severus, my lady."

"Well, he is here and so tell him. You do not mind if a woman listens, do you?"

He was no fool and he shook his head. "No, my lady. He said to tell Severus that he has captured Vinovia and he is heading north in the morning for Coriosopitum."

Caronwyn flashed a questioning look at Severus. "It is the next fort along the road. There is nothing between it and the wall. He has done well," he added, grudgingly.

"You and your men stay here. That way I know that our rear will be secure."

Lady Flavia gave a petulant look to Caronwyn, "As I pay him surely that decision should be mine?"

Lady Flavia did not recognise the maliciously cold look in Caronwyn's eyes, she saw the smile only, "Of course, my dear. Do you want him to come with us?"

"We have no guards."

Caronwyn waved her hand at the twelve priestesses who followed them everywhere. "These priestesses are all trained warriors. The Mother Cult does not differentiate between male and female warriors. If you wish to see them armed then it can be arranged. Severus, find some auxiliary armour for my women."

Severus nodded and left. He had seen the women training and the old witch was not lying.

"Well if you think we will be safe…"

"I promise you that we will be as safe as in Severus' hands." When they left the next morning, any watching scout would have been confused as the column of auxiliaries headed north up the Via Trajanus. The auxiliaries were all kitted and armed as normal but the long flowing hair hanging down their neck and the lack of facial hair looked unusual.

Caronwyn was pleased. Her plans, thought out over the years since her mother's death were finally coming to fruition. Radha's sacrifice had worked. Roman Britannia was divided in two and they would soon be able to spread the word to the southern half of the province. The Romans were defeated.

"Well Legate, that was damn close." They had watched the Votadini trudge northwards. They were a defeated tribe.

"Don't forget Livius that the Votadini only came into this rebellion because we angered them. They were not a committed tribe. The Selgovae and the Carvetii are."

Just then they heard the sound of the sentry at the southern gate shouting a challenge. By the time they reached the gate there were two exhausted despatch riders. Both were Thracian auxiliaries.

"Sir, we were sent by the Prefect. He said to tell you that Morbium has fallen to the Brigante."

There was a hesitation as he looked at his comrade.

"Well spit it out man! You won't get into trouble for reporting the truth."

"As we left Vinovia sir, well, we barely got out alive. There was a huge warband of Brigante and Carvetii. Two thousand or more sir. I am not sure if Vinovia would have been able to resist the attacks."

Julius' face fell. To lose Morbium was bad enough but to lose Vinovia meant that the thin line of men at the wall were all that stood between the province and disaster. "Livius, send a turma down to Vinovia. Tell them to be careful and report what they see. I want a sound decurion; take nothing for granted."

Decurion Lucius Marcellus Garbo had been with the ala for five years. He had fought in all of the major battles and he was an obvious choice for Livius. He was experienced and dependable. This was just as well for he had the most inexperienced troopers in the ala. That was another reason they had been sent. They had had the least action and had the freshest mounts.

Garbo rode swiftly down the road. He aimed to reach the fort in four hours. His Chosen Man, Julius, was also experienced. He had him riding at the rear. The signifer, Cassius, rode next to the decurion. These three were the ones that the decurion would depend on. Rufius had tried to tell Decurion Garbo that he ought to trust his men more and delegate. They would be better troopers in the end. Decurion Garbo liked and respected Rufius but, as he had told him there were many ways to run a turma and he had chosen his. He had been successful but, as he rode down the well-travelled Roman Road he wondered if he had taken too much upon himself.

He constantly scanned the horizon as he headed south. He could see the tell-tale smoke from burning buildings. He had been told that the fort might have fallen. Certainly, the signs were not good. He suddenly raised his hand. Cassius reined in straight away but the two young troopers were a little slow and their horses ran into the rear of the decurion's. "That is a week of shit shovelling for you pair!" He pumped his arm and his Chosen Man appeared. "Take charge here. I am going with Cassius to investigate those birds ahead." He had seen a flock of carrion birds swooping, climbing and fighting. It might be an animal but, equally, it might be something else.

They left the road and entered the tumble of trees to the east. It allowed them to see the road but not be seen. The presence of the birds suggested that man was not present but he would take no chances. Garbo saw the birds through the trees as they squabbled over the corpses of the Thracian turma who had been killed there. He could see no sign of barbarians and he led Julius through the undergrowth to the road. He saw the head of the Prefect on the top of a spear. He had seen him once before and his broken nose was distinctive. It appeared to be the only part of his head that was not bloody.

"Well signifer, we know what happened to the Thracians now. What we need to find out is what has happened to Vinovia. Bring up the turma. I'll get rid of this. It'll upset the lads."

As Cassius rode off he took the spear and walked to the Prefect's body. He pulled the gory trophy from the spear and laid it next to the dismembered corpse. "Go to the Allfather, Prefect. You died a warrior's death."

When the troopers rode up he heard the retching as one young trooper took in the scene. He would need to be on the frontier a little longer then he would become used to such sights.

"Follow me and keep your eyes open."

A small voice from somewhere behind asked, "Aren't we going to bury them, sir?"

He turned in his saddle trying to discover the owner of the voice. "Son, when you die we will remember you but you will have to be a lucky trooper if we actually bury you. So don't die!"

The decurion knew what he would find. He led them from the road so that they could approach the fort from the east. He did not want to be highlighted in the setting sun. It was still an hour or so before dark but he was cautious. He also reasoned that if the fort had fallen then they would be looking to the road for the Romans. He knew that the river ran along one side of the fort and the bridge there controlled the passage of the Vedra Fluvia. He took the troop to the woods some five hundred paces from the northern wall. He could see the fort and the road.

When he stopped his heart sank. The fort had fallen. The line of heads atop spears told him that in an instant. He turned to Chosen Man. "Ride back to the Legate and tell him that the Thracian Prefect is dead and Vinovia has fallen."

The Chosen Man hesitated, "We could all go back sir. We can't do much here."

"I know, but we can watch and we can follow. Unless I miss my guess, we are in a world of trouble. We have lost forts north of the wall before now but never south."

The rider from the south reached the fort at the same time as the wounded from the west. To Legate Julius Demetrius it was though all their disasters had arrived at once. To have lost so many troopers was a worry. To have his best leaders trapped and trying to fight an army was even worse.

He now had a dilemma. There were two enemy armies. The one to the south he knew was capable of capturing Roman forts but the one to the north potentially had more warriors. For the first time he did not know what to do. He sent for Livius. He liked talking problems through.

After he heard the problem Livius said, "The way I see it sir is that it is too late to do anything tonight. By the time our cavalry reach either Vinovia or Luguvalium, it will be the middle of the night and the men will be tired. I think that we can leave just before dawn. We will be there in the morning."

The Legate smiled, "That doesn't help me Livius. Where do we send your ala?"

"I thought that was obvious sir, to the west. Decurion Garbo is the steadiest of leaders. He will shadow the warband and keep us informed of their movements. We should send his trooper back and tell the decurion he has to watch the barbarians."

"You are right, that makes sense but this Brigante army can gather more men at will. All those who are unhappy with our rule will join them. This is not the Dunum where the Brigante support us. This is the land of the Vedra Fluvia and the Tinea; here we are hated." He stood, "But you are right. Have the ala ready to ride before dawn."

Far to the north, the sun was also setting. Rufius and the Cohors Equitata had watched the warriors as they had held a meeting of some kind. Rufius had deduced that they were debating what to do next. So long as the horse warriors guarded the Stanegate they were helpless.

"I think, Decurion, that they will try something at night. Let's get the men out to create some trips and traps. It won't stop them but it will prevent us having our throats slit."

The Batavian was happy for it gave his men something to do.

Rufius sought out Marcus. "I want you and Gnaeus to play at being Explorate tonight. Position yourselves out there in between us and the barbarians. Watch out when you return for we are laying some trips." Marcus nodded. It was what he would have done. "Be back before dawn."

"Sir."

"And Marcus, be careful. That sword does not grant you immortality."

Marcus waved Gnaeus over. "We are scouts tonight. I saw a hollow over there." Marcus pointed to the west. "We can move closer to the Selgovae along the dead ground and remain hidden. If we approach from the east we will be in the dark."

Roman Wall

Gnaeus looked to the north, "Remember what happened to the
Decurion Marius sir. One of these barbarians might well fancy another
horsehair plume."

"Then you will have to be my mother for the night and make sure he
does not get it."

The banter was just to ease their nerves. What they were about to do
was risky but they were the best that Rufius had and Marcus took it as a
compliment that they had been selected.

It helped that they were approaching from the dark that was the east.
Even so, they dismounted as they turned to head west and the hollow
which would take them close to their enemy. They both had well trained
horses that picked their way silently across the turf. They were like
shadows as the edged closer to the barbarians.

Once they reached the hollow they tied the horses to a gorse bush and
left the animals to graze. Taking off their helmets they put them next to
their spears and shields. They would only get in the way. Drawing their
swords, they slithered up the side of the grassy hollow. Their ears were
attuned to the sounds of the evening. They could hear voices to their
front but they saw nothing. The mound running along the partly built
vallum gave them an indication of their location. They moved slowly and
silently across the undulating ground. The soft turf deadened any sound
they might have made. After a small dip, it began to rise and the two
Romans could now make out the voices. They moved so slowly as to be
almost stationery. When they crested the rise, they saw that they were
just thirty paces from the barbarian camp.

There was a sentry at the edge of the camp and Marcus could make
out the glow of a fire hidden behind the bodies of the warriors. The mood
appeared to be quite bullish. At first, he could only pick out one or two
words; it was some time since he had heard their language but he heard,
'*Victory*' and '*Roman Slaughter*'. The two of them settled down to watch
and to listen.

Numbers were hard to estimate but as the barbarians moved around
Marcus saw that the camps were spread all along the edge of the Vallum.
He knew that Rufius had been right to attack them. Had they not done so
then this camp would now be many more miles inside Roman territory.

Marcus suspected that they could return to their own camp without hearing more. The warriors looked to have settled down and they would gain little more information but Marcus would stay. He could suffer a night without sleep if it brought victory one day closer.

The talk went on for some time and Marcus wondered if they would ever sleep. A sudden shout in the camp yielded silence. A single voice spoke. This time Marcus found that he could understand more words for the warrior was speaking slowly so that all of the tribes could understand him.

"Warriors, we have victory within our grasp. All that stands between us and the rich land to the south is the handful of horse warriors. They are not to be feared. When we attack, on the morrow, follow your leaders. I have told them how we can defeat these Romans and then we drive on to meet our Brigante and Carvetii brothers. They, too, have defeated the Romans in the south! The priestess was right! The Mother is with us!"

The camp erupted in a huge cheer. Marcus knew that the sentries at his own camp would be worried when they heard the shout in case it preceded an attack. He wondered what plans the leader had put in place. He also wondered if the words about the Brigante were true. He worried about his family but he could do nothing about it.

They waited in the dark listening to the sounds of the camp diminish. Within a short space of time, all that they could hear was the snores of sleeping men and the stamp of the sentries' feet as they struggled to keep warm. Marcus was about to lead Gnaeus away when they heard steps approaching. Marcus pulled Gnaeus down the slope. A pair of shadows appeared above them. A quick glance showed Marcus that the two sentries were going to relieve themselves. Although they were not looking down yet, when they did so they could not help but see the two Romans.

Marcus tapped Gnaeus on the arm. He rose and plunged the sword of Cartimandua into the chest of one warrior. Gnaeus slashed his sword across the other sentry's throat. Even while the two warriors were dying, the Romans turned and ran towards their horses, hidden in the dark. They were unfortunate in that the spears the men were holding clattered against a rock as they fell and shouts of alarm erupted from the camp. It would not take them long to find the bodies.

They donned their helmets, grabbed their spears and shields and mounted their horses. They could hear the barbarians behind them as they sought their sentries. The hollow hid them but as soon as they crested the rise a precocious moon peered out and illuminated their silhouettes. The roar told them that they had been seen.

"Well, that has torn it. We had better go steady Gnaeus. There are traps ahead." Marcus dismounted. He glanced over his shoulder and the warriors were hurtling after them.

Marcus was peering into the undergrowth to look for the tell-tale signs of a trap when he heard a low whistle. He whistled back. "Over here, sir, to your left." Titus' voice was like music to the decurion's ears.

The barbarians had disappeared into the hollow but they could only be a few paces away. He saw Titus' relieved face. The signifer had his javelin ready. He said, "Down sir!" Marcus and Gnaeus both ducked as the javelin flew from Titus' hand and thudded into the chest of the Selgovae warrior.

The three troopers quickly disappeared behind the bushes and waited. They did not have to wait long. The four young barbarians threw themselves into the undergrowth to get to grips with the Roman spies. The first one set off the spring trap and the wooden stake tore into his middle. A second one tripped over the piece of rope and he was propelled into the wooden spike sticking out from the tree. The other two stopped. Behind them were another handful of warriors. One of them shouted, "Tiernan says you are to return to camp and stop chasing shadows."

Seagh and Darius are both dead!"

"If you do not return now then you will join them."

The last of the pursuers turned and reluctantly followed the other warriors back to their camp. As Marcus followed Titus through the maze of traps he thought about this Tiernan. He was not the reckless barbarian they were used to. He had some sort of control over his men. They would have to take them seriously when they attacked for there was a plan behind this attack.

Rufius had asked to be woken when Marcus returned. He was waiting for them at the fire. They told him what they had heard. "It sounds to me like they are going to try some sort of trick tomorrow. You have done well. Get some rest. Tomorrow may be even more testing."

Chapter 19

Felix had also had problems reaching the fort at Cilurnum. There were small bands of Votadini who had managed to scale the wall and they were looting the Roman settlements south of the wall. It was late in the afternoon when he reached the bridge. He had waited in the woods south of the river when he had heard the hooves leaving the fort and he had only emerged when he saw it was a trooper from the ala riding south. He was cautious. The guards were, naturally, equally wary and the optio on duty sent for Livius.

"He is our scout, let him in."

Livius feared the worst. "Report, Felix."

"Sir, the decurion sent me because the Novontae have crossed the wall. He has taken command of eight turmae from the Cohors Equitata."

"Good work Felix. Does the Prefect at Vercovicium know of the danger?"

"Yes sir, I told him."

"Then get some rest for tomorrow we will go to the aid of Rufius and Marcus."

It was a damp and dismal dawn. The clouds had been scudding across the skies since the moon had set and the spring rain drove from the north. It was as sharp as needles. The horse warriors had been standing to since before dawn. They were already all soaked to the skin. Rufius was taking no chances, however, better to be damp than to be dead. He and Marcus sat with Decurion Albius. "We need to be flexible today. We have no idea what is happening on the rest of the wall and we just need to slow down the warband. I am sure that the Legate will have plans in place. We must buy him time." Rufius was not as confident as he sounded. He knew how few men they had. At best the Legate would be able to send a couple of turmae. The rest would be needed, now, to protect the fort at Cilurnum.

Tiernan had more men under his command than he had ever had. His brother besieged the fort at Luguvalium. They did not want the auxiliaries there to come to the aid of the horse warriors. The two brothers had decided that the horse warriors were the biggest threat. If that could be eliminated then they could run amok in the land to the south of the wall. Tiernan was using his large numbers to gain the advantage. He had watched in horror, the previous day, as his men had attacked piecemeal and been picked off easily. The advantage he had was that he could attack from three sides. He divided his army into four warbands of five hundred men. The front two ranks were armed with a spear and a shield. The warriors in the third rank had a shield too.

Three of his warbands began to move south. Each one had a leader who stood in the third rank. The Roman Severus had told them of this tactic. It went against the grain for the barbarians to march in straight lines but Tiernan had a powerful personality and a fiery temper. It would take a brave man to question him.

Rufius frowned when he saw their advance. This was not the barbarian horde he was used to. Decurion Albius asked, "Do we attack as we did yesterday?"

"No, for that would do no good; they have shields."

"Suppose we threw them beyond the front three ranks. It would disrupt those at the back."

"It is not worth the risk Marcus. The troopers throwing the javelins would have to be close to the barbarians, we would risk losing them."

"Then what do we do?"

"We fall back slowly."

They still had time to perform the manoeuvre for the warbands were still three hundred paces from them. Rufius frowned. The two warbands at the edge of the formation were moving ahead of the centre band and looked to be angling their line of attack.

"I think they are trying to flank us. It is time to move back." He turned to Titus. "Order about face."

As the buccina sounded, each turma began to turn to the right. Bizarrely the carnyx also sounded at the same time and the warbands began to move at double speed. They were not running but they were moving swiftly. The two wings began to envelop the ends of the Roman cavalry. The about face meant that the barbarians were moving quicker than the Romans. The carnyx sounded two calls and fifty warriors erupted from each of the warbands. They wore neither helmet nor armour. Half of them carried javelins, taken from the dead horsemen and the other half had slings. The rear rank of the Batavian Cohors Equitata was struck by slingshots and javelins. Horses and men went down. Every trooper was struck. Some of them only suffered a stone to the arm but others were thrown from their saddles by either the lead ball or a javelin. The warbands, miraculously, kept their pace. They did not make the classic barbarian error of charging.

Rufius had seen the attack. "Signal trot!"

The remaining turmae began to move away quicker now but, even so, the rear turmae had to endure the rain of death. By the time Rufius had managed to extricate them from the missiles twenty-five troopers had been lost. They could hear the screams as the wounded troopers were emasculated by the warriors at the rear of the warband.

Decurion Albinus was shaken. He said, quietly, to Rufius. "My men will not take much more of this. Yesterday was a good one for them but they have lost too many friends today."

Rufius was uncertain what to do. How did you counter such an attack? They were outnumbered and had few options.

"Sir, do you mind a suggestion?"

"Anything would be welcome, Marcus."

"We still have one advantage sir, we just used it. We have more speed than they do. If we split into two groups we can ride east and west along the Stanegate."

Rufius was confused. "That will get us nowhere."

Decurion Albius said, urgently, "This debate brings the barbarians ever closer!"

"They will think we are running away and that they have won. Half a mile down the road, we turn and charge their flanks. Their shields are with their front ranks. We use the Batavians' javelins and whittle them down again. I bet their best men are at the front!"

The warbands were less than a hundred paces away and Rufius made his decision. "Marcus, take your turma and half of the Batavians. Go east. We will take the rest and go west."

The decision made, they acted swiftly. Marcus yelled, "First three turmae follow me. Gallop!"

As they headed east they heard the jeers mixed with cheers from the barbarians and when Rufius did the same it became a chorus of victory. They rode hard to give the illusion that they were defeated. Marcus halted them at the mile marker. "Rest!" He turned to view the barbarians. His opinion of the leader was confirmed for the warbands did not disintegrate into a mob but continued their steady progress.

"About face." He rode to the front of the turmae. "We are going to charge the barbarians." He pointed to the decurion of the first Batavian turma. "I want you to charge and release your javelins at thirty paces. Wheel and go to the rear." He pointed to the next two. Then you will do the same. Finally, I will charge with my turma and we will use our spears. If I think we are winning. We will repeat the manoeuvre but if I sound recall then turn around and head back to this place." He saw the nods from the troopers. They were keen to avenge their dead friends.

Marcus was not happy about being in the rear. He preferred to be the first to charge but he knew that he and his turma would have a harder task and risked the highest casualties. The warband was still heading south and were crossing the Stanegate when Marcus heard the buccina. Rufius was attacking. He was earlier than Marcus. It meant that the war band's attention was to the west and not the east. He decided not to sound his buccina. He would rely on the Batavians doing their job.

One of the Selgovae had their wits about them and he shouted to his chief. The carnyx sounded and the warband turned to face the new threat. As Marcus had predicted there were only a handful of shields amongst the Selgovae who faced them. The first Batavian turma made a bloody mess of the front rank. Even as they tried to bring shields to face the new threat the second turma added their weight of javelins. By the time the last turma had thrown their missiles there was confusion and disorder in the once rigid ranks.

"Sound the charge!"

Marcus' turma charged the Selgovae. Without a spear Marcus and Gnaeus were forced to lean forward and use their swords. They were both masters of the weapons and the Selgovae were terrified of the snarling, rearing horses. Marcus' Horse punched a hole into the war band's line. They had done enough. "Fall back!"

The troop each performed the same action; they punched forward with their spear as they jerked the rein to the right. Marcus and his Chosen Man had no spear and were forced to watch. A warrior with an axe suddenly launched himself at Gnaeus. He came from the shield side and Gnaeus desperately tried to turn his horse. Suddenly the young trooper, Gaius, wheeled his horse around and speared the barbarian in the shoulder. The huge warrior roared a scream and grabbed the spear in his hands. He pulled. Gaius failed to release the spear and he was pulled from his horse. The warriors around him began to hack and chop at the helpless young warrior. As Gnaeus and Marcus extricated themselves young Gaius joined his friend Lentius in the Otherworld. He had made up for his mistake.

As they reformed at the rear of the Batavians Marcus saw that Gaius was not the only casualty. There were empty saddles. The first turma rode in again and caused devastation in the Selgovae still reeling from the previous attacks. The second turma had just charged in when Marcus heard the strident notes of the carnyx. He wondered what it meant for it came from the rear of the warband.

"One last charge and we withdraw." He saw that Titus had been wounded. As the signifer, he only had a shield and a standard. "Are you able to signal?"

He grinned and Marcus saw that he had lost a couple of teeth too. He spat blood from his mouth. "Don't worry about me, sir."

As the third turma withdrew Marcus shouted, "The Sword of Cartimandua!"

The battle cry was taken up by the rest of the turma and they urged their horses on. The disorganisation of the band and the deaths of so many had taken their toll. When the battle cry was sounded some of those at the rear began to edge back. Those at the front felt the movement and they too moved back. The result was that they were further away from the turma and that increased the speed at which they charged. When they struck there was an audible crack as spear met bone. The screams of the dying filled the air. Raven's hooves were deadly weapons and warriors were trampled beneath them. The sword carved a path of death and a wedge drove deep into the Selgovae lines. The Selgovae were breaking and Marcus began to wonder if they could defeat them with this charge.

"Shit! Sir, better fall back."

Marcus looked to where Titus was pointing. The carnyx had been a signal for the uncommitted war band which was now racing to envelop them.

"Fall back!"

The fact that the Selgovae before them were falling back allowed them to withdraw and turn their horses. The Batavians had seen the danger and taken it upon themselves to charge the advancing Selgovae and release their last javelins. It cost them a couple of troopers and barely slowed the Selgovae down. The Batavians were now reliant upon their swords.

The end of the warband now spilled over the Stanegate. Marcus wheeled Raven and shouted, "Head south."

As he looked to the west he saw that the warbands which had been there were now racing to surround him and his men. He had no idea what had happened to Rufius but Marcus appeared to have the whole of the Selgovae army trying to surround them.

The Batavian charge had allowed the Selgovae to gain ground. Ahead of him Marcus could see that there was a gap of just three hundred paces. It was closing. "Marcus' Horse, charge the warriors at the south-eastern edge of their line!" If Marcus and his men could strike the Selgovae before they had completed their circle then some of the Batavians might escape. The trouble was that the horses were tired and the warband enveloping them had yet to fight.

He looked down the line and saw that he only had twenty-three troopers left. He hoped it would be enough. Raven was stronger than the other horses and Marcus found himself at the fore once more. The

Selgovae, fifty paces ahead, could see what he was doing and ten of them formed a hurried shield wall.

"Raven let us show these Selgovae what you can do."

The warriors had not seen cavalry in action very often and knew not what they would do. They had braced themselves for the impact of the horse. Instead, Marcus sailed over the warriors. Raven's hoof cracked open the skull of one warrior while the decurion sliced down to slice into the neck of a second one. There was now a gap. Gnaeus and Titus smashed through and two more warriors died. The last of the ten were speared and trampled as the turma made a gap for the auxiliaries. Marcus reined in Raven and wheeled to see if the Batavians made the gap.

The sound of a buccina along the Stanegate brought hope to Marcus. It was the ala! Felix had got through.

"Titus, sound recall!"

Felix had brought them news of the crisis long before Metellus had heard the sounds of battle. It was infuriating for the Decurion Princeps. Those were his friends and his men being killed and yet they dare not ride too quickly for they would need their horses to have enough energy to charge. As they crested the rise they saw that the Selgovae were trying to surround the tiny beleaguered group of horsemen. The warband was huge.

"Sound form line!"

The open ground in this part of the country meant that they could do so without too much danger. There were eight turmae. Two hundred and forty men were ready to charge and each one held his spear ready. Metellus wanted the impact of the two hundred and forty men and horses to drive deep into the Selgovae line. He wanted to break it by sheer weight. He glanced to his left and saw someone jumping over the Selgovae line. That would be Marcus!

"Sod it! Sound the charge!"

The horses all leapt forward eagerly at the familiar call. Felix and Wolf stopped to watch the ala go into action. Felix's keen eyes had spotted Marcus and he and his dog hurried south to see if they could aid the decurion.

When Tiernan heard the buccina and saw the horse warriors charging he knew that his well-planned attack would fail. He remembered the words of the Roman, Severus. He had to save as many of his men as he could. The carnyx sounded again and his men began to fall back. It was at that point which things went disastrously wrong for the Selgovae prince. His men had managed to obey all of their orders when going forward but now that they were falling back and aware of the thundering horses behind them then their basic instinct took over and they began to run. Nothing their chiefs and leaders did could halt them.

"We have them! Push them all the way back to the wall!"

The troopers needed no urging. It was target practice and their spears came into their own that day. They began to kill and maim with a deadly rhythm. Punch, twist, and withdraw. Punch, twist, and withdraw. The barbarians had little or no armour and they fell like wheat being harvested. One or two Selgovae dropped to the ground to avoid the spears but they were trampled by the horses. Ironically it was the Roman defences which stopped the complete annihilation of the barbarian army. The Vallum was intended to stop everyone from crossing and the horses had to slow to negotiate the steep banks and then the ditch. The Selgovae found energy from the fear of the Romans and, as the ala wearily climbed the last ditch and headed for the wall they saw the barbarians scaling it and running north and safety.

The ala did not need to rein in. Their horses could go no further. "Chosen Man, ascend the wall and see where they have gone."

Metellus took off his helmet and rubbed his shaved head. They had thwarted one attack but what of the forces to the east?

Chapter 20

By the time Caronwyn reached Vinovia, the Brigante had finally satiated their blood lust. Caronwyn was annoyed. She did not mind Romans suffering but Briac and his men should have gone north to keep their sword in the backs of the Romans. The whole plan had been devised so that they outnumbered the Romans.

"This is not well done Briac! You have let me down!"

Briac quaked before the verbal onslaught. Elidr was annoyed by it. Caronwyn might be a priestess but she was still a woman. "We are warriors do not try to tell us what to do!"

When Caronwyn turned on him Elidr felt as though she had been transformed into a wolf so fierce was her look. "I tell you what to do because we have financed this rebellion and we have planned it. If it was not for my priests and the Lady Flavia you would still be ambushing despatch riders and talking of the good old days. Do not anger me, Elidr, or you will regret it!"

Elidr dropped to his knees for he had suddenly seen her guards. He had taken them to be men but now he saw that they were women and the fierce looks on their faces told him in no uncertain terms what they would do to him if he continued to question their leader.

"Get to your feet and get this rabble moving. I wish to attack Coriosopitum tomorrow!"

Briac turned to Pedair, his nephew. "You heard the lady get the men prepared to march!" Briac, too, was annoyed. He had wanted to gloat in the glory of taking the fort without the aid of Severus and his men. He had used cunning. His men had hidden outside the walls, and when the gates had opened to admit the Thracians his oathsworn had swarmed through and held the gate until the whole warband was through. It had been a glorious combat but now he would not have the joy of telling the tale and receiving the plaudits.

Decurion Garbo had seen the arrival of the priestess. He had been confused by the Roman horsemen until he realised that they were women. Even Garbo was surprised by the effect they had. Within half an hour the Brigante army began to decamp.

"Mount up lads. I reckon they are moving north."

He led his troop so that they could see if they returned south over the bridge or headed north. As soon as he saw them take the Via Trajanus north he wheeled his horse around. "Trooper Marius, ride and tell the Legate that the Brigantes are moving north and they look to be ready for war again."

Metellus rode through the sea of littered bodies that had been the Selgovae. Marcus had dismounted and he and Gnaeus were standing over the butchered body of a young warrior. It was Gaius who had atoned for his earlier error of judgment. He had paid a high price. "You have done well Marcus."

He shook his head, "This young warrior gave his life for Chosen Man. He has done well. We, well, we just survived."

"Do not disparage yourself. I watched as you charged many time your number. That was true courage."

Marcus shrugged and changed the subject. He disliked being the centre of attention. "How goes the war?"

"Not so well. They have captured Morbium and Vinovia." Metellus saw the look of horror which briefly flickered across his decurion's face. "So far we have not heard that either of our families has suffered."

Marcus nodded with a neutral expression. Inside his head his mind was in turmoil but he was a decurion and would play the part. "It is not finished here."

Just then they saw Rufius and the remnants of the Batavians as they trudged eastwards towards them. "I am relieved that Rufius lives still."

"How, I do not know for he has been in the most dangerous of places since we came west."

It was obvious to Marcus that Rufius and Decurion Albius had suffered as much as they had. Their ranks were thinned. Rufius clasped Marcus' arm. "That was bravely done my young friend. I know we sounded the buccina early but..."

"It worked out in the end."

The Decurion Princeps looked around the battlefield. "This has barely started." He pointed west, "Decurion you had best return to Luguvalium. Your men need rest and when the Selgovae and Novontae have licked their wounds they will come back for more mischief."

"What if the Selgovae still surround it?"

"Your presence will worry them and give heart to your comrades inside. The VIth will be here soon I expect. It is always darkest before the dawn. Have hope. You have done well here."

He nodded and then clasped first Marcus and then Rufius' arm. "Thank you. I have learned much. Perhaps we may not achieve the glory of Marcus' Horse but we shall try." He raised his sword. "Batavians!"

The three turmae who had ridden with Marcus all raised their swords and shouted, "Sword of Cartimandua." Then they sheathed their weapons and the survivors headed west and safety.

When they had gone Rufius asked. "Now what?"

"In a perfect world we would stay here and ensure that the Selgovae and Novantae did not return but we live in the real world and there is a Brigante army at Vinovia. We return to Cilurnum."

As they headed east Marcus asked, idly, "What of the VIth?"

Metellus shrugged. "The last message we had was that the officers had been poisoned and First Spear was in command."

Rufius laughed, "Then that is good news for Quintus Licinius Brocchus is the best man for such a situation."

Marcus' mind was not on the VIth. He was thinking about the men in his turma who would not be at the muster in the morning. They had all died well but they had all died and that saddened the decurion.

It was well past night when they reached their fortress home. To Marcus, it felt like months since he had slept. Before he did so he made an offering to the gods for his fallen friends; it did not do to forget those who had died.

First Spear Quintus Broccus left Eboracum with an equally heavy heart. He had the best men in the legion; the five double strength centuries he took with him could handle anything the Brigante could throw at them but he did not like leaving the northern capital with just a centurion in command. He had tired of waiting for the governor to send replacement officers. The lack of news from the north was disconcerting. He was also unhappy about the auxiliaries he had with him. There was just one Thracian turma and a century of Tungrians. He would have preferred more mobile men to protect his flanks but Quintus Broccus was a soldier. There were no others available. He would adapt.

"Right then, Centurion let's get this lot moving. We have a rebellion to put down!"

The tramp of the caligae on the Via Trajanus was a comforting sound to Broccus. It was the sound of Rome and it was heading north to put the world back to the way it was meant to be. He put aside the thought of the knife in the night which had so nearly ended his life. The gods kept him alive and he would do what he did well; he would be a soldier. Had he known that Caronwyn and the Brigante were some way ahead of him he might have risked having the men move at double speed. Instead, they marched at their normal pace.

Caronwyn's presence added urgency to the Brigante and Carvetii army. They had purpose and their leaders urged them northwards along the well maintained Roman Road. The priestess and Lady Flavia rode at the head of the column flanked by the fierce warrior priestesses. Briac and the other leaders were reduced to following the horses and the women.

The captured horses of the Thracians were used by Briac's scouts. They had reported the turma of cavalry which shadowed the army. As much as Briac would have liked to drive them off he knew that his own horsemen were not as good as the Roman horsemen. They had defeated the Thracians by trapping and tricking them. He knew that would not work now. This troop of cavalry was too wary. They had already seen the evidence from the bodies of the four scouts who had come too close to the Roman horsemen and paid the price.

Elidr still brooded about the priestess' treatment of his cousin. "Women should be at home looking after children."

Briac shook his head, "Quiet cousin. Do you want the women to hear? These are not as ordinary women. Look at these who ride before us.

When did you ever see an armed woman? And these women look like they can fight. Caronwyn has made wise decisions up until now. My concern is that Severus is not here. He understood how to fight his former comrades. I am not certain how we will take Coriosopitum."

"We take it as we did Vinovia."

"We surprised them at Vinovia. Here they know that we are coming. Those Roman horse warriors will have told them. We have been lucky once when taking a fort and we had Severus and his cunning for the other. This is a different prospect for this fort is bigger and they will be prepared."

The Legate did not share Briac's optimism. The garrison at Coriosopitum was not at full strength. They had used some of the cohort to bolster the garrison on the wall to the east. It was as large as Cilurnum but there was a large vicus outside. Those people relied on the fort for defence and he could not abandon civilians to the rabble approaching from the south. That could be a problem too; supplies were not as plentiful as they should have been. Hunger was a distinct possibility.

"Livius I am going to have to use your ala once more. I want you to escort me and a century taken from the garrison here. I will take command at Corio."

Livius looked up from the map he was studying. "Sir, that is dangerous. What if the Votadini return? We barely held them last time and who will command in your absence?"

"I think the Votadini have been cowed, for a while at least. Had this Brigante army arrived a couple of days earlier then I fear we would have lost all but we have had a reprieve. You will command in my absence. Your ala is mobile and you can threaten the Brigante. Rufius and Marcus showed at Banna how to use cavalry. You will prevent the Brigante from having a free rein. Coriosopitum is a well-built fort and it is, unlike here, finished. They have stocks of food and ammunition for just such an eventuality. Not as much as we would like but enough for the civilians from the vicus and the garrison for a few days at least. More importantly, it is on the Tinea. With luck, the Navarchus can send a boat from Arbeia. I would know what is going on in the outside world."

Livius could not argue with the Legate for his assessment was accurate. They headed down the road to Coriosopitum. It was a mere seven miles and they soon reached the former frontier. The Brigante who lived in the vicus had already been told to either seek sanctuary in the fort or move further up the Tinea Valley. Most had sought sanctuary within the fort.

Leaving Metellus in charge of the ala Livius accompanied Julius into the fort to receive his last orders. "Sir, we have prepared the defences as best we can and your eighty men are welcome but when will the VIth arrive?"

"I am sorry, Prefect. I have no answer to that question however I intend to find out. Are there still boats close by?"

"Yes sir there are a couple of river fishermen. They have sought sanctuary in here."

Julius was relieved. "Good, send them to me. Livius I want one of your troopers. Someone reliable. I need them to go with the fisherman to Arbeia." He saw the doubt on Livius' face. He was loath to lose a trooper on an errand such as this. "It could be one of your wounded troopers." There were twenty or so troopers that they had brought who had been wounded in the recent actions. These were the ones deemed fit to ride but some would find it difficult to fight.

Livius went to the main gate. "Decurion Princeps, I need one of the wounded troopers. He is to be detached."

It was Rufius' Chosen Man who was given the duty. Gaius was dependable and Metellus chose him for his brain. His left arm was still in a sling and he would not be able to defend himself in a battle.

When they reached the Legate the fisherman and his son were there. "I want you to take this officer down to Arbeia. There is a Navarchus in command of the fleet. I need aid from the Classis Britannica and I need news of the rest of the province. Is that clear Chosen Man?"

"Yes sir." Relieved that he would soon be able to return, Gaius and the two Brigante descended into the frail looking fishing boat and headed down stream.

As Livius left the fort the slamming doors seemed ominous.

Decurion Garbo was also a relieved man when he and his men encountered the rest of the ala just south of Coriosopitum. "Sir, I am glad to see you."

"And you, Lucius. You have done well." The decurion nodded. "Now, your report, please."

He pointed south down the road. "The rebels are heading north. They have a few horsemen; nothing to worry about. We estimate the army to be in excess of two and half thousand." He shrugged apologetically. "You know how hard it is to count them. The buggers never march properly. The army is led by a couple of women and they have a turma of women warriors. It looks like they have looted some of our armour."

Livius was worried by that. He had encountered the priestesses of Manavia before and they were dangerous. If they were involved, however, it explained much. "Ride back to Coriosopitum and report to the Legate and then rejoin us here. Oh, and suggest, tactfully, to the governor that he might think about defending the southern end of the bridge over the Tinea."

"Yes sir!"

After he had gone Livius explained to his officers, "I know that they can ford the river but if the Legate could slow them down a little there it might help."

"So, sir, what is the plan?"

"We keep the ala between the Brigante and Coriosopitum."

"That might not be so easy, sir. From what I saw and Rufius reported the barbarians look to have adopted some of our ideas."

"I know. I spoke with Rufius and Marcus but they also had some interesting ideas too. A mixture of javelins and spears could well work. We will try Marcus' idea of three turmae attacking with javelins to soften them up and then a fourth to attack with their spears. We will divide the ala into three. Rufius, you lead one vexillation, Marcus a second and I will take the third. Garbo can join mine when he returns. You watch the east, Rufius the west and I will stay in the centre."

"And the orders?"

"Keep attacking until you are flanked and then pull back. Keep an eye on me. Send Rufius to me so that I can explain it to him."

202

While he waited Livius was grateful for such experienced officers. His orders relied on a quick brain and a confident leader. He knew that his officers had both of those qualities.

"Sir."

"Rufius, you are to command four turmae. Harass the Brigante from the west. Use Marcus' method of three turmae charging with javelins and then the fourth with spears. Do not get trapped. Watch me for the three of us must move as one and pull back slowly towards the fort. If the bridge is under attack then we will ford the river."

"Yes sir!"

The four turmae trotted down the road and took their place to the west of it. Marcus and his turma were at the rear with their spears at the ready. Having borne the brunt of the losses Rufius' and Marcus' turmae had been the ones to benefit from the disbanded reserve turma of the prefect. There were new faces for Marcus to get to know. He was just grateful that Titus and Gnaeus, although both wounded, had survived. When they went into action then he would be able to rely on them. Felix waved as he loped off up the hill to the west and headed south.

The prefect had sent Felix and Wolf to scout Vinovia. It was important to know what forces the Brigante had left there. Was there a reserve or was this band the only one they had to defeat? The prefect had wondered at the wisdom of abandoning the two fortlets at Vindomora and Longovicium. Had they been occupied then the Brigante would have been slowed down in their advance. It was some miles to the fort but Felix had time and merely had to avoid the Brigante. He had his bow and he had his dog. He needed nothing else. It was thirty miles but he would be able to make quicker time once he had reached the road.

Caronwyn knew from Briac's scouts that the Romans were waiting for them at Coriosopitum. She halted her army, for she now felt it was hers, a mile south of the waiting horsemen. Briac's behaviour at Vinovia had disappointed her. He was not proving to be the leader she wanted. She imperiously waved for the chiefs to join her. She did not dismount. Acutely aware of the effect of making the chiefs look up at her she used every trick to her advantage.

Roman Wall

The ten men who looked up at her were all dressed in mail and each had a fine helmet. Lady Flavia's bounty had enabled Caronwyn to realise her dream of a rebel army. Their weapons were now the weapons of warriors. What Caronwyn wanted was the commitment and the discipline which she knew would reap rewards.

"The scouts have told me that the horse warriors wait for us below the fort. These are the last warriors who can stop us. Beyond the horsemen lie the garrisons of the wall. Already our Votadini and Selgovae brothers will be assaulting the wall and, even now, may be approaching Coriosopitum from the north."

At the back of her mind was a doubt for Marcus' Horse would not be waiting for them unless the wall was safe. Something had not gone to plan. The priestess was still confident for she meant what she said. Her army outnumbered the horsemen by over three to one.

"We will use our superior numbers to defeat them. Elidr you will take a thousand men and head to the west. You will outflank the horsemen and destroy them. Briac you will do the same to the east. I will lead the rest along the road."

The chiefs looked at each other. This was not right. A woman did not lead an army. When the Queen of the Iceni, Boudicca, had done so then eighty thousand had died. The gods did not approve. Elidr looked at Briac and willed him to speak. Briac was the putative king of the Carvetii and the Brigante and it was for him to speak. He cast his eyes down and the moment passed. It was at that point that Elidr decided he had had enough. Briac had cost him his son. He would support him no longer. When this was over he would wrest the crown from him. He was, however, no fool. He knew that they had to defeat the Roman horse warriors first.

Caronwyn's eyes narrowed. She had seen Elidr's reaction. He was dangerous. She would have to watch him. Briac was clay in her hands but Elidr was immune to both her charms and her magic. When this was over then he might have to disappear. He would be a dangerous enemy.

Elidr led his men over the gently rising ground to the west. There were bushes and trees dotted all over it. Hollows and rises meant that the distant Romans sometimes disappeared from view. One good thing which Caronwyn had brought to the barbarians was Severus. Elidr might not like the arrogant Roman but he wished he was with them now for he had brought ideas and strategies which would defeat the Romans.

The men that Elidr led were all Brigante and the chiefs who led the men from his land were well known to him. He remembered Severus saying that spears were the best defence against horses. He did not move in a wide line, instead, his men moved forwards a hundred abreast. It was a narrow front. The front four ranks all had spears and a shield. The front rank all had helmets and some had mail. Most of them had been taken from dead Romans. They moved in a loose line with space for two horses between each warrior. That was deliberate. As they moved north each man was waiting for the carnyx to signal close ranks. He wanted to tempt the horsemen to attack.

His fifth rank had his best warriors. All of them were armed with a sword and a shield. Half of them wore pilfered mail. They were his secret weapon. They were his horse killers. He marched in the midst of them. He was not afraid but when they attacked he would be with them.

Rufius saw the warband as it crested the rise before, briefly, disappearing in a hollow. They were trying to outflank them. "We had better realign to face these warriors."

Marcus left his turma to come to Rufius' side, "This is not the way the Brigante fight. This is the way that the Selgovae fought the other day."

"I know. I see the hand of that Roman we saw in all this. We will be cautious."

The cavalry charge which Marcus would use involved a trot for a hundred paces and then a gallop for fifty. It was efficient and did not tire the horses out. His men had put markers at a hundred and fifty, two hundred and two hundred and fifty paces respectively. He would charge at the perfect moment.

Over to his left he heard the carnyx as the other two warbands attacked. The warrior who led the band closest to them was more cautious. Marcus looked along the front rank which was oddly spaced out. He sought the leader but there appeared to be none who was giving orders. The formation was tempting them to attack whilst negating the effect of their javelins. Rufius had no other tactic to hand. In a perfect world, he would have had a turma equipped with bows but this was the real world.

At two hundred paces he shouted, "First turma prepare!"

Each trooper adjusted his shield and took out his javelin. The other two would remain in the sheath. With the reins in their left hands they waited for the sound of the buccina.

"Trot!"

As soon as they moved forward the carnyx sounded and the open formation closed ranks and a hedgehog of spears prickled from behind Roman auxiliary shields.

"Charge!"

The Brigante braced themselves for the impact. The troopers all wheeled to the left when they were twenty paces from the tribesmen and released their javelins. They threw them high to descend on the ones in the middle. Even as they released them they turned and headed east. Cassius led the second turma to perform the same manoeuvre.

Marcus had watched the attack and he could see the effect of the javelins. It had been negligible. If they had hit anyone then Marcus could not see them. "Gnaeus I am going to aim the line at the warriors on the far right of the barbarian band. Our men have been wheeling left and they will expect that. We will wheel right. Troopers hold your spear like a javelin. Lower it only when we strike."

"Sir!"

By the time Septimus and the third turma had loosed their javelins Marcus and the fourth turma were ready.

"Trot!"

As they moved forward each trooper held his spear at shoulder height. Marcus hoped to fool the Brigante into thinking that they would throw the weapon.

"Charge!"

When they were fifty paces from the line Marcus and his turma lowered their weapons. The slightly western alignment of the troop had deceived the Brigante. He saw the fear and confusion on the faces of the men on the extreme left of the warband. They watched for the wheel and it never came. Each trooper pulled back his arm at ten paces and then punched forward with the long, sharp spears. Every spear struck a face and part of the left flank disintegrated.

"Again!"

Pulling back each trooper repeated the strike and men in the second rank fell.

"Recall!"

Titus sounded the buccina and they wheeled away from the Brigante. The riderless horse told Marcus that they had paid for their success. Glancing over his shoulder Marcus saw that the Brigante had stopped to make good their losses.

Rufius was waiting for Marcus. "Well done Marcus. That was bravely done." He returned to his men. "We will attack the left flank of this warband too. Wheel right after releasing your javelins."

Elidr was annoyed. They had been doing so well until the last attack. He recognised the decurion. He had been the one who had visited him in Stanwyck and he was the one with the sword of Cartimandua. His oathsworn were close by him and he said, quietly, "The officer who led the last charge has the Sword of Cartimandua. I will have that blade!"

He watched as the next turma came at his left flank. Although the dead men had been replaced those in the second rank now had no mail. Some in the fourth rank had no shield. When the javelins fell amongst them, this time, they caused casualties. The next two turma attacked the same place and Elidr became worried. He watched as the fourth turma prepared to charge.

"Oathsworn with me." He led his oathsworn swordsmen, all twenty of them and they slowly filleted down the line until they were in the second rank. "You men without mail stand behind us."

Marcus frowned when he saw the movement. They were trotting and it was too late to adjust their line of attack. The warband had reinforced the left of their line.

"Charge!"

Once again, they plunged into the front rank which crumpled. Suddenly the second rank began swinging their long swords as they quickly advanced through their comrades. Three horses died in a heartbeat.

"Recall!"

As they wheeled right another two troopers and their horses fell to the deadly blades. This time Rufius was not smiling as his friend returned. The cheers of the Brigante filled the air as they butchered the wounded troopers.

"We have a clever opponent." Once again, they had a brief respite as the Brigante realigned. "Cassius, take your men and attack their left flank. Try to hit those swordsmen. My turma, prepare spears. Marcus, take charge here and wait for my return."

"Take care, Rufius. We cannot afford losses like this." He looked at his depleted line. He had lost six of his thirty-two troopers. A fifth of his men had died!

Rufius and his men used the same tactic as Marcus. Punching at the front two ranks with their spears they made the right flank reel. At the same time, Cassius and his men released their javelins. Two of the swordsmen fell but, more importantly, the turma withdrew without taking casualties.

As Rufius headed back Marcus noticed that the barbarians were much closer now. They kept steadily advancing. To the left, he could see the prefect was closely engaged with the main warband. Rufius looked at the river. It was less than two hundred paces away.

"Form line!" As the four turma dressed ranks Rufius said to Marcus, "We will charge and throw our javelins. I intend to withdraw towards the bridge. We are in danger of becoming isolated and trapped besides which the horses are tiring."

"Suits me, sir!" Marcus and his men were on the right of the line. Marcus turned to Gnaeus. "We are going to use javelins. I want those swordsmen dead!" Marcus realised that he was allowing revenge to rule his head but he also knew it was important for the morale of his men that they avenge their comrades.

"Trot!"

They moved forward. Marcus hefted the javelin to the horizontal. He saw that they had done well on the left flank of the Brigante. The well-armed warriors who had been there were replaced by lighter armed warriors. The swordsmen in the second rank were still the main threat.

"Charge!"

Marcus saw the leader of the swordsmen. He recognised him as the headman from Stanwyck. It made it even more personal. He aimed his javelin at the man's head. He was a cool customer and, as the missile headed towards his head he moved it slightly. The Brigante behind him took it full in the face.

They wheeled and began to ride away. "Roman coward! Fight me like a man!"

Marcus recognised the voice and he reined Raven in. He turned. "Why should I fight a deceitful liar such as you Elidr of Stanwyck?"

His use of his name told the Brigante that he had been recognised. Marcus was not being foolish. He was not doing as Macro or Macro's father might have done and risked his life foolishly. While they talked the warband was halted listening. He was buying time.

"Because I give you my word that we will not attack until you and I have settled this.

Rufius had reached their start point and looked at the scene before him. He saw that Marcus, along with his signifer, Titus, had not retreated. Was there a problem?

To his horror, he saw Marcus dismount and walk towards the Brigante while Titus held Raven.

Chapter 21

As Marcus handed his reins to Titus the signifer said, quietly, "Is this wise, sir?"

Marcus shrugged, "It buys us time and that is worth the risk."

Elidr walked through his men. He could not believe that the Roman had acceded to his request. He would make short work of him. This would increase his chances of leading the tribe. Briac would not dare to do as he was doing. He strode towards the Roman. His eyes lit up with envy when he saw the sword in the Roman's hand.

"And when this is over, Elidr, what then?"

"I will take your sword and we will slaughter your men."

Marcus nodded. He understood the rules of the combat. "And if I win, what then?"

Elidr could not comprehend failure and so he spread his arms and smiled. "Then my warriors will carry my body to yonder hill and burn it."

"Do your oathsworn so swear?"

Elidr frowned, the first hint of doubt entering his mind. This Roman understood the Brigante psyche. He nodded and the leader of his oathsworn said, "We swear."

Marcus dropped his cloak and went into his fighting stance. "Then let us get on with it, Elidr of the Brigante."

The Brigante was a bigger man than Marcus and his sword was also longer. He decided to use both to his advantage. He brought the sword over his head and swept it towards the Roman's neck in a diagonal sweep. Had it connected then the contest would have been over. Marcus flicked up his shield and angled it so that the Brigante blade slid harmlessly down the side.

Marcus' right hand darted out in a steel blur and the tip went directly for Elidr's eye. He jerked his head to the side but the sword cut a long gash in his cheek. There was a groan from the Brigante. It was first blood to the Roman.

Elidr was warier now. He swung his sword horizontally at Marcus. This time the blade would not angle down the shield. Marcus braced himself with his left leg as he waited for the blow. At the same time, he feinted with the Sword of Cartimandua. Elidr thought it was coming for his eye again and he moved back slightly. The result was that his sword cracked weakly against the Roman's shield. The decurion did not wait for his opponent to regain the initiative and he punched with his shield making the Brigante tumble to the ground as he tried to keep his balance. There was another groan.

Marcus stepped back. He could have leapt in and finished off Elidr, it would have been easy but he did not do so. He needed to win well. He wanted the Brigante to lose heart. He gestured with his sword for the Brigante to rise. Anger filled Elidr's face. This was not the way it was supposed to happen. He would finish off the Roman quickly.

Once on his feet he roared at the Roman and swung his sword with every muscle in his arm, shoulder and chest behind it. Marcus stepped to one side and the sword flashed through fresh air. He took the opportunity to slash at the Brigante's head. He was slow to raise his shield and the blade cracked against the helmet. The dent the sword made in it was matched by the ringing in Elidr's ears.

The Brigante knew that he would have to use cunning to defeat the Roman. He was a skilful swordsman. Using his left hand, he pulled his dagger from his belt. It was hidden from view by his shield. He swung his sword, once more, at the Roman's head. As Marcus countered with his shield Elidr's left hand darted in with the dagger. It caught on some of the mail links but still penetrated. It came away red.

Elidr grinned, "We are even now Roman!"

"No, we are not for you have no honour and now I will kill you."

Marcus' calm voice and the icy look in his eyes told Elidr that he meant it. As Elidr swung his sword Marcus blocked it with his own sword. As they came face to face Marcus pulled his head back and butted Elidr in the face. He heard the crack of bone and cartilage. He punched with his shield and, as Elidr stepped back, swung with his sword. Elidr had to counter with his own blade but his size and weight made him over balance and he had to step back quickly to keep his feet. He was now but five paces from his oathsworn who were watching in horror as their leader was given a lesson in arms from the young decurion.

In a blur Marcus feinted with his shield and as Elidr tried to adjust his feet the sword of Cartimandua darted out and pierced the Brigante's throat. Marcus held it there for an instant. "The Sword of Cartimandua has dealt out her justice! Die rebel!" He twisted the blade and pulled it out. Dark arterial blood spurted out like a fountain and as Elidr fell backwards it showered his oathsworn.

The ala began to cheer and the oathsworn's hands went to their swords. "Remember your oath." He held up the sword of Cartimandua. "This is the sword of the Brigante. Think before you break an oath."

The leader nodded. He and his brethren picked up the body and slowly began to carry the corpse to the hill. The rest of the warband followed leaving Marcus and Titus alone.

"Well, sir, you never do things the easy way, do you?"

They mounted and rode back to the waiting, cheering turmae. Marcus could see the anger on Rufius' face but he would not reprimand him in front of the men. Marcus was saved by the rider who galloped over to them. "Sir, the Prefect says we are to pull back over the bridge. He says can you cover the withdrawal and then use the ford?"

"Tell him aye." As the messenger rode off Rufius shouted, "Javelins at the ready. Skirmish order."

There were no warriors between them and the road. They trotted forward. The Brigante on the left of Caronwyn's column were suddenly aware of the cavalry approaching. They partly turned. Caronwyn had no idea what had happened to Elidr. His warband appeared to have disappeared. She was incandescent with rage. Her warriors had forced the Romans back. The corpses of the horses and the troopers marked their withdrawal. Briac too had had success. Now her men were halting. She saw the troopers who had been facing Briac use the hiatus to flood back across the bridge to the safety of the fort.

"Forwards! Victory is within our grasp!"

Before her men could react Rufius and his four turmae charged in and hurled their javelins. The Brigante held their shields above their heads. A second shower of javelins followed. A buccina sounded and Caronwyn cursed as the Romans she had been fighting fled across the bridge. All of her anger and hatred were now directed at the four turmae who had suddenly attacked her. Her men now held the end of the bridge. The last horse warriors would be slaughtered.

"Kill them!"

Rufius had done enough. "Sound the recall!"

The four turmae wheeled to the right and followed the decurion as he headed directly for the river. Caronwyn wondered what he was doing. She and her amazons galloped after them. When she reached the bank, she saw the eighty odd troopers swimming the narrow river. Already the first ones were clambering on to the bank. They had evaded her!

Julius Demetrius had watched the whole battle from the southern gate. He had not been idle and two Scorpios had been man handled from the east and west gates to double the artillery pieces protecting the bridge. Every available man was now on the southern walls. He had no idea what had just happened although he had seen Marcus fight a single combat with a barbarian. He did not know what had made the warband leave but it had saved the day. The Prefect and the rest of the ala had been restricted by the land and were not as free to manoeuvre as Rufius and his men. He watched the ala ride to the east and west gates. It would have been madness to try to enter through the southern gate.

Caronwyn reached Briac and his men. They were cheering and celebrating as though they had won. "Your cousin had better be dead, Briac, or he will wish that he was. He has cost us a quick victory." Before the warrior could reply she snapped, "Now take the bridge and attack the gate!"

Briac nodded and turned to the warriors closest to him. "Make a wedge and advance across the bridge. Make sure that you are covered with shields."

The hundred men closest to Briac eagerly began to line up. Pedair was amongst them in the front rank. He would show his uncle what he could do. They would march six abreast across the bridge and they knew that their shields would be effective. The vaunted Romans were going to lose!

Roman Wall

The Brigante warriors had not faced bolt throwers before. The Legate allowed them to reach the middle of the bridge before he ordered his four machines to release their deadly bolts. He did not do so all at once. There was a count of five between each one. It was a clever move for the cracks as they were released rolled together like thunder. The bolts themselves carved a line through shields, metal, flesh and bone. The four bolts cleared the bridge of the sixty men who had just stepped on to it. Not all died immediately. Some were thrown into the river while others merely had deep wounds and broken limbs. Pedair was one of the few who survived and stumbled backwards, still shaking from the shock of the wall of death which had struck them. The first attack had failed. They had, however, no respite for the Legate continued to send bolt after bolt across the river making the barbarians move further and further away. Even when they moved from the bridge itself the deadly machines tracked them and continued to plague them. Finally, the Brigante took shelter out of sight of the fort and the artillery. Caronwyn had been thwarted.

Banquo and his warriors had spent a day watching the routine of the men on the wall. They knew now of the dangers of the ditches and they also knew of the dangers beyond the walls. In the forest, overlooking the wall he gathered his men around him. His brother's style of leadership had been to tell just the chiefs of his plans. Banquo knew, from his oathsworn, that young warriors liked to feel part of the plan.

"Brothers, we will scale the walls tonight. If we have to kill the Romans on the wall we will do so but I hope that we can be as the shadows of the night and move through their land unseen. I want us to march south and join our Brigante friends and the priestess of the Mother. The Votadini gave their word. My brother might have broken his oath but I am a Votadini and I keep my honour!"

They were the right words to say and the young warriors were all committed. They would follow this valiant young prince and the Votadini would be honoured once more.

As night fell they slipped like wraiths across the ditch. The two sentries who might have alerted the mile castle were slain by arrows.

Once over the wall they disappeared south and by morning had crossed the Vallum and the Stanegate. Unknown to any Roman a warband of armed Votadini was south of the wall. The Parcae were toying with the Romans.

The VIth were being pushed hard by First Spear Broccus. He turned to the centurion of the 1st century. "Just keep them moving Servius. We have waited too long as it is to move. I know some of these auxiliaries are good soldiers but they can't handle a rebellion on their own."

Almost on cue one of the Thracians galloped in. "First Spear, the decurion sent me. The bridge is held. They are wearing Roman uniforms."

There was hesitation from the trooper. First Spear snapped, "Well get on with it! If they are our lads then we can slow up, can't we?"

"Sorry sir, the decurion reckons they are deserters or barbarians in looted uniform."

"That's better sonny. Now ride back and tell him to report everything."

"Er, sir, there is a boat moored next to the fort. On the other side of the island."

First Spear sighed, "A report in three parts! How refreshing!"

The trooper leapt on his horse, threw a quick salute and galloped back to the relative safety of the fort. First Spear scared him.

Turning to his cohort First Spear shouted, "Right boys. A quick double march up the road and we can see if can make these deserters shit themselves and give up!"

The men cheered. They were in the mood for action.

The auxiliaries guarded their flanks in case the Thracians had missed an ambush and they made double time to reach the bridge.

Inside the fort, Severus had seen the Thracians. He hoped that they were the only threat but he was not certain. He and his men had not bothered to follow Caronwyn's orders and destroy the bridge. It would have taken them too long. Once their friends and their boat had reached them then they had an escape route. He turned to his number two. "Get the treasure in the boat and stand by. If this goes wrong we will head out to sea and Gaul."

"It could be just a turma of cavalry."

"I know but it could be the VIth. I do not intend to risk a run in with them."

He went to the gate and watched the Thracians as they dismounted and tethered their horses. They had done their part. Severus had his fifteen Romans and forty-two barbarians. Most of the Brigante had been wounded and all of them were useless. He knew that for if they were warriors of any standing they would have gone with the army north. Severus knew that they could hold the fort against the Thracians and even a second auxiliary force. He hoped that was all that would be coming. When he saw the eagle, he knew that they were doomed.

He summoned Ragdh. "They have sent the legion. I have a plan. I want you and your men to keep the bridge clear with the bolt throwers and I will take my men to attack the legionaries when they manage to cross. We will use my boat to cross the river downstream."

Ragdh was suspicious. "Wouldn't it make more sense to all wait in here?"

"If you like you and your men can attack them and we will use the bolt throwers. We are better than your lads anyway. My boys have fought the legion before. If you keep the bridge clear of large numbers we can deal with any who get through. We have to protect the gate, don't we?"

Ragdh could not see any advantage in what the Roman was doing. It seemed both brave and foolhardy. He and his warriors were happy to use the bolt throwers. It would be good to kill Romans in large numbers. He nodded to Severus. "When do we begin?"

"Wait until the first men try to come across the bridge. When they get half way over let them have it. That will give us time to get in position and to hide." He pointed the small island in the middle of the river. "We will come down from that direction. The island will hide us."

Ragdh had to admire the Roman's cunning and his bravery. He watched as they left the fort through the east gate and then he returned to the southern gate. "Get ready with the bolt throwers."

First Spear saw the Roman helmets disappear from the walls. He wondered what that meant. He had seen the bolt throwers. They would make the bridge a slaughterhouse for anyone who tried to cross. He summoned the Tungrian centurion. "I want twenty of your lads to run across the bridge."

The Tungrian said, "That will be suicide!"

"Not all at once, you halfwit! One at a time. If they go all at once then they will be slaughtered. I want to see if they have archers. If your boys use their shields then they should be safe. They can shelter beneath the walls. If they get across then my slower legionaries will try it."

"Very well First Spear." In reality the centurion had no choice. He was outranked and he knew it; he had to obey.

Ragdh saw the Romans running across the bridge. The warrior on the bolt thrower asked, "Well?"

He chewed his lip. The Romans were not doing as Severus had said. He wondered if they would kill the soldier. A second and a third followed. Ragdh was about to order the bolt thrower to be used when one of warriors shouted, "The bastards are leaving sir. They are in the boat!"

Now he knew that he had been outwitted. "There are more Romans coming over."

He saw the legionaries with their huge shields as they lumbered across the bridge. "Use the bolts."

To their horror, the two bolts they released flew too high and more Romans sped across the wooden structure. As his men fought to adjust the machine even more Romans flooded across. They released another two bolts. One speared a legionary in the leg while the other buried itself in the bridge itself. Ragdh saw a hand appear over the wall as the first of the Tungrians was hoisted up to the fighting platform. He knew then that it was over.

First Spear was the fourth man over the wall. He laid about him with his gladius. The long swords used by the Brigante were of no use in such a confined space. Quintus Broccus had killed six before he realised that

217

they had taken the fort. It had cost them one man. The Allfather had
watched over them!

Inside the fort at Coriosopitum Livius, Rufius and Metellus faced
Marcus. The Legate sat at his desk watching and listening.

"But sir, I did not disobey any orders!"

"Nonsense! Standing orders forbid such a thing!"

Marcus sighed, "There was a risk, sir. Perhaps it was a gamble but it
worked. A third of their men were out of the battle at the end. You taught
us to use our heads. I was using mine."

Livius could not argue with that. The three of them were more upset
because they could have lost the popular young decurion and the
talismanic sword. "Suppose he had defeated you?"

"That never occurred to me, sir."

Metellus wagged a finger at Marcus. "One of these days a young
warrior will face you who will defeat you."

Marcus nodded although he did not believe it. The sword would keep
him safe. If he had not had the Sword of Cartimandua then he would not
have accepted the challenge.

The Legate stood. "Let us put that in the past. What will these
Brigante do now?"

They all looked at Marcus. He was half Brigante and, as he had
shown with the combat, understood the mind of the enemy. "They will
cross the river and attack us tonight. There is no honour in dying to a
bolt. They will make a sacrifice to Icaunus the god of the river and then
they will cross."

"Will they swim or use rafts?"

Rufius pointed to the south. "There are many trees. They will use
rafts."

The Legate rubbed his chin. If they crossed the river then there was
nothing to stop them bypassing the fort and heading for the thinly
defended wall. The Votadini had been cowed but the sight of a Brigante
army might rekindle the fire of rebellion in their breasts.

"We must stop them at the river." The Legate jabbed a finger at the
map on the wall.

"Easier said than done, sir. They could cross anywhere. Upstream they could probably ford the river." Livius had patrolled this land for years and knew the Tinea well.

"We will concentrate our efforts on stopping them here. If they move upstream we will deal with that problem later for it will take them some time to reach us. There are a couple of hours until dark. I suggest you rest your men for we may need them after dark."

As they turned to leave Livius said, "Sir, if I might suggest having the garrison measure accurately to the river. The onagers might discourage them."

"Thank you Livius, that is a good suggestion."

Chapter 22

The legionaries quickly disposed of the bodies of the Brigante. They were hurled into the river. The Thracians were not given any respite. First Spear sent them north towards Vinovia. He spoke urgently to the decurion. "I am worried that we have heard nothing from the north. Your lads were patrolling this road but so far, we have only seen you. Where are the others?"

The decurion was equally concerned. Once the fort at Morbium had been captured he knew that his comrades would be cut off but he had expected some scouts to be watching the captured fort from the north. The fact that they were not there was unsettling. "We can reach the fort quickly and find out if the garrison holds there."

"Be careful. The handful of men we just killed couldn't have taken this fort. There is a much bigger army out there somewhere and, at the moment, you are our only cavalry."

Felix and Wolf spotted the Thracians as they approached the fort. The young scout had found the fort empty and hid close by. He and Wolf needed rest. He looked on approvingly as the decurion sent in two men and waited with the rest. Felix mounted his horse. These were Romans. They were not deserters or Brigante in disguise. He made sure that he waved as he approached. The Thracians were suspicious and twenty javelins were aimed at Felix. Wolf growled at the new soldiers.

"What is your story boy? That is a Roman horse you are riding."

"I am Felix the scout of Marcus' Horse. Legate Demetrius sent me south to see if there were any Brigante here. There are not."

The decurion was relieved. "Right lads. He seems genuine; you can lower your weapons. We are safe. The dog won't attack us. What is happening here, son?"

"The Votadini, Selgovae and Novontae have attacked the wall. There is a large Brigante army and they are attacking Coriosopitum."

"Did you see any of our lads?"

"There are some in Coriosopitum." He pointed at Vinovia. "Many died there and there were some on the road as I came south." He gestured at the plume on the decurion's helmet. "There were decurions' bodies there. I am sorry."

"Not as sorry as me, son." He turned to a trooper. "Cassius, ride to First Spear and tell him what the lad just told us. We will head north and keep an eye on the Brigante." As the trooper galloped off he asked, "Can they hold out?"

"There are many Brigante but it is Marcus' Horse and they have the sword. They will hold out."

"I hope that you are right."

Caronwyn and her priestesses stood on the banks of the Tinea. Behind them were the serried ranks of the Brigante. They were all out of range of the bolt throwers. The walls of the fort were lined with the garrison. The captured trooper had been stripped naked and bound. One of Caronwyn's amazons held a knife to his throat. The trooper had been captured when his horse had been killed and his body pinned beneath it. He had expected death but to stand shivering on a riverbank with baying barbarians all around him was not the death he had expected.

"Great Icaunus take this sacrifice that we may safely cross. Take the body of this man and let his death be payment for our transgression."

She nodded and the knife was ripped across his throat. The blood spurted and the lifeless corpse thrown into the waters. It disappeared for a moment and then the current picked it up and it emerged in the middle of the river and began to head towards the northern bank. The priestesses all gave a wild and terrifying shriek. "The god accepts the sacrifice!" Caronwyn stared at the fort. The Romans thought that they had thwarted her with their machines. She would show them that they would use the waters of the land to defeat these defilers of her land.

As night fell both sides put their plans into operation. Livius sent our four turmae under Rufius and spread them out in the woods close to the river. Armed with javelins their orders were simple; they were to slow down any Brigante who breached the Tinea. Another four turmae waited under the command of Metellus. They were the shock force which would meet any force which evaded the river guards. The rest of the turmae now manned the walls. Marcus' Horse had lost too many men and horses

221

to be considered an effective ala. The defenders had braziers burning ready to hurl incendiary missiles at any barbarian who tried to attack the fort. The Legate prayed that help would come soon. All that they had done was to slow down the enemy.

Caronwyn and her Amazons went to the river with the twenty Brigante warriors. They had all volunteered to serve the priestess for their task was dangerous. The overcast night meant that they were almost invisible. The six priestesses who would cross the river were naked and armed only with a short sword strapped across their backs. They were the secret weapon which would unpick the lock of the fort. They slipped silently into the water and began to swim to the northern bank. They had chosen this spot, just forty paces from the bridge for a number of reasons. It was close to the bridge and yet the steep bank hid them from view. There were trees nearby for cover but, most importantly, there was a muddy beach. The six warrior priestesses rolled in the mud and then smeared it over each other. They drew their swords and blackened them too. They became invisible. The only sign that they were human and not animal was when they opened their eyes. Caronwyn would use Mother Earth to help her defeat the Romans.

The six women slithered their way to the top of the bank. There were some Tungrian sentries in the woods watching for just such an attack. The Legate had anticipated warriors emerging from the river. The other sentries at the bridge were equally well hidden.

The four sentries in the woods suddenly saw a movement but it was not human. It was a shadow; a shadow which moved without human form. Their senses alerted them to something strange, supernatural. The sacrifice at the river had unnerved them. They could fight warriors but magic was something else. One turned to his companion. "I must be going mad. I can smell a woman."

"It must be that priestess."

Suddenly two eyes appeared before him and all four men died as the six women plunged steel deep within them. The six swords ensured that they died silently. The women laid the bodies down in the woods. They slipped through the trees barely disturbing the air so light was their movement.

The last two sentries before the bridge had their attention on the river. Each eddy and bubble made them think it was a swimmer. They felt a sudden sharp pain and then they died as silently as their comrades. The six invisible killers were good at their work. There were four men at the bridge. They were just eighty paces from the wall. If any Brigante tried to sneak across the bridge they would kill them and raise the alarm. If the whole army came across they would raise the alarm as they raced back to the gate. All four were watching the southern end of the bridge. They cursed the cloudy night which made their job doubly hard.

The six priestesses stepped from the woods and walked silently towards the Tungrians. One turned at a strange smell and a slight sound. He saw shadows with eyes. The woods had come alive! He was the first to die and then his companions followed.

On the far side of the bridge the twenty Brigante volunteers had been watching. They sprinted across the bridge keeping as low as possible. At the gate one of the sentries thought that he had seen a movement but when none of the guards made a sound he put it down to the nerves of night duty. He looked again, hard. Where were the sentries?

The Brigante and the priestesses made their way to the gate. Once they reached its shadow they were all hidden from view. The warriors made a pyramid and began to climb. Once they were just a body below the ramparts the six women clambered over them. Across the bridge Briac watched the shadows creep up the walls. He had chosen the two hundred warriors who would assault the gate personally. He felt he had to make up for Elidr's mistake and he could not afford to let down Caronwyn again.

The sharp-eyed sentry approached his optio, "Sir, I can't see the guards at the bridge?"

"Did you hear anything?"

"No sir!"

"If they are shirking I will…" He walked back with the sentry to the walls.

The six priestesses slipped over the walls and, once again, their appearance stunned the guards into silence. Three died with barely a murmur but the optio was made of sterner stuff. He smelled the mud and the blood on the blade and turned as the steel was thrust into his side. He grabbed the blade and, with his dying breath shouted, "Alarm!" as he and the Amazon plunged to the ground below.

The Legate and Livius had been prepared for an attack. They raced from their quarters already dressed for battle. The troopers who were on duty joined them. They could not believe their eyes as they saw the Brigante climbing over the walls. Some of them appeared to be naked!

"Livius secure the gate!"

Julius ran to the ladder. The first of the priestesses was descending to open the gate. He swung his spatha across his body and felt it jar against her spine as he sliced her slim form in two.

Livius shouted to the four troopers who followed him, "Kill anyone who tries to open the door. Sound recall!" He knew that there were four buccinas within the fort and he hoped that a signifier would hear him.

Julius was being assaulted by a naked priestess and the first of the Brigante. The Legate was no longer a young man and Livius winced as the Brigante sword scored a red line against the body of the Legate. He lunged and his sword struck the back of the naked priestess. She gave a primaeval scream and turned on him her eyes boring into him. She screamed a death curse as she launched herself at him with her sword. Livius was no fool. He had wounded her and he stepped back as her body overbalanced and she tumbled to the ground. He sliced down and decapitated the woman.

Julius was struggling to defend himself. The wound had weakened him. Out of the corner of his eye, Livius saw more Brigante pouring down the ladders. He ignored them. His men would have to deal with them. The Legate was his priority. The Brigante knocked Julius' sword to the ground and he raised his own to finish off the leader of the Romans. Before he could do so Livius hacked at his leg for it was the only part of the Brigante's anatomy he could reach. The savage cut to the bone made the Brigante turn to face his new enemy. Rather than stepping back Livius stepped closer. He grabbed the warrior's beard and pulled

224

him forward. He smashed the pommel of his sword into the back of the Brigante's neck. Falling to the floor the Brigante put his arms out and Livius took his chance. He stabbed down and the Brigante died.

Julius was lying, bleeding. "Capsarius." Livius stood over the Legate. "Hang on Julius. Help is at hand!"

"Forget me! Defend the fort. We must not fail!" The effort was too much and the Legate rolled on to his side.

The capsarius ran up, his bag at the ready. "See to the Legate! Do not let him die!"

Livius turned to assess the situation. Brigante were pouring over the wall. "Marcus' Horse to me!" His strident tones carried over the sounds of battle. The troopers who had responded to the sound of the buccina formed up behind him. All had their spatha and their shield. Many had on their mail.

"Form a wedge behind me!"

His four beleaguered troopers were desperately trying to hold the gate. One was already down and a second was about to join him in the Otherworld. Livius did not wait for the wedge to form. He headed purposefully towards the Brigante. He hacked down on the skull of the warrior before him. With his left hand he pulled him away and stabbed forward to kill the naked vixen who was trying to kill the trooper at the gate. With his left hand he grabbed the hair of the last of the priestesses. As her head came back he ripped the edge of his sword across her throat and her lifeless body fell at his feet. His four troopers had held the gate but they had paid the price with their lives.

Livius looked at the troopers in his wedge. There were eight of them. "You eight hold this gate at all costs. No matter what happens here do not leave until I tell you so."

The Chosen Man who was with them said, "If they pass it will be because we are in the Otherworld."

The whole of the garrison had now emerged from their barracks. The fight was suiting the Brigante for it was man to man and the Romans could not use their disciplined ranks. He saw a signifer. "Sound reform!"

As the notes rang out the troopers stopped and stepped back. "Form two lines behind me!" He was helped by the fact that Roman soldiers were used to obeying orders no matter how strange they sounded. Forty men formed two lines. They were a mixture of horsemen and infantry but they all had a grim determination about them. If they did not drive the Brigante from their fort then they would all die.

Metellus had heard the buccina and feared the worst. The Legate had assumed they would come from upstream. The noise of battle told him that they had come at the bridge. "Marcus' Horse, follow me!"

They were forced to ride in a column of four for the trail was narrow. As they emerged at the bridge they saw that the bridge had been taken and Brigante were scaling the walls. There was no time for delicate and subtle action; direct force was needed.

"Charge!"

As the buccina sound, the barbarians looked west. Metellus and his men thundered in. They did not halt at the edge of the barbarian line. Every trooper hurled his first javelin and then used his second like a spear. The press of men at the bridge meant that many Brigante could not bring their weapons to bear. The horses of the ala simply smashed through them. One horse stumbled throwing its rider but the horse's body formed a barrier at the end of the bridge. The trooper died when his head smashed into the bridge.

Metellus headed for the ladders which had been placed against the wall. The crudely made siege weapons had served the Brigante well. Metellus put his spear in his left hand and rode along the ditch smashing the ash staff against the flimsy ladders. They cracked and broke throwing the warriors to their deaths in the spike filled ditch.

Marcus had seen what Metellus intended and he led his turmae to the end to the bridge. The press of men was intense. His turma jabbed and stabbed with their spears. The Brigante could not make progress because of the bodies of their dead comrades.

Livius and his hastily formed century had cleared the ground around the gate and he now ordered them up the ladders to clear the ramparts. Surprisingly there were still auxiliaries fighting for their lives. They took heart when they saw the Prefect leading the troopers to their aid. With no reinforcements, the Brigante began to edge back to form a wedge on the wall. The troopers picked up the discarded and used spears. They hurled them at the Brigante who died on the ramparts. It was the only part of Rome they had claimed as their own.

As the men cheered, Livius realised that they had not won. The battle was still in the balance. "Get the bolt throwers ready. I want the bridge cleared!"

The cheers and roars died as his men quickly threw the dead Brigante into the ditch and began to aim the bolt throwers. Livius turned to the signifer who had followed him. "Sound fall back. Prepare to loose javelins. I want the Brigante to bleed on the bridge!"

Marcus heard the buccina and knew what was to come. "Fall back! Spears at the ready!"

They backed their horses towards the wall keeping the wall of spears towards the Brigante who were still reeling from the attack of the horse warriors.

Metellus had cleared the wall and he and his men formed a second line behind that of Marcus. Their javelins waited for the order to rain death upon the enemy.

Suddenly there was a double crack as the two bolt throwers sent their deadly missiles towards the bridge. Neither the tension nor the aim was quite right, for the original crews had died, but, even so, the two bolts still carved a path of death along the bridge. In the hiatus between bolts a few hardy warriors tried to race forward. Metellus and his men threw thirty javelins and the putative attack faltered.

An almost instantaneous crack signalled the next two bolts. They had been aimed more effectively and the tension was right. Two files of eight men all fell to the bolt. That was more than enough for the Brigante warriors who fled south to safety. The men of Marcus' turma followed them across the bridge and formed a human and equine barricade. Marcus raised his sword and shouted, "Brigante! Advance on the Sword of Cartimandua at your peril! The rebellion is over!"

To Caronwyn and Briac's horror, some of the warriors slumped their shoulders and began to trudge south. They had come north with the promise of victory and the sword of their ancestors had defeated them. It was in that moment that Briac realised he had lost. No matter what Caronwyn said, he knew that the rebellion was over.

Banquo and his men had headed south-east towards the Roman Road. Banquo had the natural leader's instinct for action. His men moved through the woods quietly and cautiously. In the distance they could hear the sounds of battle. Banquo would not make the same mistake of rushing in to something. He sent his scouts ahead and he waited. When they returned he knew that he had been right.

"There are horse warriors ahead and they are watching the river."

It was perfect! "I want the men to move south in one line. When I sound the carnyx the Romans die!"

Rufius and his turmae had heard the recall in the distance. His decurion had wanted him to follow the horn. Rufius had shaken his head. "We wait here until the barbarians come! We have our orders." He wondered at the wisdom of waiting in these woods but if more warriors came across the river his was the only force which could hurt them.

It was a mistake but one made for the right reasons. He could not know the danger behind him nor could he know that the threat to the fort was over but Rufius would wake up, for months to come, sweating and fretful, wondering if he could have made a better decision.

When the carnyx sounded to the north poor Rufius was confused. As his Chosen Man fell to an axe between the shoulder blades he yelled. "Fall back to the river!" The natural leader in the decurion made the right decision. The remnants of the turma fell back to the wild Tinea. Many of their comrades lay dead. The Votadini, hidden in the dark, outnumbered them. The spears and arrows from the elated barbarians began to thin out the troopers. Rufius could see but one solution. "Into the river and swim downstream."

As Rufius leapt he felt a blow to his arm but he ignored it as he fought to control his mount. The wild river took them east and towards the bridge. Rufius counted on the fact that the bend was close to the bridge and the bridge itself would save them.

He held the reins and lay along the saddle to make life easier for his
horse. He watched in horror as a trooper lost his grip on his reins and
sank to his death beneath his weight of mail. As soon as he saw the
bridge, he yelled, at the top of his voice. "Head for the bank!" He jerked
the head of his horse and angled his legs so that it was easier for his
horse to move left. As soon as his horse's legs found purchase on the
river bottom he breathed a sigh of relief. He had made it. He struggled
from the water and released his horse's reins. He returned to the river
where he stood, waist deep in the bubbling foam and held out his arm for
his comrades. Marcus and the others saw what he was doing and leapt
into the water to help. Soon all that could be saved were plucked from
the water but many horses died a foamy death. The troopers could not
save them. Many tears were shed that night for faithful mounts which
died and were swept down to Arbeia to be food for the gulls.
    "What happened, Rufius?"
    "We were attacked from the north. It was not the Brigante. We have
another enemy! They drove us to the river." He pointed west. "They are
there in the woods!"

Across the river Caronwyn was reflecting on how close they had
come the previous night. When she had seen the warriors on the walls
she had been convinced that they would win. Her disappointment when
the men began to retreat was counterbalanced by the joy when she saw
the horsemen in the river. Briac had been confused.
    "It is our allies. They have come at last. Today we finally defeat them.
We have them between us and there is nowhere for them to go. They
cannot withstand another attack."
    Briac was not certain but they still had many men left. The Roman
mail had saved many. He began to organise his forces so that the freshest
and better-armed men would attack. They would wait until their allies
had attacked first before they risked the bolt throwers.

As dawn broke Livius surveyed the bridge and the area around the
river. They had survived but only just. They were now, effectively,
surrounded. There were Brigante to the south and someone else to the

north and west. Livius had assumed command when the capsarius had
told him that the legate was too weak for command. He had lost too
much blood. He ordered hot food for the garrison and a roll call. He had
no idea how many men he had lost. The dead barbarians were thrown
into the river while the Roman dead were laid, reverently, in an empty
barracks. They had died well and would be honoured when time allowed.

Livius was tired but he would sleep when the war was over. "Marcus,
take your turma and ride to the wall. Be careful. If there are enemies
from the north then it may have been breached."

Metellus was about to say that Marcus was tired until he realised that
they were all tired. Whoever drew the duty would be exhausted.

"Sir!"

As Marcus led his exhausted turma north Livius began to shift his
defences. "Decurion Princeps, I want four turmae west of the fort. Now!"

There was little point in Metellus telling Livius that he had barely
seventy men left. He knew the Prefect was right. Their backs were to the
wall!

Banquo and his men were elated. They stood on the northern bank of
the Tinea and watched as the river swept their enemies away. His
decision to leave his brother had been vindicated. He had defeated the
vaunted horse warriors.

"Do you see, my brothers, it has come about as I said. We have been
victorious. The priestess was right; the land and the waters will help us to
defeat the Romans."

The scout he had sent east returned. "The Brigante are fighting at their
fort!"

"Come! We end Rome's rule this day!"

A damp and dismal dawn saw the area around the fort littered with the
dead. No one had had the time or the energy to move any. The wounded
barbarians had had no help and all had succumbed to their wounds in the
night. It was a pitiful sight. Livius had come from the Legate. He was
alive and he was awake but he would not be making decisions. Livius

was the only senior officer left. There were his decurions and a handful of centurions and optios left. The others had gone to the Otherworld.

He found the walking wounded. "I want you men to get some hot food for the men on the walls."

"But sir we can fight still!"

"I know you can, soldier, but the men on the walls need the food first as do you. When we are fed then you can fight." With such an attitude Livius knew that the garrison would fight to the last man.

In the fort the auxiliaries were busily repairing the damaged bolt thrower. "Manhandle the ones from the northern gate here."

Rufius wondered at the wisdom of that. "Suppose there are more Votadini to the north of us. We are leaving ourselves vulnerable to an attack from the north."

"Marcus will warn us. We must trust our men."

Rufius suddenly remembered Felix. "Felix and Wolf should have returned before now. I fear that we have more enemies in the south than we thought."

Both men were thinking of their friends and family in the Dunum valley. That had been a safe haven but now it could be a devastated charnel house of the dead and the dying. Emperor Hadrian had thought to make a defence against the barbarians. Now it looked as though the wall was a weapon to be used against them!

Marcus was relieved when he found the gate and the fort at Cilurnum intact. The Camp Prefect was anxious for news. He frowned when Marcus told him. "I cannot understand where the barbarians came from. We were not attacked. Perhaps they came from the west."

"Rufius said that they were Votadini. I thought we had sent them home. Perhaps we were wrong."

Just then a messenger ran to the Prefect. "Sir, the centurion from the western mile castle sent me. They have found the bodies of four of our sentries."

"There is your answer, Prefect. They have slipped over the wall. I will take my turma and see if we can pick up their trail."

"And I will shut this stable door and increase the patrols along the wall."

The tracks across the spongy turf were clear to see. They had found where the Votadini had crossed. Had they had Drugi or Felix then they might have been able to accurately ascertain numbers. As it was Marcus just followed the tracks. He knew there were a large number. He saw where they had entered the woods; the broken branches and littered leaves were clearly visible.

"Gnaeus, make sure the men have their weapons ready and Titus, keep the buccina handy. We may need some help."

Metellus and his four turmae were spread in a thin line from the bridge towards the north-west. Metellus dared not risk over extending his line but the gap between each trooper was still five paces. Their red-rimmed eyes showed their lack of sleep but they still peered through the foliage to search for the enemy, they knew, lurked before them.

Banquo and his warriors were moving silently through the woods. They moved cautiously for they knew not where the fort and the Romans were. Ahead one of the horses in the waiting turmae neighed and Banquo held up his hand. The Romans were close. He had with him some twenty boys. They were armed with a sling and a short sword. They had been desperate to be used but, hitherto, there had been no opportunity. Now Banquo knew that he could use them. He waved them forward and they slipped through the woods like wraiths.

The first that Metellus knew of their presence was when Marcus, one of his new decurions was struck in the head by a lead ball. He fell from his horse and Metellus instinctively raised his shield. It was none too soon for a crack told him how close he had come to being felled. He risked a glance over the edge of his shield and saw the Votadini slingers. He kicked hard and his horse lurched towards the nearest boy. Startled, he looked up as Metellus hurled his javelin to skewer the boy to the tree.

Banquo knew now where the Romans were and, shouting their war cry, the Votadini raced through the woods. This was their time. The horses could not manoeuvre well in the woods and their movements would be restricted. Even as Metellus stabbed at another slinger with his spear he saw his men dropping from their horses.

"Fall back!"

If they moved closer to the walls then the garrison could support them with their weapons.

Livius heard the sounds of battles from the woods and he raced to the western gate. There was just one bolt thrower in place there and it was an under-strength century which defended its ramparts. Livius saw his Decurion Princeps and his men as they backed out of the woods fighting for their lives. The Votadini swarmed over them like ants over a corpse.

"Rufius bring your men to this wall!"

Rufius and the survivors of the night attack had been the reserve. Livius was forced to commit it.

Across the bridge, the movement of the defenders and the sounds of the battle to the west encouraged Briac and Caronwyn to begin their own attack. They had been constructing since before dawn some shields which were draped with mail shirts from the dead. Twelve brave warriors now carried these across the bridge.

The crews of the bolt throwers did not need orders. They recognised the danger and they released their bolts. One of them pierced the metal, the wood and the man but two of the others spun off. A Brigante ran from cover to pick up the dead man's shield. Once in place they continued across. It cost them three more warriors but once they reached the other side of the bridge they were able to drag dead bodies and built a barricade.

More Brigante joined them; this time they had bows and they began to pick off the crews of the bolt throwers. As their rate slowed down warriors raced to the shelter of the walls and the body filled ditch.

Livius heard the cries from the dying crews of his artillery. He had committed his reserve now. Metellus and his men were fighting for their lives below them and Rufius and the defenders were hurling their javelins as fast as they could. They were trying to stem a tide which would soon become a flood. They were losing the battle to hold the fort. The Legate had gambled and it looked as though he had lost.

Chapter 23

Marcus and his men heard the sounds of battle ahead. "Skirmish line!"

He had an under strength turma but Marcus could not let his friends down. They moved as quickly as they could through the trees. When he saw the backs of the Votadini ahead he shouted, "Titus, sound the charge!"

With his spear held overhand Marcus led his turma towards the Votadini.

There was dismay in the Votadini ranks. They were so close to slaughtering the horsemen before them and then they heard the sound of reinforcements coming from behind. Some of them turned to face the new threat. Metellus heard the buccina and took hope. "Sound the charge!"

It was a desperate gamble but Metellus reasoned that the weight of the horses might just make the difference. They were aided by the bolt thrower. The crew had just found the range and a bolt took out ten men. The stunned warriors around them looked in horror at their dead comrades and Metellus went for the gap.

Marcus thrust his spear into the face of the warrior who screamed his war cry and tried to decapitate Raven. He saw another warrior racing at him from his right and he stabbed at him. The spear went through the man and pinned him to a tree. Marcus released the spear and drew his sword. He could see the walls of the fort ahead through the thinning trees. There were still many Votadini between him and safety but, with the Sword of Cartimandua in his hand he felt no fear. He drew his arm back and then swung it forward. It sliced across the chest of a mailed warrior. There was a crack as his breastbone broke. The sound of Metellus' buccina spurred them on. Some of the Votadini on the end of the line raced towards the bridge to join the Brigante who were now flooding across. Their defection made a hole in their line and Metellus exploited that.

Banquo found himself fighting horse warriors on two sides. He had lost many of his men and he now saw his only salvation in joining those of his men who had made the bridge.

"Follow me!"

With his oathsworn around him, he began to hack towards the bridge. The horses suffered the worst of the attacks. The Votadini swung their long swords at the horses' legs. Riders were flung from dying horses as the desperate Votadini carved a path towards the bridge.

It cost Banquo fourteen of his oathsworn but he and forty warriors reached Briac and the bridge. Behind him, his warband was being slowly but inexorably hunted down and slaughtered. They had, however, served their purpose. The Brigante now held the bridge. The bolt throwers had been silenced and there were just two centuries of defenders left on the walls.

Caronwyn, still defended by her remaining females, ordered forward the twenty men with axes. Once the gates were destroyed they would flood in and they would massacre the defenders. The sacrifice had worked and the Mother had aided them. The fort was about to fall.

"Rufius, take your men and get to the south wall. Metellus and Marcus can finish off those in the woods." He nodded and took off his men. "Centurion. I want you and half of your men to come with me. We have to defend the gate."

The weary centurion nodded. "One man in two, follow me. Optio, take charge!"

The sounds of the axes on the gate were like the cracks of doom. The whole gatehouse shuddered. Rufius and his defenders hurled rocks and javelins from the gate above as they attempted to stop the Brigante but they were well defended with shields held high above them.

Livius picked up a shield and a spear. The centurion took his place next to the Prefect of Horse. There were just thirty men ready to attempt to repel the Brigante who would soon be pouring through the shattered gates. The Brigante were determined. They had been given impetus by the arrival of the Votadini. Despite the failure of the attack it had diverted some of the ala from the defence of the fort. Caronwyn and Briac could almost taste victory.

235

Banquo made his way across the bridge and gave a slight bow.

"Well done, young Votadini! Where is your brother?"

"He returned north. I am my own man now, my lady, and I serve you!"

Lady Flavia took his hand. "And we shall make a king of you too." The two women knew how to manipulate young men and Banquo was their slave from that moment.

Briac had a better view of the battle from the back of his horse. "There is daylight in the gate. They are almost through!" He turned to his reserve war band. "Demne, take your men and support those at the gate!"

The last warband trotted over the bridge. The bolt throwers had ceased to be effective some time earlier and the warriors were able to cross with impunity.

The remnants of the ala had fought themselves to a standstill. Their horses were exhausted. Metellus had suffered a wound to the leg but he was still in command.

"Ala, dismount. Wounded warriors hold the horses. The rest of you follow me." The southern gate was hidden from view but the Decurion Princeps could hear the sound of axes and he knew what it meant. He saw that only Marcus remained unwounded from his decurion. "Column of fours, follow me."

He and Marcus led the dismounted cavalrymen along the western wall of the fort. They reached the corner as two things happened. The gate was breached and Demne crossed the bridge with his warband. Metellus knew that they had to disrupt the Brigante attack. If they made the interior of the fort then all would be lost.

"Charge!"

Marcus lifted the Sword of Cartimandua high above him. The clouds broke briefly and a shaft of sunlight sparkled on the blade. It gave the troopers heart and they charged into the side of the advancing Brigante. Marcus brought down the mighty sword and he split open the helmet and skull of the unsuspecting warrior who was closest to him. He pulled back the blade and thrust it forward. It went through the eye of the next man and into his brain. Titus and Gnaeus were behind him and they formed a wedge which drove deep into the warband.

To their left they heard a mighty cheer as the gate was shattered and the Brigante poured into the fort. Livius desperately led his small force to counter the attack. Marcus and Metellus had split the warband in two making the battle a series of individual combats. The Brigante were fresh and they were unwounded; the tide began to turn. Marcus watched as weary troopers succumbed to blows from the Brigante and he saw them die. It felt as though all hope had gone when he heard the sound of a buccina, and it was from the south!

Hearing it Metellus shouted, "Help is to hand! Back to back boys!"

Marcus glanced over his shoulder. There was a Brigante there and he was about to strike Metellus. The decurion reversed his sword and stabbed backwards as he stepped back. The Brigante fell dead and the remaining Romans fought back to back. They were a thin line of red horsehair plumes but they were brothers in arms and they fought for each other. If it was their day to die then they would die together.

Rufius, standing on the gate, could see what they could not. It was Quintus Broccus with the VIth and the Thracians. They were sweeping towards the bridge. He shouted, at the top of his voice. "It is the VIth! Hold on!" Then he turned to the troopers who had followed him up to the tower. "We will go down and reinforce the Prefect. If we can hold on for a short time we will prevail!"

Caronwyn almost screamed when the Roman reinforcements arrived. She recognised them. They were not auxiliaries. They were the legion. Briac, too, knew that they had not enough men to stand against these well drilled and trained soldiers of Rome. She mounted her horse. "Come Briac and Banquo. We will depart south and begin again."

Banquo looked at his warriors who were still fighting with the Brigante. Could he desert them? The eight of his oathsworn who had crossed the bridge looked pleadingly at their lord.

"Come Banquo and live or stay and die."

The Roman cohort had turned and was now heading for the bridge with a screen of Thracians and Tungrians in front of them. Banquo knew that she was right. He turned to his men. "Come with us and we will begin again."

Four of them shook their heads and began to run back to the fighting. "We came here for honour and we will have it in life or in death!"

With just the bodyguards of the two leaders and the female warriors Caronwyn and Flavia headed south. The Thracian decurion saw their departure but dismissed the group as too small to be of concern. They headed for the bridge.

Inside the fort, the extra soldiers brought by Rufius had swung the balance in favour of the defenders. The centurion, although wounded, was a mighty rock. His spear darted out to skewer his enemies and he used his shield as a weapon too. Inexorably they began to push the Brigante back to the gate. There was a mighty press of Brigante and Romans entwined in individual combats in the space between the river and the fort. No quarter was given.

First Spear took it all in. He had witnessed scenes such as this before and he knew what to do. "Decurion, protect our flanks. First Century! Double time! Charge!" With interlocked shields and pila held high before them they ran towards the bridge. The Brigante and Votadini were brave and they were not stupid. They turned to face this new threat and they locked their shields.

The 1st Cohort had the best warriors in the legion and the 1st Century the best in the 1st Cohort. First Spear yelled when they were twenty paces from the waiting warriors, "First four ranks! Release!" The sixteen pila flew high and cracked into flesh and wood. The soft metal bent and the heavy spear pulled down the shields of those who had not been struck. The gladii of First Spear and his men punched through the men at the bridge as though they were not even there.

They went into their killing rhythm: punch with the shield, rip up with the gladius, step forward, punch with the shield, rip up with the gladius, step forward, punch with the shield, rip up with the gladius, step forward. They were across the bridge before the Brigante and Votadini could catch their breath.

"Halt! Two lines! Now!" Knowing that the auxiliaries could mop up any warriors left behind them Quintus calmly dressed his ranks. A brave warrior ran up to First Spear as he stood there. He swung his long sword at the centurion who flicked up his shield to deflect the blade and then eviscerated the man with his gladius. He shook his head. "Stupid bugger!" When he was satisfied that they had a straight line he shouted, "Forward!"

The warriors who moments earlier had outnumbered Metellus, Marcus and their men were now outnumbered themselves. It was as though a machine was scything down wheat. The Brigante and Votadini fought bravely but they were no match for these well-trained soldiers. When First Spear reached Metellus he saluted with his sword. "Sorry we are a bit late Decurion Princeps. If you and your lads would step through our ranks we'll finish these bastards off." He stopped and shouted, "Halt. Open ranks!"

It was like a well-oiled lock. Every legionary turned to the left, their scuta protecting them and the troopers walked between the two ranks.

"Close ranks!"

The solid wall of shields faced the Brigante once more and the troopers caught their breath as they watched the VIth Victrix slaughter the last rebels south of the wall.

They weren't quite the last rebels. There was a small party heading south down the Roman Road. "We will head for Morbium and Severus. With his men to protect us we can cross over to the west coast and take a ship for Manavia."

Briac was annoyed that he wasn't being included in the conversation between Caronwyn and Lady Flavia. "There are still many Brigante to the south. We can raise another army!"

"That may be true, although I doubt it. However, we have no arms for them. The army we have just seen destroyed were paid for by the Lady Flavia here. How will you arm them?"

Banquo was confused. He had thought they were going to find more warriors. Perhaps his four oathsworn were correct. Perhaps there was no honour in this. "Are we running away? Why?"

"Because we have hurt the Romans this time and we can build an army once more. We know their weaknesses and we can exploit them."

Banquo reined his horse in. "I will not run away. The Selgovae and the Novontae fight yet. I will join them."

Roman Wall

Caronwyn was pragmatic. As much as she would have liked the handsome young warrior to be part of her plans it also suited her for him to join the other rebels. He would be able to rally the Votadini beneath his banner. "Very well but if things do not go well for you then you can come to Manavia and join us there!"

He was touched by the affection in the priestess' voice, "I will and I promise that I will continue to serve the Mother."

The five Votadini turned off the road and headed west along the valley of the Vedra. Caronwyn turned and looked at the remnants of her army: ten warrior priestesses and five Brigante. She would have to begin again. Her mother had taught her to be patient. The burnt-out fort at Vinovia which they passed was a reminder of what they could do to the Romans when warriors followed her plans. When they reached Severus, they could use his clever mind to plan for the future.

First Spear left the clearing up to the auxiliaries he had brought with him. They had merely been bystanders up to now. He took off his helmet and scratched his stubble. Livius was having his arm bandaged by a capsarius. Quintus put his head to one side. "Considering you boys are donkey wallopers you did quite well."

Livius laughed at the insult. He and Broccus knew each other from campaigns past. "We have to, now that the legion has left us."

"I am sorry about that. You know it was not my doing."

"I know. Come we will see the Legate. He too was wounded and we can tell you the situation here."

The Legate was sitting up and Julius Longinus was feeding him. "Legate, at your age you should be letting the younger warriors fight."

"And I would have First Spear save that we were badly outnumbered. It is good to see you and I thank you for your timely arrival."

"Thank that scout you sent to us. He made it clear that our errand was urgent. Now, how stand things on the wall?"

The Legate pushed the bowl of food away with his good arm. "All of the tribes revolted. We sent the Votadini away but one band remained. Their bodies lie beyond the wall."

240

Livius wondered how Julius knew what had happened outside the fort. The Legate smiled at the quizzical look on his face, "Your clerk is a mine of information."

As he left the roof clutching the food bowl the clerk said, "I fight with my mind!"

"The wall was breached but we held them. The problem lies in the west at Luguvalium. There the fortress is surrounded by three tribes and I fear for their safety."

"Then I will suggest that we abandon this fort and head for Cilurnum. I will take the Thracians and the cohort west. The auxiliaries I brought can make good the losses on the wall."

It was a suggestion for the Legate still commanded. "He is right Legate. The door is damaged, the ditches are no longer functional. Cilurnum is the best option."

"Very well. Get the wounded on wagons and let us go now."

Quintus liked the Legate for he was decisive. It took less than an hour to clear the fort. The legion and the Thracians marched ahead of the wagons and then the garrison, the ala and the replacement auxiliaries followed. Marcus was the last to leave. He and Felix watched as the weary soldiers on exhausted horses trudged up the road to march the seven miles to Cilurnum.

"You did well, Felix."

"Thank you but I wish to go home, sir. I miss Drugi and the Dunum."

"Wait until the morning. We will discover our fate then."

Mavourna was delighted when Rufius arrived back at the fort. Although wounded he was still able to ride. To his acute embarrassment, she threw her arms around him and showered him with kisses. Quintus roared a laugh so loud the horses started. "I can see the advantage of being a horseman when you get a welcome like that from a beautiful woman."

Rufius just blushed. The Thracian Decurion said, "That reminds me; who were the women riding south when we attacked?"

Livius and the other officers stopped and stared at each other. "I had hoped that they died."

"No, sir, there were women who were armed and some Brigante warriors on horses."

Livius looked at the Legate. "Then this is not over."

First Spear looked confused. "What harm can a handful of women do?"

"They are the ones who organised the poisoning of your officers. They are the ones who planned and financed this rebellion. If they are alive then this is not over."

The Legate nodded, "Livius we need to pursue and capture them."

Livius looked at his officers. He had one who remained unwounded. "Marcus, I want you to take Felix and every trooper who has no wounds. Take spare horses. Follow her and bring her back!"

Marcus nodded. The Legate added slowly, "If you cannot capture her then kill her for she is deadlier than a warband of Brigante."

"Sir!"

"My wound is not so bad, sir."

"No, Metellus. You and Rufius will be needed here."

By the time Marcus was ready to ride he had his troopers ready with new javelins, five spare horses and food. Titus was not fit enough to travel but he had Gnaeus as his Chosen Man. The decurion was happy.

Rufius offered one piece of advice before the young decurion left. "She is cunning beyond words. Assume nothing and trust to Felix. He can sniff them out."

Felix beamed at the compliment.

With just a few hours of daylight left they headed south as quickly as their weary mounts could manage. Livius and the Legate watched them leave with heavy hearts. There was a huge amount of responsibility on the young officer's shoulders.

Chapter 24

Caronwyn and her band approached Morbium just after dark. The crucified defenders and the smell of the dead were a shock. The fort was in darkness. Briac sent his Brigante to examine the fort. When they returned it was with the worst news. "It is empty. Only the dead lie within!"

"Light torches and let us see where our friends lie."

They spread out and searched every uncia of the fort. Caronwyn sent her women to examine the crucified bodies. The only dead they could not find were Severus and his men.

"Perhaps they escaped." Flavia desperately tried to see good in all of this.

"Then they would have joined us or sent us a message."

"They could be hiding nearby."

Caronwyn shook her head. "The Romans have deserted us. We are alone!"

After they had made a meal Caronwyn outlined their options. "We could try to go west along the Dunum valley and take a ship as we planned."

A silence followed her words and Briac said, "That sounds like a good idea to me."

"Except that we will be pursued. The Romans will have patrols hunting us and they know where we will head. With Severus and his men, we had a chance, now..." she shrugged.

"What else can we do?" Flavia was becoming a little more hysterical and less composed now that Severus appeared to have abandoned them.

"What about Eboracum? We could take a boat from there." Briac, in contrast, was actually thinking.

Caronwyn looked at Flavia. "Do you have any boats on the river?"

"I may do but I am known there. It would be dangerous."

"We appear to be trapped and without a way out. I must communicate with the spirits."

Briac had no idea what she was talking about but he knew enough to remain silent. Flavia did know. "This is not the place for that, is it? The Romans have destroyed the life of the river by building a bridge across it."

"You are right. But a day's ride south of here is a cave over a holy river, the Nidd. The cave is high above the water and yet the water flows through the cave." Briac was about to ask how and then wisely kept his mouth shut. "We will ride there tomorrow and I will sleep with the spirits. We will have to travel cautiously for we must use the Roman Road for some way and we cannot be seen."

Briac did not mind the risk. At least they had a plan now and he spied a sort of hope. His four warriors were the best he had left and he had seen the female priests fight. They would reach the cave and then he was certain that the priestess would conjure an escape from this trap they found themselves in.

Marcus felt exhausted before they set off. As they were saddling he asked Felix. "How will you be able to track them on the road? They leave no sign."

"They leave a sign at the side of the road. When they make water, I can tell. Your nose is Roman. You cannot smell the different leaves and the soils through which we pass. When we passed through their camp I could smell them. There are many women in this party and they leave their sign wherever they pass as do the warriors."

Marcus felt happier and they pushed on south. They reached Morbium by mid-afternoon. The change of horses meant that they could travel further and faster. At the fort, Felix grinned. "They camped here last night and then headed south. I will ride across the river and see which direction they took."

By the time he returned the troopers had fed and watered their horses and eaten a frugal meal themselves.

"They went south."

"Not west towards their home?"

"No, they went south and they followed the Roman Road."

"Then we will push on and see if we can gain some ground on them."

244

Marcus looked wistfully to the west as they headed down towards Cataractonium. His home was but a few miles away. He steeled himself and forced himself to stare south. The fort at Cataractonium was still manned. They would either see those that they sought or they would turn off the road first. He guessed that they would turn off the road and head west before the fort for there was a road which headed west towards Cataractonium.

His exhausted troopers managed another five miles beyond the bridge and he ordered them to camp. Cataractonium was but a few miles ahead yet they could go no further. Even Wolf and Felix seemed tired and that, in itself, was unusual. Tired they might be but Marcus insisted on a camp. Their prey had shown cunning already. He would not put it past them to wait and then to ambush them.

Caronwyn and her party had left the road shortly before the fort. They had not headed west as Marcus had supposed but cut across ancient trails to the south-west to where the ground began to rise and the distant barrier of mountains divided this part of the province in two. Their going was slower and Caronwyn, like Marcus, was forced to halt with twenty miles yet to travel. The cave was a haven. It was a beacon drawing them to safety.

Flavia glanced north as they huddled together and ate a handful of early berries and drank the last of the water from their water skins. "Do you think they will follow?"

"They will follow. We have not left much of a trail but they will come after us. We have caused too much mischief for them to ignore. We have a day perhaps two and then they will come." Caronwyn smiled at Flavia and put a comforting arm around her shoulder. The young half Roman half native had held up far better than she could have hoped. She had thought the loss of Severus would have broken her. Caronwyn knew that without her money they would never have achieved as much as they had. "They will lose the trail when we leave the road. Once we cross the river they will never find us. I believe we still have sisters who live there. They can help us. Once in the cave, we will be safe. I can dream and we can plan the rest of our escape."

Roman Wall

Caronwyn knew of the power of the Mother. The Roman-built buildings were a defilement of the Earth. The cave would protect them. Her power would increase and they could begin again.

The three small ships moored in the river. Two of them were from the Classis Britannica. The third was the Legate's own ship. Its old captain was now retired but Furax had been a street urchin adopted by Julius Demetrius. He had grown into an excellent captain.

The Navarchus and Furax looked at the devastation of the Coriosopitum. The inhabitants of the vicus, destroyed in the fighting, now returned to rebuild their homes. The half-century of Tungrians were delighted to see the ships. They were a sign that they were not forgotten. The optio gave two horses to them and an escort. "The Legate and the rest of the staff are at Cilurnum."

Furax wondered why the Legate did not retire to his estates in Surrentum. It was the most beautiful of places and Hercules seemed to have grown years younger since he had retired there. The young captain realised it must be a sense of duty. He was a product of Rome's slums. He did not understand this duty to the state. He owed duty and loyalty to the man who had rescued him from a life of poverty and crime.

When they reached the fort the VIth had already left with every auxiliary who could be spared. Julius Demetrius was up and about but Furax was appalled at how thin and wasted he looked.

"Good to see you Furax and you Navarchus." He gestured for them to sit. "Navarchus, how many ships do you have at Arbeia?"

"The two river boats I brought and one bireme."

Julius was disappointed, "Where is the fleet?"

"It was summoned to Gaul and Batavia. There were uprisings there."

Julius controlled his anger. He turned to Livius and said, coldly, "The Emperor thinks the wall is the end of problems here and the new Governor is too far away." He shook his head. "Livius I shall appoint you temporary Legate until I return, I will travel with Furax to Rome." Furax was delighted and his face showed his joy. "Navarchus I want you to use your river boats to resupply Coriosopitum and the wall." He saw the question on the sailor's face. "I will write the orders for you. Then I wish you to patrol the river. The new legate, here, will need support until the rebellion is over."

The Navarchus did not like his orders. There was too much danger on the river. The barbarians were too ready to attack anything Roman for his liking but orders were orders. "Yes sir. And the orders…?"

"Will be ready by the time I leave. You are dismissed."

After he had gone he shook his head irritably. "Hercules and you are sailors to my taste. The Navarchus just objects to taking orders from a landsman. Julius!"

The clerk came in, "Legate?"

"Make a list of all the supplies we need and add a quarter. Make it into a requisition and I will give it to the Navarchus."

"And men sir?"

"And men. They may not be available yet but we will put our request in first."

Livius smiled, "You should think of retirement, sir."

Furax nodded his agreement. "This land is too cold." He spread his arms, "And this is their warm season!"

The two older officers laughed. "I will write your orders out personally Julius. I want you to be able to order the VIth to keep soldiers here on the wall. I have no doubt that we have snuffed out this rebellion but there will be sparks and so long as Caronwyn and the like are around then they will be fanned."

They both looked south. Livius said, "I hope that Marcus succeeds."

"You are thinking of his brother?"

"Aye, the last time they faced a priestess Macro died."

"Marcus is not his brother. He will survive."

Felix found the place where the horses had left the road. The fresh animal dung told even Marcus of their route. "I wonder where they are going. I expected them to head west. What is south of here?"

Gnaeus ventured, "It might be a long way Decurion, but Mona lies to the south-west."

"If she risks that then there will have to be a good reason. The XXth lie across her path at Deva and they keep a tight watch on the road. There is little point in idle speculation. We follow. How far ahead are they Felix?"

The scout picked up some of the dung and smelled it. "Eight hours or so."

They found the camp the rebels had used and the embers of the small fire confirmed Felix's view. "We have gained time. They will be but four or five hours ahead now." Marcus pointed south. "Felix, find them. It will be quicker than going at our pace. Use Drugi's signs to lead us."

Felix was happier to be on foot and unshackled. He handed his reins to Gnaeus. "Wolf, scout!" The dog raced off and, after adjusting his bow, Felix loped off after him.

Gnaeus shook his head. "Those two are as fast on foot as some horsemen I know."

"We are lucky to have them on our side."

The cave was on a hillside above the river. The four warriors were left with the horses by the river and the priestesses, Briac and Flavia climbed the path to the entrance. The warrior priestesses changed from their Roman war gear at the foot of the path and donned their plain white shifts. They still carried their weapons but Caronwyn would not risk sullying the sanctity of the cave with Roman equipment.

Briac made a fire and they lit some rush torches. Caronwyn would not risk anything which might make the spirits angry. When all was ready they entered the stygian dark of the cave. They had to duck beneath the entrance. Caronwyn led the way. She held one torch and, at the back, Briac held a second. Flavia shivered. It was not just the cold there was something else. The cave felt alive. She pressed closer to Caronwyn.

"Fear not child, the spirits are those of the land. They will not harm you."

Once they reached the rear they saw fantastic rock formations. The priestesses bowed their heads and stood in a half-circle around their leader. Briac suddenly said, "That rock looks like a woman!"

Caronwyn turned on him and snarled. "Fool! Leave the cave and rejoin your men! Do something useful and build a camp!" The chastened Brigante happily left the sharp-tongued priestess.

When he reached the river, he saw that his men had led the horses and tied them in a line close by a clearing where there was grass for them to graze. "We will be camping here tonight. Pedair, take Aed and you see if you can hunt some food. I have had enough of berries."

Carnac said, "I will put some lines in the river. We may be lucky."

The five Brigante were pleased to be doing something. It had galled all of them to flee from Coriosopitum but they all knew that to stay would have meant certain death. This way, at least, they could learn from their defeat and rebuild.

Felix and Wolf spotted Carnac as he laid his fishing lines in the river. They hunkered down to watch. He only saw the five warriors and he wondered where the women had gone. Suddenly his eye was caught by a flash of white from halfway up the hill. It was one of the women. She disappeared into what looked like a cave. Having located the men, he focussed his attention on the cave. He saw that it lay beneath a tumble of rocks. A rogue tree had grown out at an angle and held the rocks. It made the cave look as though it was crowned with hair. Felix shivered. The women in the cave were witches. The cave looked to be part of their domain. He was a brave scout but he would not risk the wrath of the mother.

His patience was rewarded when he saw the line of women emerge from the cave and descend the path. The tendril of smoke from behind the trees told him that they were camping. He could return to the decurion and tell him that their prey was close.

Caronwyn was satisfied. They would drink from the river and then purify themselves for the ceremony of the dream. It would just be her and the priestesses who would sleep in the cave. The men would hinder the spirits and she was not certain if Flavia would cope with the sometimes traumatic and unpredictable dreams which haunted such places. Her only disappointment was that the sisters who she had expected were not there; not alive, at least. She had seen the petrified bones of what looked like two priestesses. They must have died in the cave and the cave had consumed them. She knew that their spirits would linger yet in the wet gloom of the cave.

Briac appeared like an eager puppy. "We have tethered the horses and my men hunt food."

"Then you and your men can eat it. Until we have dreamed my sisters and I will eat nothing. You are to guard the cave. Once we enter then no one must defile it until we emerge in the morning." She turned to Flavia, "Briac and the men will protect you."

She looked fearfully across the river. "What if the Romans come?"

"We have lost them and they will not come. We have time. Fear not, the river and the cave will protect us."

Marcus and his turma reached the bluff overlooking the river well before dark. He went with Gnaeus and Felix to scout out the barbarians. "They are over there, decurion, you can see the cave and their camp is in those trees."

Gnaeus peered down at the river. They could cross there but it would mean they could be easily seen by their prey. "Felix, find us a crossing point upstream."

The scout and his dog trotted off west. "If they go in the cave sir we will have a hard job to winkle them out. Some of those caves can go back for miles."

"I know but that doesn't worry me. If they are in the cave then they are trapped. I want them secure. The last thing we need is to lose them. This would begin all over again."

They reached the turma. "You four stay here with the spare horses. We are going to attack them. If they try to escape then you cut them off."

"Sir!" The men he had with him were not only the ones who were still unwounded, they were also the most experienced troopers in the ala. They could all be relied upon to use their initiative.

Felix and Wolf appeared as though by magic. "There is a ford just around the bend in the river sir but you must be careful. There are two warriors hunting in the woods."

Marcus turned to his men, "Careful, weapons at the ready."

They descended through the woods to the river. Marcus handed his reins to Gnaeus. "I will cross with Felix. We will wave you across when it is safe."

The ford was just knee-deep but some of the stones beneath the surface were treacherously slippery and Marcus took his time. Felix and Wolf seemed to almost walk on the water. Once in the woods, Felix held up his hand. He moved silently up the bank to a handful of bushes. He waved Marcus forward and they crouched underneath the bushes. They saw a couple of young deer in the distance. They nibbled some hidden bush and then their ears pricked. They bounced away down the slope and then stopped. Felix mimed pulling a bow. Marcus nodded. The deer were being hunted. The deer continued to graze. Suddenly they heard the twang of two bows being drawn. The deer started towards the river. One of them fell, struck by two arrows. It landed twenty paces from where they lay hidden. The other deer escaped. Marcus watched as the two Brigante emerged from cover and raced towards the dead animal.

Marcus could hardly breathe as the two Brigante picked up the deer and headed down the slope to their camp. Marcus waited until the two men were well away and then tapped Felix on the shoulder. He mimed for him to stay there. Felix nodded and Marcus made his way back to the river. He waved across the rest of his men. There were over thirty of them. He had more than enough to do what he intended.

Briac was delighted with the kill. It was not a large deer but it would be hot food and they had all night ahead of them. Carnac came from the river with a brace of trout. "Excellent! Pedair and Aed you are good hunters. This will be like a feast."

Caronwyn shook her head, "That is the trouble with you Briac. You cannot see beyond your next meal. If you were only able to channel your mind and your spirit the way that you fill your belly, then who knows what you could achieve."

Briac felt humiliated to be spoken to like this in front of his men. Flavia touched his hand. "Men always think better on a full stomach!"

Caronwyn shook her head. "We will begin our ceremony when the sun dips below the western mountains. Do not disturb us until it rises again in the east."

His men had kept their heads down as they gutted the deer. The dead wood would burn well and not make smoke. All six of them just wanted Caronwyn gone so that they could eat.

The smell of the venison cooking had the troopers salivating. Spread out in a wide circle they approached the camp slowly. Night had begun to fall as they had slowly closed with the camp. Septimus was almost walking in the river while Lentius was a hundred paces away to the south. Marcus was taking no chances. He needed these men and priestesses dead or alive. If they escaped then he had failed.

He heard the woman talking to the warrior in the mail. "You could come with me, you know Briac. I have a fine villa across the sea. We could live well."

"And what about Severus?"

"He is either dead or he has deserted me." She shrugged, "The result is the same."

"I am not sure. I believe my destiny is here. I am descended from Venutius who was the last free king of my people. If I went with you then I would be letting down my people. I need to fight these Romans."

Suddenly Marcus and Gnaeus stepped into the firelight. "Put down your weapons Brigante and..."

Marcus got no further. His orders were to bring them back as prisoners and he had tried to do so but Briac and his men had other ideas. They grabbed their weapons and ran at the two men. The rest of the troopers stepped forward. Briac and his oathsworn knew that they would die but they would die as warriors with swords in their hands. Briac swung his spatha at Marcus. Neither man had a shield but Marcus had fought far more men than Briac. He spun and evaded the wild swing. Bringing his sword around Briac frantically blocked the blow. Marcus twisted the Sword of Cartimandua and flicked the end in the direction of Briac's side. The sword ripped open two of the mail links.

Marcus stepped back as Briac drew his dagger and came towards Marcus with two weapons. Marcus feinted and Briac made the mistake of using both weapons to block the blow. Marcus still wanted a prisoner and he did not make a killing strike. Instead, he turned and twisted his blade beneath the hilt of Briac's dagger. It flew from his hand.

Suddenly there were wild screams as the naked priestesses flung themselves at the troopers. Flavia took the momentary distraction to run towards the cave.

Two of Marcus' troopers were distracted by the naked women and surprised by the sudden attack. Both men paid for that with their lives. Briac, too, tried to use the reinforcements to his own advantage. He spun around and brought his spatha two handed around Marcus' back. Marcus was nimble on his feet and he stepped to the side and chopped down with his sword. The Brigante blade bounced off a rock. Briac tried to force Marcus backwards by pushing as hard as he could on his sword. Their faces were close together. Briac snarled, "You are half Brigante! You have the Sword of Cartimandua. How can you fight for the Romans?"

"I am half Roman and I know that the world of Rome is right for the Brigante."

Briac hooked his leg around the back of Marcus' knee and pushed. Marcus fell backwards. He had not been expecting the blow. He reached out with his left hand to stop himself falling and clutched at Briac's mail. They fell together. Marcus felt the warm spurt of blood as the sword of Brigante sank deep into Briac's heart and the last issue of Venutius died.

Marcus pushed the body from him and looked around. Five of his troopers were dead but the Brigante warriors had been slain and five priestesses lay dead. Of Flavia and the survivors, there was no sign.

"Where are they?"

"They ran to the cave."

"Gnaeus bring ten men and come with me. The rest of you see to the wounded."

This would be the end of it. He had them trapped in the cave.

In the cave, Caronwyn cursed the Romans. The five priestesses followed the hysterical Flavia deep into the cave. One of them had a mortal wound to her stomach.

"We are outnumbered. There is no escape!"

"I know. We will take as many of them as we can. Here take this." She handed them a mushroom each. She took them from the bag of potions and powders. She looked at Flavia. "Eat this and they will have no power over you." The priestesses snuffed out the torches but one and the cave became eerily blue.

Flavia eagerly took it and greedily ate it. "Thank you, sister. And when they have gone?"

"Then we will be with the Mother."

Flavia felt a sudden pain in her chest. Her breathing became more difficult and yet her head was filled with a euphoria she had not felt since her brother had died. Caronwyn eased her to the ground and kissed her on the head. "Soon I will join you!"

Gnaeus and the first four troopers burst into the cave. Their eyes were not used to the dark and they sought their foes. Marcus, Felix and Wolf followed. The dog growled and his ears went down. Like Felix, he felt the power of the cave. While Marcus followed his men Felix and the dog remained fearfully at the entrance.

Suddenly the torches were snuffed out and they were in complete darkness. Marcus yelled, "The rest of you wait at the entrance!"

He heard the clash of blades and then a shout as one of his troopers died. Marcus backed off to the side of the cave so that his back was to the damp wall. He heard more metal on metal and this time they were the screams and shouts of women as they died.

Gnaeus appeared from the dark and lurched towards Marcus. He was trying to hold his entrails in. "I will see you in the Otherworld." He slumped into Marcus' arms. Even in death, his Chosen Man did his job. The wounded priestess stabbed the corpse in the back thinking it was Marcus. The decurion ripped his sword across her throat and her dead body fell across that of Gnaeus.

Silence filled the cave. Then Marcus heard the steady drip of water from the roof. Somewhere ahead one of the wounded gasped their dying breath and then was gone.

He heard a cackle from the corner, "So bearer of the Sword of Cartimandua you have escaped me yet." Marcus said nothing. He was trying to locate the witch through the sound of her voice. He did not want to let her know where he was. "I know you live still. I can feel you breathing. You have no power in this holy place, for this is the cave of the mother."

He sensed a movement to his left and, as he turned, a wounded priestess hurled herself at him. Her eyes were wild with fury and she had bared teeth. Marcus thought his time had come until Felix's arrow erupted like a third eye.

"You have luck, spawn of Ailis, I will give you that but now I will take it away from you. I curse you and your line. I call upon the power of the Mother to make you all suffer a long and painful death. I curse your family, your mother, your wife, your brother, your children. I curse your land and I curse your animals. And when you come to the Otherworld then I will inflict the direst of tortures upon you and your issue. And I will sit in this cave until my prediction comes to pass. I will watch generations suffer until there are none left to curse." There was a pause. "I come!" The silence, punctuated by the drip returned.

Marcus waited for an age. He felt frozen to the ground. He was about to shout out when one of the troopers lit a torch and stood in the entrance. The sight which greeted him was horrific. The bodies of his troopers lay entwined with the dead priestesses. He saw Flavia lying on the ground with a smile upon her face and there, seated beneath the dripping water sat a naked Caronwyn. Her back was to the wall and on her head, she wore the crown of the Brigante given to her by her mother, Morwenna.

Marcus knew that if he did not move now he would never move. He sprang away from the wall and leapt for the entrance. Felix and Wolf preceded him. He would not enter the cave again. No-one would.

"Lentius take four men and prise those rocks from above the entrance to the cave. I want it sealed up forever."

"But sir, the men!"

"I gave an order. They died well and their bodies will not be harmed within this tomb. Let them sleep with the witches and mayhap their spirits will protect us."

The curse had worried Marcus. All those who had heard it felt the power of the words. Felix was shaking as they walked back to the horses. As they saddled the horses and laid the bodies of their men who had fallen in the camp on their mounts they heard a sound like thunder. Lentius and his men stood atop the witch's head and the rocks buried the cave. It was gone.

As they rode north in silence no-one wished to talk of the end of the line of Fainch, Morwenna and Venutius. All were thinking of their own fate. The rebellion had been ended but its effects would linger.

Epilogue

As the VIth finally disposed of the last of the Selgovae First Spear Quintus Broccus felt a sense of satisfaction. The fortress they had built had survived. The wall had not been breached and the rebellion was suppressed. He knew they could not have done it without the invaluable auxiliaries. He even felt a little guilt for he had barely forty casualties and that included wounded. He had seen, as they had marched west, the bodies which marked the defence of the wall. He had already sent a rider back to bring up the 11th Cohort. The 1st would return to Eboracum when they arrived but he would ensure that the legion had a presence on the wall. He knew that it had been a mistake to withdraw it.

Banquo and his four oathsworn made it all the way to the west coast well below the wall. Killing the fisherman and stealing his boat was simple. He decided to head north. He would seek sanctuary at the court of King Tole and he would continue his fight against the Romans. He was not the naïve warrior he had been. He had learned much and the Romans would learn of his education.

As *'The Swan'* headed south Legate Julius Demetrius wondered if he should retire. He knew that not all of his decisions had been good ones. They had won but only just. Perhaps he should consider Furax's words. He was too old to fight and he remembered when he had been a young officer in the ala how he had wondered at men too old to fight who gave orders. Perhaps it was true that the great leaders such as Alexander and Julius Caesar had all died young. Old men like Crassus led men to their deaths and not to glory. He would wait until he was in warmer climes before he made that decision but his mind was already drifting south to the sun.

Marcus led his turma towards his brother's farm. They would be arriving late at night but he would be given a welcome and he would feel safe there. Felix was silent as they headed along the track from the

Roman Road. The scene in the cave, Gnaeus' death, all of it had upset the youth. Marcus had thought that finding the last of the rebels would end it. He was wrong. He now had Caronwyn in his head. The witch had known what she was doing when she cursed him and then took her own life. He smiled when he saw the familiar walls ahead. The torches burning at the gate were welcoming and warm.

The man on the gate recognised them and shouted, "It is the decurion and his troopers!"

The gate swung open and he saw his brother advancing towards him. Behind him, he saw Drugi with his arm around Frann. There were no welcoming smiles.

Marcus dismounted and Decius walked up to him. He had been crying. He put his arms around Marcus' shoulders. "Our mother is dead, brother."

Marcus felt a chill grip his heart and squeeze. He said, very quietly, "When?"

"Just after dark. She was at the table. She stood and cried, 'It is the witch! She fell forward and she died."

Marcus fell to his knees and began to sob. The curse had begun. Who would be the next to fall victim to the witch?

The End

Maps

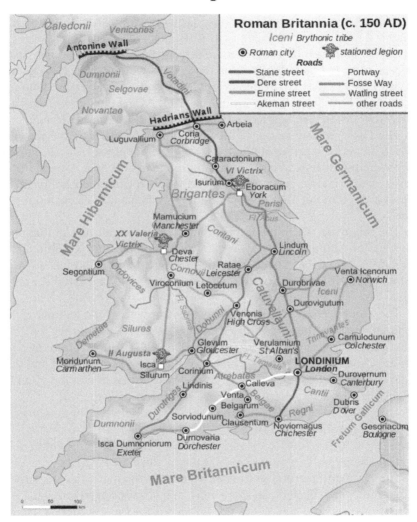

Maps Courtesy of Wikipedia

Historical Background

Aulus Nepos was the Governor of Britannia for a short time and it was his decision to enlarge Hadrian's original ideas. That proved expensive and his tenure was a mere three years. He was responsible for Housesteads and the other forts on the wall as well as those built north of the wall. His successor, Trebius Germanus, was a vague figure who may or may not have been Governor in 127 A.D. As the next governor we know for certain was Sextus Severus 131-133, I have used Germanus.

The Dacians were stationed at Vercovicium on the wall and the Syrian archers did arrive at about the time the novel was set although they were not in time to aid Julius. South Shields became Arbeia or Arab Town, when the Hamians and the river boatmen from the Euphrates and Tigris arrived in the province making the northeast quite a cosmopolitan place.

The Selgovae, Votadini and Brigante kept on revolting right up until the reign of Antoninus Pius who built the Antonine Wall to subjugate those tribes. It never quite worked out and eventually, Hadrian's Wall became the northern frontier and the Brigante finally accepted Roman rule.

The building of the two walls was the last work of the legions in Britannia and the defence of the wall was left to the auxiliaries who were sent to the northern frontier to guard it. The wall itself was built largely as described. Where there was plenty of local stone, in the east and the middle then it was made of stone. In the west, it was made of turf which is why the best sections to explore are in the centre of the wall.

The vallum was added after the wall was completed. It ran along the south of the wall, on the Province side. It consisted of two mounds with a ditch between. The only crossing points were at the forts. It would not stop an enemy but it would slow him down considerably.

I have used the term bolt throwers although the machines in question were quite sophisticated and there were many sizes: manuballista, ballista, scorpio and catapulta were all names for these weapons. Here is a picture of a modern reconstruction of a scorpio as used by the reenactors of the XXth. This photograph was taken by the author at

Cilurnum.

The sacrifice of Radha is based on evidence found all over Europe but especially in England. Lindow Man was found in a bog in Cheshire. He was not a slave and had manicured hands, traces of mistletoe in his body and was not bound. He had been struck on the head, strangled and then had his throat cut. This was a Celtic tradition. The fact that Radha was a Queen and a priestess would have made the sacrifice even more important.

The single combat between leaders was an important aspect of Celtic life. There was much honour in such a combat and the ancient writers make much of the custom. The Celts were frequently surprised when the supposedly better Roman warriors refused such a combat.

Mother Shipton's cave on the River Nidd is a famous natural phenomenon. It is the oldest charging tourist attraction in Britain and has been visited since the 1660s. There is a petrifying well inside the cave and the limestone dripping from the roof of the cave turns everything to stone.

Books used in the research:

- Rome's Enemies-Wilcox and McBride (Osprey)
- Celtic Warrior- Allen and Reynolds (Osprey)

Roman Wall

- The Roman Army from Caesar to Trajan-Simkins and Embleton (Osprey)
- Hadrian's Wall- David Breeze (English Heritage)
- Chesters Roman Fort-Nick Hodgson (English Heritage)
- What the Soldiers Wore on Hadrian's Wall- Russell Robinson

Griff Hosker September 2014

People and places in the book.

Fictitious characters and places are in *italics*.

Name-Description

Ambrinus -Gallic Prefect

Aneurin-Recruit

Appius Serjanus-Governor's aide

Aulus Platorius Nepos-Governor of Britannia

Belatucadros – a Celtic god of war

Briac-Brigante prince and descendant of Venutius

Capsarius(pl) capsarii-medical orderly

Carnyx- Celtic war horn

Cilurnum-Chesters (on Hadrian's Wall)

Claudius Culpinus-Senior centurion vexillation of the VIth

Coriosopitum-Corbridge

Dunum- River Tees

Felix-Brigante Scout

Flavia Nepos-Wife of the Governor

Frann- Marcus' wife

Frumentarii- Roman Secret Police frumentarius singular)

Gaius Culpinus-Tungrian Prefect

Iucher-Votadini warrior

Julius Demetrius-Legate

Julius Longinus-Ala Clerk

Livius-Chosen Man

Livius Lucullus Sallustius-Prefect Marcus' Horse

Lucia Scaura-Flavia's companion

Macro-Marcus' son

mansio-State inn for travellers

mansionarius-The official in charge of a mansio

Marcus Gaius Aurelius-Decurion Marcus' Horse.

Mercaut- Lindisfarne (Holy Island)

Nemesis-Roman Fate

Oppidum- Tribal hill fort

Roman Wall

Pons Aelius-Newcastle
Quaestor-Roman official or tax collector
Cassius Metellus Meridius- Prefect 1st Batavorum cohort
Quintus Licinius Brocchus-First Spear VIth Legion
Roaring Waters- High Force Waterfall
Rufius Atrebeus- Decurion and former Explorate and frumentarius
Scanlan-Brigante Warrior
sesquiplicarius-Corporal
Sextus-Marcus' chosen man, later a decurion
signifer-The soldier who carries the standard and also acts as the turma banker
Tinea- River Tyne
Titus Plauca-Camp Prefect Eboracum
tonsor-Roman barber
Trierarch-Captain of a Roman warship
Vedra- River Wear
Vercovicium-Housesteads (Hadrian's Wall)
Via Claudia-Watling Street (A5)
Via Hades-Road to Hell- Dere Street (A1)
Via Trajanus-Dere Street (A1)-Eboracum North
Vicus (pl)vici-Roman settlement close to a fort

Roman Wall

Other books by Griff Hosker

If you enjoyed reading this book, then why not read another one by the author?

Ancient History

The Sword of Cartimandua Series
(Germania and Britannia 50 A.D. – 128 A.D.)
Ulpius Felix- Roman Warrior (prequel)
The Sword of Cartimandua
The Horse Warriors
Invasion Caledonia
Roman Retreat
Revolt of the Red Witch
Druid's Gold
Trajan's Hunters
The Last Frontier
Hero of Rome
Roman Hawk
Roman Treachery
Roman Wall
Roman Courage

The Wolf Warrior series
(Britain in the late 6th Century)
Saxon Dawn
Saxon Revenge
Saxon England
Saxon Blood

Roman Wall

Saxon Slayer
Saxon Slaughter
Saxon Bane
Saxon Fall: Rise of the Warlord
Saxon Throne
Saxon Sword

Medieval History

The Dragon Heart Series
Viking Slave
Viking Warrior
Viking Jarl
Viking Kingdom
Viking Wolf
Viking War
Viking Sword
Viking Wrath
Viking Raid
Viking Legend
Viking Vengeance
Viking Dragon
Viking Treasure
Viking Enemy
Viking Witch
Viking Blood
Viking Weregeld
Viking Storm
Viking Warband
Viking Shadow
Viking Legacy
Viking Clan

266

Roman Wall

Viking Bravery

The Norman Genesis Series
Hrolf the Viking
Horseman
The Battle for a Home
Revenge of the Franks
The Land of the Northmen
Ragnvald Hrolfsson
Brothers in Blood
Lord of Rouen
Drekar in the Seine
Duke of Normandy
The Duke and the King

New World Series
Blood on the Blade
Across the Seas
The Savage Wilderness
The Bear and the Wolf

The Vengeance Trail

The Reconquista Chronicles
Castilian Knight
El Campeador
The Lord of Valencia

The Aelfraed Series
(Britain and Byzantium 1050 A.D. - 1085 A.D.)
Housecarl
Outlaw

Roman Wall

Varangian

The Anarchy Series England
1120-1180
English Knight
Knight of the Empress
Northern Knight
Baron of the North
Earl
King Henry's Champion
The King is Dead
Warlord of the North
Enemy at the Gate
The Fallen Crown
Warlord's War
Kingmaker
Henry II
Crusader
The Welsh Marches
Irish War
Poisonous Plots
The Princes' Revolt
Earl Marshal

Border Knight
1182-1300
Sword for Hire
Return of the Knight
Baron's War
Magna Carta
Welsh Wars
Henry III

Roman Wall

The Bloody Border
Baron's Crusade
Sentinel of the North
War in the West

Sir John Hawkwood Series
France and Italy 1339- 1387
Crécy: The Age of the Archer

Lord Edward's Archer
Lord Edward's Archer
King in Waiting
An Archer's Crusade (November 2020)

Struggle for a Crown
1360- 1485
Blood on the Crown
To Murder A King
The Throne
King Henry IV
The Road to Agincourt
St Crispin's Day

Tales from the Sword

Modern History

The Napoleonic Horseman Series
Chasseur à Cheval
Napoleon's Guard
British Light Dragoon
Soldier Spy

Roman Wall

1808: The Road to Coruña
Talavera
The Lines of Torres Vedras
Bloody Badajoz
The Road to France

The Lucky Jack American Civil War series
Rebel Raiders
Confederate Rangers
The Road to Gettysburg

The British Ace Series
1914
1915 Fokker Scourge
1916 Angels over the Somme
1917 Eagles Fall
1918 We will remember them
From Arctic Snow to Desert Sand
Wings over Persia

**Combined Operations series
1940-1945**
Commando
Raider
Behind Enemy Lines
Dieppe
Toehold in Europe
Sword Beach
Breakout
The Battle for Antwerp
King Tiger
Beyond the Rhine

Roman Wall

Korea
Korean Winter

Other Books
Great Granny's Ghost (Aimed at 9-14-year-old young people)

For more information on all of the books then please visit the author's web site at www.griffhosker.com where there is a link to contact him or visit his Facebook page: GriffHosker at Sword Books

Made in United States
Orlando, FL
05 December 2022